Susan Delle Cave lives in South West London with her husband and has five daughters, all of whom live close by. She speaks three languages and has taught various subjects in a range of schools.

Her many interests include the opera and theatre, genealogy, Sudoku for relaxation and spending time with a growing number of grandchildren.

She would have liked to become an archaeologist.

For dear Tommaso, without whom this story would not, and could not, have been written.

And for my brother, William Clive, whose short life touches me still.

Susan Delle Cave

IN SEARCH OF CAMEOS

AUSTIN MACAULEY PUBLISHERS™

LONDON * CAMBRIDGE * NEW YORK * SHARJAH

A CIP catalogue record for this title is available from the British Library.

ISBN 9781528900164 (Paperback)
ISBN 9781528901901 (Hardback)
ISBN 9781528903585 (ePub e-book)
ISBN 9781398418257 (Audiobook)

www.austinmacauley.com

First Published (2021)
Austin Macauley Publishers Ltd
25 Canada Square
Canary Wharf
London
E14 5LQ

I wish to thank all my 'teachers'—past, present (and future), far too many to name.

Chapter 1

Star House

A good few years before the parakeets had arrived and turned the sky a screechy green, a rather unusual woman resided at Star House, alone. It was an elegant house, a tangible echo from a distant epoch; a past age of gables; drawing rooms; servants' quarters and decorative brickwork; an age which had inadvertently been wiped out by a terrible war and had made way, so they say, for a more tolerant, fluid and equal society but then came yet another terrible war.

Visitors to the house came and went, some repeatedly, others only once or twice. This included a regular stream of young people, and, of course, the Parish Priest, Father John. But some years later, a family moved in. The young woman remained, keeping a wing of the house for herself. Life appeared to go on as usual.

The house was located down a lane, in a tiny concealed pocket of the world, though a busy high street beckoned insidiously from a short distance. It was the kind of place very few knew existed, a place no one ever actually stumbled across. Star House was nestled amongst lofty horse chestnut trees, secular oaks sturdy in their own importance; flirty camellias and magnolias and the woman's own personal favourite: a luscious fig tree.

This solitary tree occupied one of the few patches of earth at the front of the house. It generously yielded up twice yearly vast quantities of fruit, and so the many tentacle-like branches were forced to curve and bow low. Its owner loved the huge-leafed tree; the deliverer of vivid proof that summer was on its way or had already arrived. She also relished its anomalous position in the garden and for the poetry of its gently swaying green canopy.

Its produce – the figs – were sweet and fleshy. Year upon year, the woman continued to pick and savour these earthy treasures with a childlike delight, in all their sweet, gritty stickiness, which oozed in trickles from pink-tinged flesh.

Yet unsuspecting visitors remained less favourably impressed, as at such times of year, they were invariably attacked by the overgrown monster, while trying to enter through the silent black gate of wrought iron.

Newly fallen leaves, ample as outspread male hands, some like crumpled paper, others a bright yellow…a colour which always reminded her of her father's Strega liqueur had to be cleared daily, together with remnants of squashed or discarded fruit, which left a dark treacly mess on the surrounding paving stones.

Planting such a tree, in such a position, would have been unthinkable in the distant place her family had come from, a symbol of fallen women residing within, like a medieval advertisement for a certain type of pleasure house. No one here would or could have known. She possessed her own wry joke against a system; a green and hidden counterattack; a cowardly act perhaps, yet necessary all the same.

Casa Stella – Star House – had been given to Giulia by her father, together with a few other bits and pieces, which once belonged to a former owner. This assorted collection had included some coloured glass drinking goblets, which she hoped had been hand blown in Murano. But with no visible mark of proof, she had concluded that it was of no consequence, as she loved them anyway. They remained unused, awaiting that special moment. There was also a Raffaele Monti bust; mother Mary dismissing, with her downward gaze, all the beauty of an Aphrodite bestowed upon her by her sculptor. Spode bowls took pride of place in the oak dresser, occasionally catching the careless glances of guests with their pretty Oriental design covering base and rim.

The house also came with a huge Bible in three volumes, printed in Italian, her mother language.

Giulia had chosen the name of Star House because her father had been born in a road called Via Stella, in a house where the humans lived upstairs, and their animals below. It also tied in nicely, so Giulia thought, with the nativity story.

And it was books, especially fiction, which had begun to take root all over the house, in ever-increasing numbers and somewhere Rimbaud sat uncomfortably next to Jane Austen; precious volumes of *The Golden Bough*, next to Butler's *Lives of the Saints*, and Lawrence's *Sons and Lovers*. One day, there would be time enough to read them all, to sort them. The heart of her world was in fact fixed deep within Casa Stella; an imposing building, which she had over time, lovingly draped and swathed with silks, velvets and damasks. From its high ceilings she had hung (second-hand) crystal chandeliers, whose pendants nightly trapped the light's golden drizzle, transforming rooms into temples of white. And she had littered the floors with patterned rugs, which transposed ancient fables and histories from far-flung places for those willing to read into the woven worlds beneath their feet.

To visitors, her drawing room opened its doors onto a giddy boutique of pretty watercolour princesses; faded roses on bone china; trapped seascapes spread out in gilt frames; black and white photographs of 100 bemused schoolgirls; veiled Madonnas; tiny lacquered and enamelled boxes; pink and red handmade thankyous; books in towers; books in rows; glass bowls of tiny sweets glistening in their wrappers. The whole room – a mother's womb with the mother tightly clasping her universe. Each object, grand or simple, with its own history; its individual right of occupancy; its emotional links with its owner.

And from the drawing room it was possible to make out a large garden to the rear. This garden had known both long periods of silence, and over the years, the buoyant laughter, shouts and protests of many children. It had survived the winds, hail and rain of winter months and had absorbed the seasonal sun and birdsong. There the world of adults had not really made its mark. Did the grown-ups ever wonder just how the children might have arranged their time here? Probably not. So all the better for them; the garden remained their secret, yet temporary space, their place to explore and inhabit, deliciously free of the shadow of adult intervention.

Yes, it was a place that coincided with the stories they read, the plays they devised and the dreams that invaded their heads at night, when life on Earth is a very different creature. A place where human flying is the norm and the poison of evil can be destroyed with the casting of a few well-chosen spells. They would possibly all, one day, look back on those garden adventures and this would provide an alternative escape route from the overwhelming harshness of everyday living.

Some of these children were destined to become Giulia's students.

There was one corner of the house, however, which didn't exude the same quasi-Bohemian feel of the other rooms. Even insects, both the flying and crawling varieties, were said to avoid it! It was a spacious square-shaped room, which Giulia had chosen to be her study. It was located just off the entrance hall. In here, she inhabited a more organised and regimented world. Here the books occupied shelves and were also arranged in a coherent order, thus quickly identifiable and within easy reach. There were a few classic novels among them and several slim volumes of poetry but by and large they were schoolbooks, consisting of a range of dictionaries, atlases, encyclopaedias and textbooks, as well as the necessary foreign language courses. For her younger pupils, there were also some large colourfully appealing picture books.

And occupying the very centre of the room sat an oversized desk that Giulia had bought from a local antique dealer; one of her earlier acquisitions. Mrs Mogden kept it dusted and polished with due reverence. At any time of day it was possible to see arranged on its vast table top a wooden box of sharpened HB pencils: blue, black and red biros, straight as soldiers; a set of coloured pencils, rainbow perfect, and her own precious dark-green fountain pen. All exercise books and sheets of paper were kept out of the way in the deep desk drawers. On the walls hung a collection of meandering Fielding House school photographs, presented in chronological order, and a series of pictures of some of her creative heroes from the past including: Raphael, Michelangelo, Mozart, Shakespeare, Alexander Pope, Jane Austen, Saint Catherine of Siena, Oscar Wilde, Marie Curie, Albert Einstein, and her latest exhibit: a photograph of Sylvia Plath.

She didn't want a wall clock or any other kind of visible timepiece in her study. Even though each lesson lasted a precise 60 minutes, she always set out to create a timeless, other-worldly atmosphere in which to weave the desired magic. *How irritating,* she mused, *to catch sight of a student's wandering eyes as the last remaining minutes of the lesson were being counted!*

Each week of the academic year Giulia spent many an hour here. She gave lessons in English, French and Italian to a range of students. In effect it was her way of transforming the many gifts and blessings life had already bestowed upon her. She was completely aware she wouldn't have survived a single day as a school-based teacher, with all its constraints and rigours. She was not interested in school rules, correct uniform, staff meetings or setting detentions in fact any kind of brutalising, institutionalised learning. One teacher for one student at a time was her precious way of doing things.

First and foremost, she felt her principal task was to open up her students' hearts and minds to the wonder of knowledge, the creative arts and the beauty of the world around them. An impossibly tall order but there had also been some minor successes. Of course most of their parents were far more interested in examination results and getting so-called value for money. She fully understood this expectation; in a society such as ours, no one wanted to take the risk of jeopardising the future chances of their own beloved children. However, this had to be balanced against her own idea as to the true meaning of education: the magic key which opened a box of irreplaceable treasures.

It still caused her great sorrow, sometimes bordering on a quivering yet silent rage, that so many adults of her acquaintance had forgotten the enquiring minds of their own childhoods. Up until a certain age, every child in the world asks the infuriating BUT WHY again and again. It is, of course, part of the child's need for attention and subsequent enjoyment of the frustrated parent's inability to deliver up, at best, some half-baked answer. But surely, they had already become little experts in that field! No. The child wants to know and then know more and more still. And at some point, this deep yet fundamental desire gets put out, turned off, extinguished.

Perhaps most of us take out of life no more than we think we need for everyday survival?

Each summer, Giulia's teaching year would end magnificently with her students performing, for her and their parents, an eclectic mix of poem recitals in various languages, violin pieces they had practised over again, songs delivered a cappella, and once in a while a magic show!

Chapter 2
The Piece of Paper

At St Raphael's Catholic Church, it was the priest's day off, if such an event were possible. Many years ago, he had taken Holy Orders, in The Vatican itself, and a while before that, the much-discussed Vow of Celibacy, which would free him up entirely for God, his future parishioners, for the good of all mankind.

The training in Rome had been long and arduous but he had never once questioned the path he believed God had chosen for him. He had also made some deep friendships there. He had struggled with the acquiring of Latin and had also learned, with great difficulty, how to deal with the natural longings which surged all too regularly during his seven years in the Eternal City, which churches aside, was also a place full of beautiful women.

For some unfathomable reason he had been picked out, chosen to live differently, to serve God in each waking moment, all of which would manifest itself in the love he would show his fellow man.

It was also during this time in Rome he took to smoking quite heavily as did many of his contemporaries. It was often a night-time activity helping them cram and revise for the barrage of examinations they regularly faced. Cigarettes and thick black espresso coffee served up in those tiny white ceramic cups.

His parents in Ireland were proud of their son, John, a pride they managed quietly to the outside world. They had little idea as to the reality of his day-to-day life far away in Italy, even though he did manage to write to them each month.

Receiving and replying to John's letters took on an almost sacred dimension. It was not, of course, an age of instant communication. And much care was taken regarding the written word for letters of a personal nature: the handwriting had to be clear and the content often drafted, edited and then re-written. Such letters were received with a mixture of joy and pain; pain for the reminder of physical separation. They were read by each family member dozens of times and new discoveries came to light on each reading.

They had a telephone, but this was only used for very serious matters, perhaps only a few times a year. The sound of the telephone ringing at home would cause a general shudder and call for a deep intake of breath before the receiver was lifted. The arrival of a telephone call usually meant bad news. And this was why their son very rarely rang them.

John's brothers and sisters were in awe of him and the choice, they still believed, he alone had made. Would he really see it through and become a PRIEST in the years to come? This was the question that had often spun around their young heads until the day in question finally did arrive the day of their revered brother's Ordination.

So Father John, unlike his Anglican counterpart who could take a wife and have children, would never have to choose between family and the wider community. He was, in theory at least, available to all at any time, day or night.

Let us just say that for the last few years a Wednesday had become the most convenient day of the week for him to 'disappear' for a few hours, once mass had been celebrated for the early morning faithful. (Though it would have been unusual for Giulia to make an appearance mid-week.) He needed a little dose of 'otherness', unlike a priest friend of his, whose character seemed much more in keeping with his vocation; man and role becoming (and staying) one. Whereas for him, it was not at all seamless; it was a daily yet beautiful struggle and with by now years of experience, he had learned it was doable all the same. On this particular Wednesday, he had already greeted Mrs Sullivan, his part-time secretary, and had left clear instructions to his housekeeper regarding the new curate, Father Paul.

The tall, once imposing figure, whose upper back had only recently started to curve a little, would very soon be slipping quietly out of the side door of the sacristy as he looked towards the new day, already unfolding. But first his habitual quick check of the pews and even quicker tidy up of stray missals and other left behind paraphernalia. The church building would then stay open for the following hour for the purpose of quiet reflection and private prayer. During mass that morning he had been aware of a few 'unknown' faces, floating forward from the distant reaches of his church. Not a completely unusual situation…but one that often caused him to smile to himself in that the owners of such faces, believing that their semi-hidden state protected their identity, stood out all the more.

He had already carefully wound the checked lambs-wool scarf a parishioner had given him a few birthdays ago around his neck and had noticed that his jacket, kept for walks and always at the ready on the hat stand by the Presbytery door, was looking a bit over grubby and frayed at the cuffs. It also smelled of months of nicotine absorption but Father John, as a fairly heavy smoker, was totally unaware of this minor detail. All in all he was satisfied that this jacket with its beige colour, so efficient at disguising general grime and minor stains, kept him warm and dry. It still had many years of wear ahead, but did he?

The jacket was thus in line for a happy and probably seldom to be cleaned future, but as for John, the bathroom cabinet mirror had once again greeted him with the daily reminder that he certainly wasn't getting any younger: his cheeks were looking more sunken; his once forget-me-not blue eyes seemed more weighed down by the side folds of his eyelids; his jowls more slack. Of course should he decide to smile back at his reflection, then he had instant proof that his face could still be salvaged, redeemed, transformed. The power of a smile (you can even pick your favourite) and a clean shave!

On reaching the back of the church, his eyes were drawn towards a piece of paper, pristine white and probably twice folded, which had been left on the shelf where the hymn books were stacked. He picked it up, deciding that though not as urgent as a wallet find, it should be checked over all the same and only then discarded.

His few hours of Wednesday freedom had just come to an abrupt end.

Father John O' Flaherty's plans would suddenly have to wait. His one impulse was that someone, not too far from where he was standing now, might be in need of help and was possibly even asking for it, asking him in particular. He made a quick dash outside the church looking right and left, right and left repeatedly. It was still quite early and the street practically empty. So John crossed the road and entered the little park opposite. He made a couple of rounds. Nothing. No one who might fit the bill. Disappointed, though still hopeful, he sat down on his favourite bench, put on his glasses and reread those painful, nihilistic words over and over.

All afternoon he was drawn back to the piece of paper among his many other duties.

He was seated most of this time at his round multi-purpose table, which over the years had seen human life in many of its facets: used for (mostly) solitary meals; the writing of homilies; heated church meetings; and once, on the night of the Easter Vigil, a certain baby had had his nappy changed upon it, just before he was due to be proudly carried into the church, a vision of innocence and fresh hope, ready for the Sacrament of Baptism, enveloped in a white gown, lovingly hand embroidered by a sentimental aunt.

But in all probability, Father John had never actually been made aware of this particular usage!

A nagging sixth sense warned him, whether he liked it or not, he would one day be meeting the desperate creator of those rambling lines and stark images. He spent a good while reading them over to himself and then out loud, ultimately arranging them as lines of poetry but otherwise leaving them as they were, free of any punctuation. He had very little experience of literary criticism, he greatly admired the work of Heaney and some of Hughes' poems had once cast a powerful spell over him yet now, he found himself counting how many words started with the letter 'b' and reflecting on the explosive effect of all those angry 'b' sounds when read aloud. He had become more aware of the many references to death and destruction, torture and insanity, the futility of life, suspended between each line.

Having concluded early on that it was not a matter for the police, he would have been laughed out of the police station; he was on his own looking for clues, as to the identity of the writer. John had, in fact, spent a couple of afternoons off and on, playing detective, and a morning or two looking out for whom he thought he was searching. The only way to proceed, albeit naively, was to continue believing that there had been in his church, two or three days beforehand, a lost and demented soul. And Father John's only option was to locate him or her (but guessing the writer was male), before it was too late, and get him the help he needed; medical, spiritual or a combination of the two.

Needless to say, the possibility of it all being a ruse; a sick joke played out to test John's true colours, never left his thoughts. And if genuine, why hadn't the writer just turned up for help at the Presbytery or his family doctor?

Here are some of the lines which had in turn caused our priest such torment:

The big bang. Was it just one or did I fall into others?

A black hole barnacle black interminable black black in the bottomless blackness black pain back pain knots of barbed wire black chasm falling blind backwards downwards bog thickness of black burnt and blistered blackness brittle brutal.

Being not living buoyed broken heartbeats bone cold bone beaten below zero blind blackness belsen brutal life bruised blueblack and battered bedlam beached and bleached of the life force blown out belched out blackbelted and back bent not whole broken bits blowing away hells bells bats wings beating bees in the blackness buzzing in life's bleak house backstreet black bombs in the blank bank account of individual identity.

Black bermuda hole of broadmoor branded and burned by blackness belched out by Beelzebub bitter breath life bankrupt bradyblack bleeding blossoms of black blood, black bile no life business here blacks bed is no bed the bulging black balloons blow and burst like giant berries in the blizzard.

The barracuda bride in black bridal gown bears me down brain dead.

18

Chapter 3

The Healing Angel

St Raphael's had twice been John's home and during each residency he had delved into the mists of its history and had, in a modest way, added to it. Yet he'd never managed to uncover the origin of the choice of its name; this particular Archangel; Raphael's link with his Parish; someone's brainchild never recorded for posterity. It was enough for the priest to know, however, that their angel's business operated within the realm of healing.

Father John's mind was by now immersed once again in the past life of his dear parish.

The past 80 or so years had been a time of enormous upheaval inside and outside of the universal church, but here at a local level, it had all started with the buying of a nondescript piece of land, once part of a grand Victorian estate, for the sum of £500. As the years went by, and after much scrimping and saving, a church, school, presbytery and convent were erected upon that land, populated by a fairly closed community of priests, curates, nuns and lay teachers serving the increasing numbers of local Catholics, often the sons and daughters of immigrant families and over the course of time coming from a range of ethnic backgrounds. A growing community which saw and survived a devastating church fire, two World Wars and Vatican II. The Parish of St Raphael's was born.

The coming of the railways to this part of the world had brought with it teams of Irishmen, digging and laying track, who needed to find a place of worship in what was then a mere village. In fact the nearest chapel, where Sunday Mass was celebrated, required a four-mile walk there and four miles back. Many of the men were beginning to settle here and even bring their families over the Irish Sea. Consequently, the very first 'church' erected on the piece of land in question was a glorified hut made of corrugated iron; a result of much faith and fervour nonetheless; a huge feat also because for hundreds of years, Catholic worship had been outlawed in England, instigated by a world famous (and local) sovereign, King Henry VIII, once a devout member of the Catholic Church himself.

As everyone knows, however, laws can be repealed from one day to the next, but it can take the passing of many generations for people's hearts to be touched, moulded and then gradually transformed.

In spite of some sporadic local opposition to this new parish springing up in such a central position within the village, a phenomenon taking place in many English towns, those strange newcomers, who took their moral orders from the Pope, Peter's representative on Earth, said prayers in Latin, and confessed sins they knew they would soon be recommitting, were generally left alone in all their misguided ignorance.

Returning to present realities, Father John had fallen into that very human of traps, having conjured up in his mind a picture – an identikit – of the person for whom he thought he was searching: male in his 20s or early 30s, somewhat unkempt, a wild look in his eyes and probably under the influence of illegal stimulants. He wasn't even certain there had been such a specimen at mass that morning though to be fair, there had been several 'new faces'.

About ten days later, however, he was approached by a quietly spoken, mild-mannered individual, who wanted to meet with him in private. John asked him what it was about and said he could spare him half an hour at 2pm, that same day.

The young man did, in fact, return at the established time (not always the case in his experience.) John ushered him into his study and beckoned him to sit in one the incongruous armchairs, arranged for visitors, which faced his desk.

"So what can I do for you? Father John, by the way."

After a somewhat awkward silence, the stranger managed to squeeze out a reply that he was very anxious to speak in depth to someone trustworthy but didn't know where to start. Father John decided therefore to ask him some generic questions about his life, believing that was the only safe and effective method of breaking the ice and then broaching complex or sensitive subject matter.

"Let's begin with your name then."

"James Newhouse," came the faint reply, with his face angled in such a way that he could, at least for the time being, stare out of the window into the garden and thus avoid any of the priest's own facial reactions to his replies, or make eye-contact.

The priest, gentle and patient by nature, did his best to encourage James to take his time and only answer questions he felt comfortable with. He also called out to his housekeeper, both men by this time becoming painfully aware of the ghastly singing, drilling holes into the walls of the downstairs rooms (and no doubt also upstairs) to make them a pot of tea.

"So, James, do you live locally? Can't say I recognise you."

Their meeting spilled over into the next hour, and without any heavy-handed probing, John was able to form a sketchy portrait of the young man in front of him. 33 years of age; older sister he hadn't seen in quite a while; parents, whom he had always thought of as 'elderly' and somewhat 'remote', who had both died quite recently, a few weeks apart. James tried to explain, albeit with great difficulty, that at this point in his life, he felt totally isolated; that life had isolated him but that he had done nothing to halt the process. He had had friends at school, and later at university, but none of these relationships had ever blossomed into lasting friendships or even looser arrangements built around say twice yearly phone calls. As his life progressed (or rather as the river of months and years flowed by), he took nothing or no one with him from an earlier stage. He had never felt compelled, not even on a whim, to get back in touch with a former acquaintance but only now was becoming aware this was a strange and possibly unhealthy state of affairs.

However, that which totally set him apart from the outside world, according to Father John's inner thinking, was the fact that James didn't have to work for a living; his parents had left him a huge fortune, but as their son saw it, he had neither dependants nor a future to invest in. A rare late 20th century equivalent to an early 19th century gentleman lifted from out of the pages of Sense and Sensibility, John mused to himself. If he needed something, he bought it; if he wanted to take a walk, he just went; if he felt like going to the theatre, or flying to Paris, he just took himself off.

The two men agreed to meet again a couple of days later. The piece of paper had not been mentioned.

After John had made the finishing touches to his next homily and had jotted down a few more points to raise at the forthcoming parish AGM, he sat down with a glass of whiskey in one hand and his pen in the other and scrawled down a few notes about the meeting with James, to keep afloat its momentum and to mull over what had transpired: seems uncompelled by urges; emotionally immature; little past structure to learn from or build upon; 'No man is an island' phrase sprang to mind; still holding a lot back; seemingly unaware of the implications of his economic privilege; intellectually advanced; not uncivil but unable to show much in the way of appreciation; didn't appear to know love but now showing signs of anxiety; a greater awareness of his situation. Could this already be a turning point?

Dear Father John, forever full of optimism.

On the day of their second meeting, John was able to watch James' arrival from his upstairs sitting room window, as the young man made his way up the private road which led to the presbytery. He now noted further details about his appearance that had escaped him during their first encounter: the fact he was quite tall, had a full head of darkish hair, walked rhythmically, though free of swagger, was modestly dressed (and yet on later and closer scrutiny, revealed the wearer's innate good sartorial taste, perhaps inherited from his parents.) As James came more clearly into view, John was reminded of his regular features, somewhat downgraded by the intense expression, his face never once breaking into a smile.

The previous meeting had not then been a waste of time; somewhere deep in James' psyche, he believed that for the time being at least, John could be of some help. At this revelation, John was suddenly filled with a warm rush of contentment, bordering on quiet joy. A parish priest's rare and fleeting reward, wholly emotional.

James and John continued to meet regularly over the next weeks, which ran quickly into months, both men looking forward to the time spent together but for entirely different reasons: for Father John it provided an opportunity to get to know someone who lived a life totally outside the Catholic domain; moreover, James was deep, intelligent and yet also a little elusive, which greatly appealed to the priest's investigative interests. When on holiday, he loved nothing more than devouring a stack of whodunnits with their tortuous plots and subtly (or not) placed red herrings.

He also felt their meetings were having a positive effect on James, and in a very small way, contributing to the healing process.

For James, on the other hand, it was more a case of having found some structure in his life and a purpose almost; nothing revolutionary but in John he had found a highly decent human being, who was absolutely trustworthy and non-judgemental. He had even started to enjoy John's rambling stories about his childhood years spent in Ireland and laugh at his quirky little jokes, delivered more often than not in a played down and deadpan style. And most important of all, John actually listened to him. Was he on the road to recovery? It was probably far too early to tell. James was taking one day at a time and trying out some of the very basic tasks John sometimes set him.

After a couple of months, John felt it might be useful to step up the pace; at their first meeting, James had mentioned a sister. Perhaps now was the time for him to start thinking about the possibility of a reunion. They talked about the Holy Family, families in general, their purpose in communities and society; family ties; John spoke of his own experience of family life; his brothers and sisters. He asked James what he hoped would emerge from a future meeting with Harriet. James replied that he wasn't ready to see her yet. He couldn't even begin to imagine what they might say to each other after all this time but that he would give the matter some thought. Father John proceeded very cautiously from this point and gave James the necessary time to reflect and generally get used to the idea. It would be interesting to see if James would be the one to make reference to it.

Chapter 4
Safely Delivered

It wasn't that Giulia lived predominantly in the past or that she ever deliberately dipped her mind into the warm sea of memory, as Father John was prone. It was more a case of her future, past and present continuously merging and reforming. In fact, some of these memories returned without warning and with such force, they attacked her senses so that the event in question became an actual reliving of each delicious, terrifying or mesmerising moment; moments that burst the ordinariness of day-to-day existence and that punctuate our lives with meaning. Most of the remembered scenes of her childhood centred on her formative years at Fielding House Convent School for Girls. And it was for the most part train journeys which suddenly caused her head to fill up with such flashing images and interconnecting thoughts.

Her father had deposited her at Fielding one fresh May morning fairly soon after their arrival in England. She remembered quite clearly the intense numbness, an emptiness that engulfed her after being left alone in a cold but beautiful room, which she later discovered to be referred to as the Marble Hall. She could sometimes dredge up at will the sweet smell of the lavender perfumed beeswax, which sealed the bannister rail of the mahogany staircase and other pieces of sturdy furniture which occupied the room. She still felt the comforting effects of the painted cherubs cavorting on the ceiling; remembered picture reading the vivid Bible scenes leaping out from the blue-tiled walls, cautionary parables retold in bold primary colours.

After what seemed like hours – each one strung out like stretched elastic – her father finally returned with Sister Agnes at his side. He kissed his daughter first upon both cheeks, left, right, then placed a longer kiss above her forehead, as he clasped her chin in one large deliberate hand.

Giulia's life with nuns in Italy was now transposed into a life with nuns in England.

Her father was a taciturn man, who had never, she believed, been unkind to her, but one who preferred to deploy looks and gestures, rather than utilise verbal communication. She accepted him just as he was, like most children of her age. With few family members or close friends, no other points of reference, she was never tempted then to ask herself if other fathers were any better or worse, more or less affectionate, more or less present in their children's lives.

They had travelled together by train to England, a seemingly endless journey to the young Giulia and yet it was probably then that she started to learn how to make the most of any trivial object that came her way and how, even more importantly, to cope with the boredom that fills up much of our waking hours. At one point she had involuntarily picked up a folded map which had been discarded on the opposite seat of their carriage. It turned out to be a map of England. She had been told very little about the faraway place with the strange name Inghilterra/ENGLAND, but here it was, spread out on her lap; her new country, a mere splodge of green.

She squeezed her eyes shut and clenched her fists to try and conjure up exactly what she did know about it. All she could come up with was that it was ruled over by a king, the weather was always wet or foggy and that English people ate fish and chips (coming out as one word in her head). This was the sum total of her knowledge.

However, back to the map. After having turned it around and upside down a few times, having studied it for its alien place names, totally unfathomable in most cases – her first proper discovery was that ENGLAND was detached, totally separated from the European land mass she had learned about in Italy. Knowing nothing about Scotland, Wales or Ireland, she saw her new country as a green island floating in a sea of blue; sad and desolate. And the more she scoured the map, the more she noticed and fantasised upon. For example, she saw that the English coastline had been designed in such a way, that it looked as if once, in a fit of frenzy, it had taken leave of its senses and made a deliberate choice to flee the continent in the space of a few moments. It had turned its back on its lifetime home with its big upturned bottom positioned in a very rude gesture, and with its feeler hands and feet stretching out for dear life in the opposite direction, far out into the Irish Sea and Atlantic Ocean; a cold watery world, surely far less welcoming. It did later cross her mind that in a much smaller way, she was doing exactly the same.

There would soon be a new language to master. Who would teach her? How long would it take? Would there be a friend for her in ENGLAND? She hoped that the more often she whispered its name, the happier she would become, as regards the reality of her future situation. This map interlude had also left an indelible impression on her young and molten mind.

Giulia eventually discovered that a ferry would be carrying them and their luggage across that steely grey stretch of water (definitely not the blue of the map) called the English Channel, followed by a much shorter series of train journeys than the one which had snaked its way through Italy and France with them on board after which they would arrive in London, England's capital. Her father told her that London was a vast City and that many parts of it were still having to be rebuilt as a result of the bombings of the war. He also told her that it had been founded by the Romans about 2000 years beforehand and they had named it Londinium. England then would have been covered in dark green forest.

This was the news she had been waiting for; a connection. She was not from Rome and it was a long time back in history, but that lone dry fact gave her the fine golden thread she craved, linking her own Italian past and English future. *How strange that a few words, a randomly dropped fact, can make a world of difference,* she thought.

On arrival in the former city of the Romans, Giulia, with her own very Roman name, still had no idea that her father had arranged for her to become a full-time boarder at a Convent School for Girls, or that visits he would pay her after that would become sporadic to say the least. Back in Italy, her aunt had got her ready for that final journey and Giulia arrived on English soil as she had departed her native country, wearing a blue pleated skirt, white blouse and grey V-necked cardigan. Her hair had been plaited with military precision, as it had to stay tidy till London.

She had never liked her aunt, whom she called Zia, but felt guilty as this was the sister of her own father. Giulia had been brought up to accept that all adults had to be shown an unquestioning respect, and that if they were family members, even more so. She found this very difficult. She could certainly play the part of the polite young girl, a near faultless performance, but afterwards didn't live comfortably with herself and the continuous hypocritical act she carried forward.

When she did once broach the subject with her father, he just brushed the matter aside with a shrug and an outward wave of his hand: "Oh you know what she's like; she doesn't mean it; she's had a hard life; she's your aunt."

About three or four times a year, her Zia would pay her a visit at the Collegio Sant' Antonio where Giulia was being educated by an order of nuns, and which was, to all intents and purposes, her only home. The woman did, however, usually take her niece a bag of homemade biscuits and the inevitable packs of ground coffee for the sisters. Surely proof she wasn't as bad as Giulia made out, which only served to make her feel even more guilty.

They didn't make conversation as such but a typical visit would start with Giulia asking how she was, which would be met with a litany of complaints about her incompetent husband (Zio) and how she had to struggle with certain tasks, that men had been put on God's earth to carry out, but never mentioning the fact that Zio, poor man, had problems with mobility and, thought Giulia, was probably suffering from nervous exhaustion as a result of having to live alongside such a horrible woman! She would then mention her daughter, just slightly older than Giulia, (whom Giulia only remembered seeing a couple of times) and be told how well the girl had learned to embroider, how helpful she was around the house and then during the final ten or fifteen minutes of their meeting, Zia would eventually remember Giulia's presence and that her niece would no doubt benefit from another outpouring of her wisdom and advice; her father above all, needed his daughter to remain a '*brava ragazza*' (a good girl) at all times.

Giulia would then sometimes catch sight of her aunt having a private chat with whichever sister was available through the half open door of the visitors' room. Yet, she could never prise out of them what Zia had said about her, or what information her aunt had tried to wheedle out of them. In fact, she had given up asking, as such an impertinent question would inevitably lead to a penance, such as toilet cleaning or extra kitchen duties.

There was, however, one such visit which, following the usual pattern of complaints about Zio, reference to her daughter's common sense and general usefulness, the hard and huffy advice, ended slightly differently allowing Giulia just for a brief moment to catch sight of Zia with her guard down. On saying goodbye, she held Giulia tightly by her wrists, and let out, involuntarily, the word '*magari*' in a strangely whispered and wistful way, realised her mistake and swiftly swept out of the building. Now the word *'magari'* in English means 'if

27

only'. She also thought she had spotted a single tear welling up in one of Zia's eyes! Though perhaps by now that extra detail could have been a mere figment of an untamed imagination.

The two passengers travelled with a couple of slightly battered brown leather suitcases, Giovanni already having arranged for the rest of her possessions – clothes mainly, different sets for the changing seasons – to be sent ahead.

The sisters at Fielding House had kindly agreed to his request to organise a full uniform for his daughter, and had welcomed his generous donation, which was to become an annual offering, over and above the cost of equipment, visits and termly fees always paid for in advance. Giulia had hardly begun to contemplate her new life, as she took in her first gulps of English air.

The lingering smell of her father's tobacco smoke as it rose out of his old pipe would stay with her forever and she would be able to magic up all the interlinking remnants of past Italian memories whenever it wafted her way in the years to come.

Chapter 5
Anglicisation

By the time Giulia had lived about eight or nine months in Fielding House, she felt happy enough. She had made at least three close friends and was growing bilingually with each passing day. It had seemingly all been a success even though no one had ever bothered to explain to her exactly WHY she was there in the first place.

The first few weeks and months, however, had passed by very slowly, each minute nightmarishly painful. In a closed and regimented world where very little happened, the new arrival was constantly stared at by the other girls; girls who launched her way poisonous darts of sneers and seething hatred; she was excluded from their cosy groups and giggles; excluded by her own shameful lack of language; punished for the crime of being new; her foreignness. They gave an ongoing masterclass in group cruelty, and she lacked the sophistication and maturity to see that the reason they were investing so much time in her clearly showed they had a morbid interest and were possibly envious of her good looks, which in turn, made it even easier for them to be nasty. They shut her out but at the same time gave her lots of attention. She allowed them to make her feel worthless; she concluded she was worthless; abandoned and unlovable.

Her nights were even lonelier with no lessons to distract her. She cried herself to sleep in secret until her salty eyes ached raw and her only comfort was that sleep (and possibly dreams) would provide a temporary respite from her suffering. Prayers to God the Father seemed to go unanswered; repeated thoughts and images of Jesus on the road to Calvary convinced her, temporarily, that her small sufferings were nothing compared to Christ's human agony but then came the next day and the next and the deftly targeted cruelty cut and continued without end. She had also tried to conjure up a series of plans involving dramatic escapes from Fielding, yet all the while knowing she had nowhere to go; she didn't even know the whereabouts of her father, that darkly strange man, who appeared and disappeared in and out of her life.

When Giulia did start to speak English, the other girls continued to make fun of her, especially when she mixed up her expressions. She spoke of, making the table and laying the bed, which incidentally she had problems with, especially when tired, for the rest of her life, long after she had fully mastered the English language. They also spotted her bizarre eating habits; how she filled a mug with milk, dropping in a few cornflakes at a time or how she dipped biscuits into the milk, eating the wet bits before they became too soggy to savour; how she would never spread her bread with butter nor try to tap out salad cream onto the side of her plate; how she never bit into an apple or pear, but would always peel and slice it first.

Incidentally, the food was yet another alien adventure for Giulia: no pasta, no olive oil, no garlic or herbs; that awful tasteless sliced bread. Neither did she cope well with the limp, overcooked vegetables. And so many things came out of tins! No one ever seemed to comment on the taste or the preparation of the food at table, unless when on occasion, it was particularly unpalatable. Everything just got wolfed down regardless.

Desserts, however, were far more varied than back in Italy. Giulia soon managed to distinguish bread and butter pudding from rhubarb crumble; spotted dick from apple pie and custard; blancmange and ice cream from lemon meringue. These and other twice-daily culinary treats came to be her only comfort; edible friends, softening if only for a few minutes each bleak and difficult day.

There was no obvious turning point as such, no breakthrough moment, no apparent Divine intervention, just a slow and steady journey towards normality. One by one, the girls eventually bored by their own constant teasing and victimisation of the New Girl, began to accept and acknowledge Giulia as a decent, interesting and attractive fellow student. Neither could they fail to notice just how quickly she made progress in lessons and how she had never reported their questionable behaviour to any of the sisters. They didn't feel quite so pleased with themselves now; not quite so superior; but neither did they feel compelled, whether as individuals or as a group, to ponder too long on their own cowardly contribution to the situation.

At school all the girls were kept incredibly busy, so there was hardly any time for Giulia to miss her father but when a wave of Italian nostalgia did sweep over her, she was usually capable of dealing with it very efficiently, brushing it swiftly out of the way. She enjoyed her lessons and unlike many of her friends, did not find the strict regime of the Fielding House nuns intolerable. In fact, she found it all far more relaxed and the nuns far more docile than those she had shared her life with in Italy. And they had been kind enough to arrange advanced Italian lessons for her at the convent and had accepted her decision NOT to change the spelling of her name to Julia, even though she was beginning to pass as an English girl.

However, she did miss Suor Chiara and Suor Maria Luisa, and wrote to them regularly.

Giovanni always promised to write soon especially when visits became difficult, but these were promises often broken. There had been a couple of letters though to treasure and reread many times. His photograph stood proudly astride a rather narrow bedside table, and it was the last image her mind processed each night before sleeping, and the first image she absorbed on waking, heralding all the hope of a new day. She was determined this face would never become a mere smoky shadow! Like the examples of still life which would one day decorate her walls in paintings, the emotions of her early life were also trapped in photos, mementos and mental images.

The English seasons arrived, merged and passed.

During this time, Giulia's all round progress allowed her to become privy to bits of Fielding folklore, a time she was later to refer to as her Gothic period, which usually manifested itself in talk of supernatural happenings, dangerous staircases and unexplained early deaths at the convent. There was one enticing convent legend which told of a nameless young nun, who had taken a fall on the library steps and had broken her neck, resulting in her death. In the wake of this tragic accident, the stairs were thoroughly checked and examined for any clues pointing to the likely cause of the fall. However, nothing tangible came to light; no slippery steps; no missing bits of stone; nothing poking out. To make matters worse, a chain of identical incidents was to follow, always when the victim was on her own, and it was said, falls always took place on the fourth step. And the body was always found in an embryonic position at the bottom of the staircase…

There hadn't thankfully been any such accidents for many a year, but lingering phenomena, such as creaking stairs, humming noises, circles of light, misty patches, a chair that rocked spontaneously had all been witnessed by a number of staff and girls alike.

31

There was also a tale which surfaced regarding a different part of the school. Giulia learned there had once been two nuns in the convent, who despised each other, in spite of their holy vocations and daily prayers offered up to become more Christ-like. One day, a blazing row erupted between them and one nun felt compelled to push the other over the bannisters, the young woman falling the full drop – three or four flights of stairs. She was inevitably killed outright. A small statue was later commissioned in her memory and placed in an alcove above the entrance to the building. One day the 'killer' nun who had lied about her part in the tragedy, walked past the alcove and was instantaneously flattened by the securely fixed statue, which had flung itself at her in an act of vengeance. The statue was consequently removed, wrapped in a blanket, and put away forever – thus not destroyed – in a large wooden chest. The permanent space in the wall left an empty, forbidding chill in the air to all those who passed by, especially those of a sensitive disposition.

Such school myths, legends and stories were the lifeblood for the pre-hormonal Giulia and her friends, who willingly drank down in gulps the dangerous cocktail of romance, horror and adventure.

The girls' uniform happened to be a universal navy blue, a colour which suited everyone and one still used widely to this day. But in those days, there were a few extra accoutrements which could best manifest the high standards the nuns promoted for the turning out of such fine young ladies. The younger girls wore socks, and later stockings held up by garters. The capacious dark blue knickers came complete with side pocket for handkerchiefs or other girlish secrets. White gloves were worn in winter and summer alike. Giulia loved all these alien customs, especially when the navy-blue velour hat was replaced in late April with the straw boater.

It was her very favourite item and testament to the fact she was gradually evolving into a genuine English girl both to herself and to the outside world. This symbolic straw hat also held precious links with the Saints' Days and school trips, mainly taking place in the long and lovely Summer Term, which signalled high teas; cakes bursting with jam and whipped cream; a day at the seaside with candyfloss and vanilla ice cream, usually somewhere along the south coast; the visit to Whipsnade Zoo; the Fielding House Feast Day, whose precise date she had since forgotten but knew was sometime in July. The pretty little convent chapel in later years destined to become a mere dining hall; her introduction to the horse chestnut tree in early autumn, and the brave new world of secret conker fights, absolutely forbidden by those strict nuns.

All this was family.

By now such memories were whirling and heaving within her; the orchard, the walks in Medleys Park, the processions around the gardens on the Feast of Corpus Christi, the huge thermometer which hung on the outer wall, other torchlight processions to the grotto, cold and mesmerising, the trees festooned with multi-coloured fairy lights, the tableaux created by the students of sacred scenes illuminating the deep significance of Christmas and Easter; the rose garden tended so lovingly by the older sisters; the cemetery; the midnight feasts.

Chapter 6
Heads, Baskets and Other Nightly Goings On

There were four houses at Fielding, dedicated to four key New Testament women:

Martha, who had stopped carrying out household duties, in order to listen to Jesus; the House which promoted the discipline of listening to the wisdom and experience of others.

Magdalen, (Mary Magdalen), who had totally transformed her life after meeting Jesus; delivering the message that it was never too late to change for the better, and that each day allowed us an opportunity of making that new start.

Veronica, who tradition tells us, had wiped the blood, dirt, tears and sweat from Christ's face on his way to Calvary. Bold active service was the focus for girls in this house, and this was where Giulia had been assigned.

Elizabeth, Mary's cousin, who had carried John the Baptist in her womb, while quite elderly but Giulia had long forgotten the connection linking this particular Gospel story and Elizabeth House's aspiration for the girls in its care.

It was not only the nuns who had lofty spiritual goals to nurture.

One spring Saturday morning, Giulia would never forget it, a group of girls from Veronica House called her into one of the side classrooms, after they had finished morning prep. They had serious looks on their faces and Giulia's first reaction, in spite of deepening friendships, was that their former behaviour was about to start up again. What ghastly ordeal now awaited her? But she couldn't think why. Within a sighful of seconds, it appeared her bravely fought new world was now once more in jeopardy. She was made to sit down, and as the girls took up their places around her, was handed a letter. Then in this uneasy atmosphere, one girl stood up, cleared her throat, all ready to make her pre-rehearsed announcement:

"Giulia, we have brought you here because we owe you an apology. A few of us went to speak to Father Murphy, when he was last here, because we were feeling awful about how we've treated you. It was quite a difficult meeting. We were embarrassed and could hardly bear to look him in the eye. He must have thought we were all really horrid. But funnily enough once we managed to get the words out, we all felt a bit better. We didn't know how to make it up to you and Father suggested that one thing we could do would be to write you a letter. Please read it later when you're on your own. Oh and here are some buns I baked yesterday in Domestic Science. I don't know if they are any good but I wanted you to have them. Sorry, Giulia, sorry for everything. Please try to forgive us," at which point the girls ran out of the room, leaving a bewildered Giulia on her own, not knowing whether to laugh or cry!

Much later that day, when the ebb and flow of twilight was magically filling the sky, Giulia sat down to write a longer diary entry than usual. She always wrote in Italian, partly to keep her written thoughts private and partly to keep a grip on her mother language, which she feared was rapidly waning. Looking back on this period of her life, Giulia realised that although she had never tried to forget or blank out such painful experiences, neither did she dwell on them, preferring to settle for the outcomes; the bigger picture.

Dear Diary,

Such a mixture of emotions today; a sudden fear that the bad days were returning and then total relief; the apology, the letter. I never ever thought they would say sorry but instead Fiona started to talk to the others about how she was feeling and this is the outcome.

Who'd have thought it? My prayers have been answered in a way I could never have imagined. I am blessed; I am a survivor; I have come out of this very strong, stronger than before; I am re-born. I think I have forgiven them; it's hard to say. I will see how I feel in a few weeks. I think they really are my friends now.

All this has brought us together; a deeply shared experience.

The nuns' own order was incidentally named The Sisters of the Divine Revelation, and the Fielding House young ladies had, behind the scenes, changed the word 'revelation' into 'revolution', which they thought was outrageously witty and modern, never believing for one minute that the nuns had ever picked up on this delightful play on their name which conjured up wild images of

35

guerrilla nuns with berets and machine guns on craggy mountain passes. But the adult world, even that of the sisters, should never be underestimated by the young, as grownups inevitably know much more than they are often prepared to reveal and this was definitely the case regarding their colourful nickname! Unbeknown to the girls, perhaps the joke had backfired after all? Giulia had reacted differently to such an act of verbal bravado; she smiled internally thinking that Jesus Himself might also have preferred the newly chosen version of their name!

There happened a period of great intensity which coloured one of the school terms. It was given over, outside of the classroom, to the meticulous planning and playing out of scenes inspired by the French Revolution. For some unknown reason, it had already become quite fashionable that academic year for the girls to adopt French expressions *mon Dieu, sacré bleu, comme ci comme ça and* so on and pepper them into their everyday English conversations, much to the annoyance of their teachers. Giulia and her friends went much further. Their own dramatic tribute to French culture dominated all their free time and private moments. Excitement was heightened further when Laura discovered from her older sister that there really had been a couple of French princesses, who had attended Fielding House long ago, two royal sisters in fact. Their presence at the school had had a connection with the political situation in Revolutionary France, not something the friends knew much about. But their energies became more and more consumed by their own dramatic production, a Gothic-style masterpiece, which they planned to show all of the girls in Veronica House with a series of forbidden nightly performances. Until then their plans would have to remain secret, their nightly comings and goings clandestine!

The event which had triggered such behaviour turned out to be a history lesson based on the life of the founder of the nuns' order, Sister Bénédicte, a courageous and obstinate Mother Superior of French origin, who had purchased Fielding House about 100 years beforehand. Her complete opposite in looks and character, Sister Bridget, old and rambling (even when she was young!), was taking the class but inadvertently ended up feeding the subversive yet beautifully turned out young students, some of the more sensational details of the bloody Revolution, describing the horrors of La Terreur, and completing the picture with the infamous '*tricoteuses*', those tenacious and feisty females, as they sat in rows with their knitting, making up a daily audience all over Paris, just inches away from the savage beheadings.

Not long after this ground-breaking lesson, cotton sheets started disappearing from the laundry cupboard, at least the smaller ones, so that some of the girls, alias unfortunate royal escapees, once decapitated, could be deftly transformed into ghosts. The two princesses, it was democratically decided, would be making their escape to England, dressed as rustics. The drama was underway, and under constant review and embellishment.

Shhhhh! Fiona's whispered yet eerie warning still reverberated down Giulia's spine whenever she relived this scene from her precious girlhood. It marked the first of their five or so nocturnal trial runs as the play matured. These special rehearsals took place every few nights in order for the girls to catch up on missed sleep. Much of their free time during the intervening daylight hours was religiously filled with the necessary planning and plotting. At night they would creep their way along the length of the dormitory towards the unsuspecting study; each girl in single file; each young heart beating much faster than usual; on occasion close to bursting point, but all worth it for the forthcoming masterpiece they had so brilliantly and conscientiously devised. So much better than last year's secret moonlit feasts, held on the convent lawn, by now a dim memory.

Laura had come up with the idea of using the wooden hat stand to double as the priest, for someone behind the scenes could easily mutter a few prayers on his behalf. So Giulia wedged a prayer book, carelessly left on the study chair, into one of the stand's prongs, serving as hands, and placed a spare piece of cloth part of their ongoing 'magpie' collection around its 'shoulders'. A separate piece was found to blindfold yet another unfortunate nobleman. Fiona too had met with a moment of genius, so much so she even forgot to get her friends' consent. With a red felt pen she had decorated a confiscated net ball, which had been staring down at them from the top of the bookcase, and had decorated it with spatters and drops of pen blood, spurting out from black penned eyes, holed out as for the cavernous mouth; her own contribution to the final royal solution.

Each participant had been allocated her own set of tasks and responsibilities. Laura, tall and willowy, had made five golden crowns, for which she also had to find a suitable hiding place. Caroline and Giulia worked on the dialogue and Fiona selected the props and costumes, having raided the real princesses' costumes box! Anne had decided upon where the gruesome events were to unfold the square-shaped study, perfectly equipped with wicker basket and sombre high-backed chair, which they could turn sideways for the many beheadings. Pat would narrate the chain of events in her evocative Irish tones.

The girls' own dolls and teddy bears would also be put to good use, showing just how spoilt the royal children had been and how they deserved to die by guillotine, while the vast peasant population had been slowly starving to death. Sound effects, part vocal, part instrumental at reduced volume of course, were to be provided by another Ann (without an 'e'). A young nun had conveniently been teaching some of the girls to knit, embroider and crochet of an evening, but it was the continuous screechy clatter of the knitting needles that best suited the girls' present purpose!

Laura played the part of the Chief Executioner and Giulia glowed proud that she, an Italian, had created the following dialogue:

"You are accused of robbing the poor; you are accused of living a life of decadence and luxury; of not caring about your fellow man; for these crimes you are guilty; no more cake for you; you are a royal enemy to your people; you have betrayed them and now you will rightly lose your head!"

And with these words, pronounced, of course, with a ridiculously overblown French accent, the homemade guillotine crashed down and each severed bloody netball-head fell into the awaiting basket.

At the first proper showing, and at the very moment, when the fake blood, the gruesome head, the crash of the knitting needles and Laura's harsh words had each member of cast and audience totally absorbed, spellbound even, in the delicious sadism of the night, no one had noticed the arrival of Sister Philomena.

"Girls," she hissed menacingly through gritted dentures, "return to your beds at once! This very serious matter will be dealt with in the morning. Leave all your props here in the study."

After each girl, with head bent in real or contrived shame, had sullenly padded their way out of the makeshift Parisian Square, the study with its grim contents, the nun quietly locked the door behind her.

Chapter 7
Vanity and Empathy

School memories continued therefore to be rich and numerous, some tinged with disappointment, others joyful.

On another occasion during her first year at Fielding, Giulia and her classmates decided to play a wonderful April Fools' joke on their young, kind-hearted English teacher Miss Hadway, not a sister, who would surely appreciate the exquisitely planned hoax. Firstly from inside their dismal classroom, they rammed the table against the door, turned off all the lights, just a few minutes before she was due to enter, and then as her even steps were heard in the cloakroom outside, the girls hid under their own individual wooden desks. Miss Hadway was, in fact, furious. Her face burning white hot with rage, they had never seen her like this. Within moments and in dead silence, the lights were turned on, the table meekly returned to its correct position and the girls' heads hung low for the remainder of the lesson.

Giulia learned a lot from this brief episode, which on hindsight revealed quite easily how she and her classmates had totally misjudged the situation and how it had brought to an abrupt end the teacher worship that had been mounting for nearly two terms. It also highlighted just how carried away a group of adolescent girls could become with a simple idea and how quickly things can get out of control!

A few years later, we find Giulia in a French literature class, the girls having been asked to read the first 20 pages or so of *L'Histoire du Chevalier des Grieux et de Manon Lescaut*, in French. Not an easy task, under any circumstances, though for Giulia, something uniquely beautiful was about to happen. After about half an hour of silent, close reading, the teacher asked the girls to shut their books and answer the following question. All the girls who thought they had read that Manon, the novel's charming anti-heroine, was fair-haired were to put up their hands, and then likewise those who thought she was a brunette. An epiphany was in the wings, with Mademoiselle Roger quietly commenting that in nearly every case, the blonde girls had raised their hands for fair; the darker girls for brown.

But the writer, l'Abbe Prevost, hadn't included a physical description of Manon at all. A magical case of empathy in action; the unconscious mind brought swiftly and deftly to the surface, after being swept up into the welcoming arms of a beautiful novel.

This newly revealed knowledge and of the power of books in general (especially fiction) was to remain with her from then on; a moment to treasure.

All these powerful experiences, starting with her own arrival in England; a motherless girl, accompanied by a sombre, distant father; a girl trying to cope with that universal need to belong to the group and yet break free at the same time. Being taken and delivered to a world within a world, of foreign speaking nuns and in the main, privileged if not totally spoilt, girl boarders. Giulia's spirit was, however, rarely broken and she had been blessed with a pleasing appearance and on the surface, an easy-going character.

She loved reading, history and drama, subjects which could transport her effortlessly to other places and epochs. Even from an early age, beauty in all its forms had never escaped her: she could see it in rain; hear it in silence, as well as taste it in music and rainbows. She also loved words; looking at them, lifting up their multi-layers of meaning, tracing their origins and journey to the present day. For her it was tantamount to examining the gorgeous, multi-coloured, many-layered petticoats of a can-can skirt or tutu for a would-be dancer. The sounds words made, their flow when put together, their cadences; rhythms, accents, fascinating in all their variations. She also enjoyed spotting connections between certain words and meanings across different languages.

However, all these little esoteric joys she kept close to her heart. She now had good friends to confide in, but not one ever hinted they experienced even a fraction of the happiness she felt when magically transported away by the beauty of human language, written and spoken.

As a punishment for her part in the French Revolution fiasco, Giulia soon discovered, first by rumour then for real, that Sister Philomena had given away the Queen of the May role for that year to a girl in another house. A few weeks beforehand she had been overjoyed when a tiny piece of paper containing her name had been lifted out of the hat. Now, locked away, her heart stung even more than the tears in her eyes, after having been summoned to sister's study, to hear the unthinkable verdict.

Her friends had often talked about the annual procession with Mary at its centre; the ancient songs and hymns dedicated to Our Lady, Queen of the May; what the girl chosen to be Mary would wear; how she would have been raised up and carried on a type of throne and about the many wild flowers strewn along the path of the procession route. She had even secretly copied out the words from a borrowed Chapel Hymnal of Mary E. Walsh's Queen of the May, entering them reverently, and in her very best handwriting, into the precious leather-bound notebook her father had recently sent her.

Refrain:
O Mary we crown thee with blossoms today!
Queen of the Angels and Queen of the May
O Mary we crown thee with blossoms today
Queen of the Angels and Queen of the May.
Bring flowers of the rarest
Bring blossoms the fairest,
From garden and woodland and hillside and dale,
Our full hearts are swelling,
Our glad voices telling
The praise of the loveliest flower of the vale.

And so on. And she had even highlighted her favourite lines:

As long as the bowers
Are radiant with flowers,
As long as the azure shall keep its bright hue.

Now she felt totally ridiculous, not only because it turned out to be a public humiliation, but also because these very words, which had previously lifted her soul, were now a permanent reminder of her sorry downfall. The haunting tune still cruelly lingered, creeping up on her when her defences were down.

Quite a while later though, she was able to re-open the notebook, re-read those words dedicated to Mary in that simple hymn, and realise that her desire to be Queen of the May that year had had much more to do with her own vanity than a special devotion towards the Mother of God. Moreover, she gradually became aware that the popular appeal of the school's annual Marian event was due more to its pagan qualities than to Christian ritual.

And although she took her punishment in a dignified and contrite manner to the outside world, she harboured no regrets about planning the revolutionary play and performing it, in the middle of the night, to the many girls in her house, sometimes wrong can be right; she felt rightly proud of the passion, sacrifice and sheer hard work she and each of her friends had poured into it. The Queen of the May could wait!

It was shortly after this episode that Giulia came to be acutely aware of her appearance (it never having mattered much before) and even more significantly of the effect it was having on others. Of course she had always checked every morning that her middle parting was straight and that her tie was neatly knotted. The sisters would have expected no less. But this became a different kind of looking in the mirror; it was lingering, admiring, self-indulgent, worlds away from the earlier girlhood indifference. She continued to blossom physically and academically, during adolescence, and girls at the school did from time to time comment on her ocean beautiful eyes, her very long dark hair and on the fact she radiated a lovely sunny smile. Now no mirror was safe; no mirror could simply be passed by; even the local shop windows acquired a secondary use, when a proper mirror was not available.

Paradoxically the original owner and resident of Fielding House, long before it had been turned into a school, happened to be a highly regarded furniture maker, specialising in the creation of huge mirrors bought by titled 18th-century gentlemen to adorn the elegant walls of even grander houses. The girls were told that about a century later Sister Bénédicte had bought the house together with the last remaining contents, and part of these included one such huge mirror, which had never been removed from an imposing dining room. The mirror was thought to have been made by Thomas Fielding himself and yet was kept hidden from the eyes of the outside world.

Giulia had also stumbled upon this room a while ago when she and her friends were still happy to play hide and seek during wet weekends. They were not supposed to enter that part of the building but the sisters were often very busy on a Sunday, attending masses, sorting flowers and ironing albs. To her amazement, she had since discovered that they had forgotten to lock its vast oak door. The room now served two purposes: a place Giulia could secretly escape to when she felt the need to be alone and it was of course where the mirror hung. She felt she looked more beautiful in that mirror than in any other. It also meant that she was now carrying around a new and deliciously deep dark secret, which made her writhe with joy and guilt in equal measure.

Of course it was bound to happen. If we repeatedly carry out a secret fantasy, it is only a matter of time till someone uncovers it. We get sloppy, less observant and even more focussed on the object of our desire. The discovery was made in this case by Sister Agnes, the first sister Giulia had encountered on her very first day at Fielding House. Giulia had always respected her and Agnes in turn had kept an eye on the once lonely Italian girl yet from a comfortable distance. Just as Giulia was leaving the dining room one Sunday morning, having spent a good ten minutes admiring her looks and fantasising about romantic fairy-tale encounters in front of Fielding's full-length mirror, she collided, sideways on, with the nun who was hurrying along that particular corridor.

"Giulia, are you alright? Are you sure, what's the matter? What were you doing in the dining room? You know full well no one is allowed to be in this part of the school!"

Although Giulia had been blessed with a wildly colourful imagination, she was rarely able to invent something (that is, tell lies) when put on the spot!

Hardly believing she was saying the words which were dropping loosely from her mouth, to a nun of all people, she told Sister Agnes the whole truth about her obsession with mirrors, her pleasure at seeing herself in them, her fantasies and how she loved the dining room mirror most of all. Poor Agnes listened patiently, probably never having come across this particular phenomenon before, and tried as best she could, to raise the young girl's awareness as to the many alternative attributes women possessed, and endeavoured to leave her with the idea that it was much better to pursue loftier pastimes; good looks were merely temporary and had incidentally caused the lasting ruin of many of the women who possessed them.

Giulia didn't really understand her final remark but this embarrassing encounter had already produced the desired result: from now on mirrors were out and she soon resolved, yet again in secret and over a period of time, to become a blue-stocking; (she simply loved that image and label!); a composite of Amazon warrior, Boadicea, Elizabeth I, the Suffragettes and Virginia Wolfe!

She also chose, but then quickly discarded, the charismatic Cleopatra, an important historic figure...a woman equally remembered, however, for her physical charms.

Chapter 8
Man and Wife

A young couple were taking a first and tentative walk around a strange and distant village somewhere in the north. It lay stretched out in front of them, haphazardly straggled and huddled along clumps and gaps; low buildings in the main, many whitewashed. The rain had only recently stopped and the air was still thick with moisture. They walked side by side, but never hand in hand, and sometimes the young woman had to take a few extra steps in order to keep up with her companion, although he was only slightly taller than her. The village was to be their home for the next few weeks only. After that they would be travelling south, where a brand-new life awaited them. These were puzzling and awkward days, and it felt as though real life had been trapped in a narrow void.

They could not speak to or understand anything uttered by the people around them. All their modest transactions had to pass through the ears and mouths of the middle-aged couple, at whose guest house they were staying, a husband and wife who had also made the journey there many years beforehand and from the same part of the world. The young woman was clearly ill at ease, completely out of her depth and totally dependent on the man at her side, never forgetting that they were both at the mercy of what God might next launch their way; life having already dealt them some major blows.

Each morning began like the one before, an ugly ritual of her being sick in the shared lavatory at the end of the landing. The young couple, in order to preserve the modesty and sensitivity of those around them, occupied separate rooms on separate floors in the gloomy house run by their compatriots. The unstoppable waves of nausea usually overcame her shortly after breakfast, brought on more by the smell and sound of the food her companion was devouring, than the two slices of toast she herself was grappling with.

There would be no problem getting into the pale blue 2-piece woollen suit hanging up outside the wardrobe door, safe under its plastic covering, a tight-lipped parting gift from her mother.

She was determined to make him a good wife; he had not abandoned her. She knew how to cook, wash, sew and clean; no lack of experience there! However, she secretly hoped that they would not have the same marriage as her mother and father.

So the long damp days passed very slowly – the young man spending them, when not eating, playing cards with fellow guests, and in the evenings watching television programmes he couldn't understand, or going for short walks just to break free from the static gloom of the guesthouse. Sometimes, the owner came to prise him out of the television room, which he often occupied during the day (when, of course, there was no daytime TV to watch) and took him into the garden, proudly commentating on the progress of his many plants, vegetables and fruit trees, in spite of the challenging weather conditions in that part of the world. The younger man listened and nodded at intervals; his day always made better by the regular appearance of the owners' daughter, who would materialise for short bursts and then suddenly vanish into the surrounding mist. She was a wild and beautiful creature, innocent and all-knowing at the same moment; part woman, part child and all the more irresistible for being out of bounds. She spoke both languages better than her parents, creating an even greater mystique. Her name was Flora.

He would lie awake at night, stuck in the same thought that she also lay somewhere under the same roof, perhaps only a few metres from him; he wondered what was going on in her mind, her dreams, and what other treasures lay hidden.

The daily walk became ever more significant for his companion. She too could escape the dull walls and heavy furnishings, breathe in some of the cold and bracing air and even try to start up little conversations. Her heart was bursting, not so much for love, but from sheer gratitude.

Back at the guesthouse, she spent considerable time with the owners, when not alone in her room, offering to help with its busy day-to-day running, and they in return passed on all their worldly wisdom and advice, acquired over the years of life here and there. Mrs Owner also told her to spend more time with her husband to be, and go join him more often in the television room.

Their next walk also gave rise to her longest proper conversation so far with him:

"Been sick again?"

"Yeh, but I'm already feeling a bit better."

"How long is it going to last then?"

"Oh only another few weeks I think, how are YOU feeling?"

"Never felt better! Know what? Just maybe everyone should have the chance of starting again."

"Yes, I suppose so; I'd never really thought of that. Look at Gino and Angela, they've worked hard and made a real go of it and you only have to look at their daughter…"

Neither had it escaped her that he was the one to initiate it. Everything would be all right.

During one walk, which took them much further out than usual, as it also involved their taking a bus, they came across a hitherto unknown stretch of water, whose view from inside the bus had been extinguished by the low-lying blanket of cloud. But upon their arrival, the sun's powerful rays had suddenly burst through, revealing a vast green sea or lake. The speed and beauty of this phenomenon took their breath away yet neither had the words nor the wherewithal to express this shared experience; she could only pull herself closer to him and he accepted her closeness. They had no idea just how long they had spent looking out towards the deep blue horizon, drinking in all the view had to give them, but eventually the woman began to feel cold and suggested they might continue their walk.

It also somehow reminded them of the 'actual' day; the reason for their presence in the faraway village. It was fast approaching, in spite of the seemingly slow wait, a day which would bind and seal their lives forever; a day which would mark the beginning of a new shared way of life in yet another unknown place, amongst people who spoke a different language and lived out different customs. But the woman had little to pine for at home, her former life having been harsh and grinding. And as for her husband to be, he had seized an opportunity, which he hazarded to believe could change his life for the better.

Within a couple of weeks, they were on their way south but to them it still felt very northerly. They would be arriving at their destination by train and a car would then be sent to collect them and their meagre luggage, delivering them to what would be their next home. However, neither husband nor wife had any idea for how long this chapter in their lives would run. It had not been a wedding with photographs or guests; feasting or fun. It just had to take place and be done with. The young woman never expected to refer to it ever again or even try to remember the minutiae of the day.

They now both felt tense and cautious in equal measure and alongside this, the woman also felt an irrational and inappropriate joy for that new life that was growing daily inside her. She did not mention this to her young husband.

But what kind of life would they be able to give a child, once on the outside? Wrenched away from all they knew, like two oversized orphans dazed and manoeuvred into a faraway world, which they found cold and unwelcoming; not even able to ask the time or the price of a bus ticket; greet fellow travellers other than with gestures or exchange opinions about the weather. In addition, neither had been blessed with a sense of adventure or enterprise. Their window on the world was hinged on service, deference, gratitude and survival which left scant vista for dreams or ambitions. They saw themselves as they had been placed up to now; unfortunate and needy, alone except for each other.

And there it was laid out and displayed in all its ornate grandeur, the building they would be occupying. They were overwhelmed by the dimensions of the centuries old structure, suspended between hope and horror and feeling even more diminished by its stature and importance. Had they been of a romantic inclination they could, if only for the few minutes the car was sweeping them up the grand gravel drive, have morphed themselves into the roles of a prince and princess returning from a sumptuous honeymoon in the Orient, about to take up their places at a Royal Palace, gifted to them by generous parents or in the shoes of a benevolent English Lord and Lady of the Manor, ready to dispense mercy and munificence upon the local villagers.

Either side of the sweeping drive ran wide verges of beautifully tended grass and beyond that, in perfect symmetry, sat rectangular ponds, edged with ornamental plant life, channels of water completing the avenue effect! And as they came closer to the main door, they managed to make out a crowd of boys, who then quickly grouped themselves into twos or threes. They were dressed in strange and identical clothing, seemingly green and dark grey and were soon heading in different directions, each boy with a strong sense of purpose, as they carried their books or satchels.

After veering to the left side of the great building, to a part which appeared to consist of many smaller structures, the driver dropped them off silently and sourly, indicating with arm and index finger the small door, by which they presumed they were supposed to enter with their luggage. *"Grazie, grazie mille,"* they called out, hoping the driver had actually heard their somewhat delayed show of appreciation and hoping once again that he might be able to understand what they were actually trying to say.

On entering a poky and somewhat damp smelling reception area, a middle-aged man in uniform arrived swiftly onto the scene and started uttering a stream of unfathomable sounds. It didn't take him long to realise they hadn't followed a single word of his detailed instructions and that their repetition of the word 'Italiano' pointed to the fact that he wouldn't be getting any further without the help of another Italian national working at the school. "Somebody go and get Albert," he called out into a side office, "and fast!"

Their new life together, as man and wife, at St. George's, an all boys' Roman Catholic College and Seminary somewhere in the north of England, was about to commence.

Chapter 9
Mrs Moggs' Monologue

"And so you see, Father, oh God, I've said it; who would credit it? I said 'Father', never thought I'd be able to, like crossing myself, can't ever see myself doing that either, but now well who knows? As I was saying, a while back I got to meet Giulia, looks like ghioolia, doesn't it, when you see it written down? And it took ages to get to know her just a little bit. But for someone like me from my background, well haha the gutter really, it was all a bit like meeting the queen. I suppose after a while I just wanted to be a bit like her, knowing I'd never be able to talk like her or read all them books she's got. Where I come from people like her are like from another planet. But the more we chatted over the weeks and months I got to see the real person, her sort of human side. She might not 'ave the money problems Steve and me has got, but she still has to watch her health, and cope with knowing she's not getting any younger. It's a crying shame she doesn't have any children, don't know about a husband! Haha! She probably gets lonely too. I know I would in that house! I can't say I know many others of her type around 'ere."

"But fair's fair. She's been very kind to me and helpful, like when she helps Mark with his homework and always asks about 'im and his brother. He calls her the Turquoise Lady. She helped my Steve to write his application for his last job and he got it too not to mention the time we had to fill out them forms, just didn't understand what those questions were going on about and she explained it all to us. Have you seen those eyes of hers? Oh and she lent me a scarf once; she called it a 'foolah' or something. It's probably Italian for scarf. It's a bluey-green colour and she then said I can keep it. Anyway, all this got me thinking about church. They're all Catholics in Star House, aren't they? And I wondered if this could help me a bit. It's like having something extra, isn't it? Or something special. I know she plans her week round going to church though she calls it mass; I don't really get that bit myself. But it was when YOU said Father ha ha, look I've said it twice now, that we are all born with a kind of gap, a bit missing deep down inside, and until it's filled we're never at peace. We spend all our lives trying to fill the void? I think that's the word you used…like with TV or drink or drugs or buying clothes or going on package holidays but none of this really works; we're only happy for a short while and then it all starts up again. I didn't really get it at first, but I think I do now.

"Do you know I've spent practically all my life now come to think of it, waiting for something else, something I didn't have at the time: like a party, the weekend, the holidays, the man of my dreams, being older no, not now; if only I was younger now! Or that, that something would come to an end, like school, for instance. And it's sort of wishing our lives away and never living in the here and now. And you said God created us like that, cos he wanted us to know the most important thing that he was our father oooh I've said it a third time now, but I'm talking about God now, not you! So like I said he's waiting for us to return to him, but doesn't force us. Like that we can be really happy.

"But it's still all a bit of a mystery isn't it?"

Gasps for breath.

"But you haven't said anything, I'm not rabbiting on too much, am I? I just needed you to know what I'm like and where my head is and that even though I don't always get things straight off when I first hear them, they do go round and round and round my head, and then it all starts to mean something."

Father John only wishing to interrupt her now, gently replied: "Mrs Mogden, I realised you had a lot to say and needed to say it to someone like me. You also needed enough time to say all those things. It was all quite illuminating. May I leave you with something to do this week? I hope you will find it useful. Try and speak these words and thoughts to God Himself or at least make contact. Choose a good time of day and try this even if you find yourself with nothing to say. Just know you are spending a few precious minutes in His presence. He can read through silence and read into your heart. He will know what you are yearning for. Come and see me again next week and you can tell me how it is going."

Father John remained immobile at his desk for the next few minutes and looked down at his watch, noting that Mrs Mogden (or Mrs Moggs as he liked to refer to her in his head) must have been talking for the better part of 60 minutes. He also realised he had a wry smile on his face, he actually felt it fixed there! However, it was not a smile of deprecation; rather one of marvel and respect. This woman, endowed with so few of life's privileges, had poured out her heart to him in a frank and artless manner, totally unaware that in the process she had perfectly described the human condition. Sometimes all it takes is honest simplicity, the biblical yet misconstrued 'out of the mouths of babes' quote sprang to mind! She had also clearly listened to his words at the recent Baptism she had attended and had tried to make sense of them. How many so-called practising Catholics actually did that?

But if she'd have repeated the words BUT or BIT just one more time, in the manner that only she knew how, he would have had to fully restrain himself from placing his two still capable hands firmly around her neck!

At that moment, James burst into his study, holding up a piece of paper. "John, I went for a walk and suddenly found myself writing a poem, all in the space of about three minutes. Can't believe it, please will you read it sometime and let me know if I'm back on the road to sanity! Have to dash now; I promised Carmela I would pick up some stuff from the dry cleaners! I'll call in on you in a couple of days. Bye! And thank you!"

Trolleys

From a pond's ringside seat
A figure muses at length,
Presumably upon
The heady combination of animated water fowl
And three drowning trolleys.

It could have been in any town,
But not at any time in its modest history;
Ex-village, now exposed
To the wild dreams of town planners
And private entrepreneurs
Who've taken it upon themselves
To interrupt the evolutionary scheme
Of creeping urban sprawl
Ripples surreptitiously leave their mark

And he thinks he hears
The twentieth century voice cry out
In the wilderness…

Okay, so not a bundle of laughs, but a good day for John nevertheless; at least no more black holes.

And Joan, his housekeeper, had just stopped singing.

Chapter 10

A Special Favour

"John, dear John, so good of you to find the time; do come in; it's been far too long; how are you? Shall I take your jacket?"

"Oh thank you, Giulia, yes it has been a while. You look very well by the way, much better than when I last saw you. What a relief, that has cheered me up no end. Thank the Lord! I actually need to ask you…"

"You don't mind coming into the kitchen, do you? It's definitely the cosiest room in the house at the moment. Have you had breakfast this morning?" She led him along the hallway and they both instinctively sat themselves down at the table.

"Oh yes, can't start the day without what I consider to be its most important meal but if you insist, I will allow you to make one of those expresso coffees of yours, haha."

"ESpresso John, eSpresso, with an S. How many times do I have to remind you?"

"I'm not one of your students, Giulia, thank goodness. You know that I'm no linguist. Actually, I've got something to ask you."

"Oh surprise, surprise, it isn't just a social call then, is it? I might have known. But you know I would do anything in my power to help you, John, so there I've already said yes. You can tell me what it is on your way out."

"Thank you, Giulia, I really appreciate that, but it's something you will need time to think about and possibly even discuss with the others."

"Whatever you say but now I want to hear about your trip to Breggan. It is Breggan, isn't it? How is your mother?"

Father John watched Giulia while she rinsed out the 'macchinetta' (that's how she referred to it), charmed by her easy movements, her naturally straight posture, her general elegance, yet none of which ever seeming to undermine the fortunate person in her company. And soon the dark aroma of the coffee was filling the whole kitchen and for Father John this was all part of the pleasure of having someone like her make it for you; you began to enjoy it before it touched your lips. Just as the coffee in question started to spurt and gurgle up into the top part of the macchinetta, Giulia shot up to push it away from the hob's inner heat circle, so that the coffee could spout out very slowly in its thickest, most concentrated form. Ristretto!

"Are you not joining me? Yes, the usual two sugars please! And yes, she's doing pretty well at the moment, never has been one to complain about aches and pains, she must get them though? I know I do and probably mention them too, far too often!"

"Well, yes you do, actually… no, only teasing, only teasing I promise! Goodness you looked crestfallen; so dejected for a moment, I've never seen that side of you before, you were play-acting, weren't you? You know I didn't mean it."

And so their conversation rambled on, a jokey mixture of genuine enquiry and mickey taking; quite different from how they behaved when others were present; both very aware how such verbal fooling around could be misinterpreted by people of a more rigid expectation as to how priests (and others) should behave.

"So my dear, I couldn't help noticing the books in the hallway, what have you been reading since I was last here?"

"I'm reading, or should I say, revisiting Sartre at the moment. It's also brought back so many memories. I probably shouldn't be having this conversation with my Parish Priest but I have to confess I worshipped Jean Paul, the writer, not the Pope haha, for a while, quite a long time ago now I suppose, but his *mauvaise foi* philosophy fitted how I then saw life, exactly. No compromises, no hypocrisy, no keeping up with appearances, just each of us carving out an authentic and individualised destiny. What people always forget is just how hard it is to put that philosophy into practice; it is of course highly individualistic but it does have its own strict code; it is very moral."

"Oh, I'm doing it again, do excuse me, I just get carried away but there are so few people these days to share ideas with! I steer clear of such matters with my students. They are at such an impressionable stage in their precious lives. I wouldn't want any of my ramblings to be misinterpreted and as for the family well, you know how they would react but what about you, John, do you ever allow yourself anymore the luxury of reading philosophical fiction? I know there was a time."

"Funnily enough, Giulia, I have been dipping into the odd collection of poetry recently; something as you know I used to do on a more regular basis. I must say rereading favourite poems from the past is a real eye-opener. It's shown me quite clearly that there are those you grow out of and then those of a more lasting, universal appeal, which you continue to learn from, garnering more insight into human nature in all its forms and that means into yourself! Which all brings me to the special favour, no, no, you really must let me explain now though it involves a certain level of confidentiality but I think I will be able to tell you enough about the matter for you to make a decision."

"What is it? You are making me anxious."

"I've been trying to help somebody, Giulia, and I believe a certain amount of progress has already been made. I was wondering if you would consider giving him a kind of home, I suppose, here at Star House, just for a short while as he continues to improve. It is certainly not my intention to put any pressure on you if you say no, that is fine. I won't even need to hear your reasons…and you have my word that I will never mention it again. Of course he knows nothing about my plan and there's every chance he won't even go along with it. I am not asking you to help him in any other way. I suppose in essence it's normal everyday life that I'm asking to offer him. Family life, different age groups, comings and goings, family meals, Sunday lunch, the odd celebration."

"I gave you my answer as soon as you arrived, John; we'll give it a chance; in fact, I'm intrigued. Who is this person? What problems does he have? I suppose he's looking for work, doesn't he have a family of his own?"

"Well, all in good time, I will tell you everything I deem appropriate and thank you, Giulia, thank you absolutely. You may not be the typical mass-going parishioner, but I'll have you know, in terms of Christianity, in action, you stand out a mile, bless you, bless you!"

Giulia and Father John agreed to meet again in a few days, after he had had a chance to talk over his plan with James himself. At least something was in place, which gave the priest a little more time to catch up on Parish business. As ever, he felt energised and invigorated by seeing Giulia again, but best not to entertain or analyse thoughts about her ongoing effect on him. He was happy enough in the knowledge she was there.

"James, I've had an idea, it's a bit of a crazy idea too but tell me honestly what you think. I think I'm right in saying that a certain amount of, let's call it progress, for want of a better word, has been made over the past weeks, even though neither of us has referred to it as such, you've come out and about with me, you've helped me a lot here at the Presbytery; you are genuinely showing a much greater interest in life; you now seem to be engaged in things around you, and it's wonderful for me to observe all this. But that also begs the question, where do we go from here? Hence my plan.

"I've been giving the matter a lot of thought and this is the best idea I've managed to come up with. For many years I've known a woman called Giulia, Giulia Cristaldi. She lives in the Parish, in a very large house, a house she shares with family. Lorenzo will soon be moving out; he's actually getting married and his going will free up even more space, though he won't be going far; he's bought something only a few houses down, along the same road. There will be a lot of noisy coming and going, general bustle I suppose and don't you agree that would be a good sort of place for you to move into during the next stage in your life? They are all so busy; they will hardly notice you and you can gradually involve yourself as you see fit. You can even pay them a little bit of rent if you wish?

"And if you do agree, if you say yes, it will be up to you entirely how much or how little you decide you want to tell them about yourself and your life. Of course I've mentioned it to Giulia already and she's happy about the arrangement. She's an incredible woman and all she knows is that I've been helping you and that moving into the house of a big busy family would allow you to take the next step. So what do you think?"

"I don't know, I honestly don't know, John. I must say you've taken me completely by surprise. Of course I appreciate all you've been doing for me, are doing for me; I'm not even Catholic, for Heaven's sake, or have any intention of ever becoming one, but living with a strange family I probably have nothing in common with, what are they? Italian? Why would they want someone like me hanging round their house? I'm in my 30s, and this would make me a lodger, a lodger, can you believe it? I must be coming across as really ungrateful but no I'm sorry, I don't think I can go along with your plan."

"I understand entirely your position, James. I thought this was probably how you were going to react. I did warn you it was a stab in the dark. Don't give it another thought. I should be seeing Giulia again next week, so I will tell her."

Now changing the subject completely, "I got in touch with Harriet, she sent me a lovely long letter in fact and even though she doesn't feel ready to see you yet either, the tone of the letter leads me to believe it's only a matter of time; she's still feeling hurt and rejected that you've made no effort in the past months and years to see her and the boys, 'innocent victims' she calls them in this sorry business. She even said that she would think about sending you a photograph of them. Of course my letter must have come as quite a shock for her, even though as you know, I tried to word it carefully, not wanting to upset her further or put her under any more strain or pressure. Let's just sit back and allow time and the Holy Spirit to work their magic!"

Chapter 11
Lorenzo il Magnifico

It had been a tiring day for Giulia and she could feel the early signs of a migraine creeping up on her. Twinges always started just above her right eyebrow and then slowly made their odious journey downwards to her ear. She took a couple of pills, having learnt a good while beforehand that just letting it go or using mind over matter tactics simply didn't work as cures. She had also learnt over time that her migraines were often followed by a short rush of euphoria, as she experienced the tail end of disappearing symptoms, sometimes up to a couple of days after they had first begun. A pure and unforced joie de vivre invaded her being, reminding her yet again, just how privileged she was to be alive; to have been selected for human life in the first place. So paradoxically, they also gave her something to look forward to.

The pills were not going to work completely, she knew that, but they did often manage to take the edge off the pain and allow her to continue functioning.

She also decided to make herself a coffee. A friend with a nursing background had once told her that coffee could help combat the overwhelming pain but Giulia had never worked out if this remedy was wholly or only in part effective as although she had become fairly expert in the management of her migraines, each one was slightly different, unique in its own horror. After installing herself in her favourite armchair in a corner of the darkened drawing room, she began sipping the coffee and warming her hands which were spread around a comforting blue mug.

She soon caught sight of a photograph, whose face was staring out at her from inside a silver frame on the dresser. It was a photo of Lorenzo, that is, a past version of Lorenzo, when he was about 11 or 12 years old, soon after she had met him in fact. His deep-set black eyes stared out blankly, and she was once again reminded of her own stupidity, another fine lesson in humility, as Father

John had described it, regarding the spiralling plans she had once concocted for him. But he had been a beautiful child. Perhaps without the classically perfect features one would expect for such a description, and yet for Giulia this made him even more beautiful, even more unique, in a wild, unfinished kind of way as though the master sculptor had been called away and had never returned to complete the finer touches. The photo revealed an already long aristocratic face partly hidden by long hair, dark and silky, which fell either side of his cheeks in naturally tight waves much to the erstwhile dismay of his father, commenting disparagingly at the time that his son was becoming a '*finocchio*'; a '*frocio*'. Whereas for Giulia, completely indifferent to possible sexual proclivities, saw in Lorenzo the makings of a poet, a philosopher, a man of letters.

For so many weeks she had taught him, coached him, advised him, steered him towards the noble future she had mentally laid out for him. And uncharacteristically for Giulia, she had shut her eyes to the swiftly emerging reality, that although he may have had the looks of a musician or aristocrat, he possessed none of the talent, intellect, originality or desire, possibly the most important component of them all, to realise her ambitions for him. She remembered that the highly respected piano teacher she had hired for him, had told her early on, and in no uncertain terms, that she was wasting her time and money on him, he lacked talent and application so why torment the poor boy?

Giulia froze at this moment, remembering the cruel and unbearable pain of being fed a hard truth, far, far worse than her present migraine. It got worse; she hadn't listened to the piano teacher, writing off his advice as the words of someone who had probably been teaching for far too long and who had lost the necessary patience and inspiration for his chosen profession. Or maybe he hadn't chosen it after all. Of course that was it! He himself would invariably have wanted to become a revered composer, a concert pianist, a famous conductor. She had by now turned the tables and written him off completely, together with his unwelcome words!

However, it was interesting she now noted that she never did endeavour to replace him and that Lorenzo never even bothered to ask her why.

So Giulia continued to refer to Lorenzo as her 'Lorenzo il Magnifico', much to the bewilderment of his family. She had once tried to explain to his parents that a man of this name and title really had existed and how he had played a key role in the Renaissance back in 15th-century Florence. However, their eyes soon glazed over, signalling a total lack of curiosity as to what she was droning on about, what could all this possibly have to do with their beloved son?

And they were right. She even once shoved a picture of the 15th-century Lorenzo under their noses, which revealed a mediocre male figure complete with squashed nose, and underneath this image, a description of him which made reference to short legs. Their Lorenzo was going to be tall and handsome!

In fact a residue of earlier hankerings concerning Lorenzo continued to lurk, biding their time, and then all of a sudden attack her sensitivities. If only she had known him as a child, from babyhood even then surely she would have been able to shape and mould him into the young man she believed he was destined to be.

Now curled up in the oversized armchair, the owner of the migraine allowed herself the luxury of musing over past failures. It would have been so much easier to block such an embarrassing interlude. However, she felt it was important once in a while to face these brutal truths, as it helped to recalibrate her own self-knowledge; eliminate any signs of rising self-importance. It certainly wasn't a wholly masochistic act. This Lorenzo madness did have its repercussions after all: it eventually gave Giulia an insight into the elusive world of parenthood and demonstrate how, that in some cases, parental love and ambition can get confused, to the detriment of the child. Years later she had even concluded that parents were much better off having children of average intelligence, who were evenly balanced; well grounded; far removed from the pathetic ambitions of personally frustrated parents. Genius would after all always find a way of seeping or bursting out if it were there at all.

And what was genius anyway, but yet another form of loneliness and isolation?

Giulia eventually dozed off, yielding to the power of the unconscious state, and didn't stir until about two or three hours later, when she was woken by the comings and goings of Mrs Mogden. Oh yes, it was her day to polish the downstairs furniture.

The joy, albeit short-lived, of forgetting what day of the week it was, or the time of day even; the slipping off life's carousel and only jumping back on when ready or rested…

All those thoughts about past personal misdemeanours gradually gave way to thoughts about Lorenzo's imminent wedding in Southern Italy. To all intents and purposes, it was an arranged marriage; a consequence of his being whisked away to Sicily by a close friend of his father. The girl in question was called

Serafina. A photograph of her had been brought over for family inspection and approval and everyone had agreed she was absolutely beautiful and, in the case of his parents, they were relieved he would be marrying an Italian girl, a Catholic, therefore an unworldly girl, who would have fully understood the sacred (and therefore permanent) state of marriage. For Lorenzo she would be giving up the only life she knew and starting a brand new one in England. One wondered whether the word love had ever been mentioned, so important an ingredient in the way marriage was perceived by contemporary English minds and those of the western world in general. One wondered also if they had spent any time at all alone together!

So Lorenzo, magnificent or not, would very soon be leaving Star House, to take up residence in a new marital home, a few doors down the lane, with a young bride he hardly knew. And the whole family with its small, tight-knit entourage of friends, neighbours and work acquaintances, would be travelling to Italy to be part of their wedding celebrations. Of course many of the guests would be combining their stay abroad with their annual summer holiday and not everyone was as well off as Lorenzo's family had turned out to be. Giulia had not enquired as to why the marriage was not going to be held in the bride's hometown in Sicily, but instead in a beautiful Cathedral on the Costa Amalfitana. This was surely an unusual break with tradition?

Both far too young to marry, Giulia mused but then, halting such thoughts in mid-stream, decided she had no right to be judgemental. As a couple, they had everything necessary to face a bright future: they were young, attractive, healthy, financially sound and enjoyed a high level of family support. They had a house nearby. There would be babies.

And then, in and out of a gossamer sleep, her thoughts drifted back in a circular motion, back to Lorenzo de Medici and the city of Florence itself, cradle of the Rinascimento!

Giulia had twice visited Florence, two completely different experiences! And she was about to revisit them now in her state of demi-sleep.

The first had been a Fielding School Sixth Form trip, lasting a couple of weeks and designed to inculcate some last-minute culture into the girls, before they left behind their formal education to take up their place in the world as mature, erudite and sophisticated young ladies. And what better destination than Firenze (Florence)? Giulia, like the other girls, had been looking forward to it for weeks. Her friends, in particular, had begun to demonstrate a sudden burst of interest in Italian and kept asking her how to say quite banal phrases, such as "I love you" or "Where is the Arno?" and how to spell Brunelleschi and Botticelli.

In fact their stay in Firenze was to take place about ten years before that sacred river burst its banks, producing the worst flood for over 400 years. Dozens of lives would be lost; the whole city totally unprepared for the impending horror and havoc. The water levels rose rapidly to 22 feet and Firenze's vast number of treasures were destined to be lost or damaged: books, illuminated manuscripts, fine art masterpieces, frescoes and so on but for Giulia and her friends, that was an unthinkable disaster wedged firmly in future time.

Santa Croce merged into the Uffizzi into Santa Maria del Fiore into the Ponte Vecchio and on into Palazzo Pitti.

How could a lively group of 17- and 18-year-old girls, all travelling around together, all set to embark on life's adult adventures, possibly take in and retain those long and romantic sounding place and people names, all those dates and religious cum historical facts going back centuries?

On the other hand, they had enjoyed looking out for the ubiquitous Medici signs and symbols as they charged around, and then arguing amongst themselves as to who had found the highest number! Their main concerns centred on when and where they were next going to be fed, trying out a new flavour of ice cream, and asking permission to visit the San Lorenzo outdoor market after the torment of the continuous flow of churches and museums. In many ways, Giulia was no different from the others; however, she did make a promise to herself that she would, one day, return to this beautiful city and take in all the sights properly and on her own, research the lives and works of her future Renaissance heroes, and sit for hours in front of The Birth of Venus; come to know Michelangelo's David, who already both thrilled and frightened her in equal measure.

Chapter 12
Paradise

Once in a while, peace spreads her gentle wings over us and for a few hours life also hovers pain-free.

The eagerly awaited day finally arrived and Giulia together with the rest of the wedding party climbed aboard La Perla Partenopea, which would carry them elegantly to their destination further along the tortuous coastline, about an hour away. As to be expected, there was a constant buzz and bustle aboard, often punctuated by loud shouts and bursts of laughter which marked the excited anticipation of the day ahead. There seemed to be a hundred children rushing about in their patent shoes all over the deck; the girls, regardless of age, all dressed like dolls with the requisite bows and flounces; the boys, like miniature gentlemen, complete with slicked back hair, lightweight dress-suits and bow ties. It was already warm and most guests had brought along their wedding outfits in small suitcases, others preferring to travel light, but also having to make doubly sure they weren't allowing unsightly criss-cross creases to attack their expensive and carefully chosen garments.

The importance of a *'bella figura'* culture, which cut through all social class boundaries, had survived the more faddy fashion-based tendency of English shores and was in full evidence. Most guests here today were after all of Italian origin, even if they had lived most of their lives somewhere in Britain.

Those guests slightly less concerned about appearance and sartorial perfection just wore linen, the perfect material for a summer's day on the Mediterranean Coast; it starts out creased and stays creased. Perfect for attracting the more intellectual, less materialistically inclined conversation companion; though definitely a minority species!

Nearly every guest would also be carrying the all-important envelope, holding a monetary gift, which years beforehand would have been pinned directly to the bride's dress, presenting by our standards today, a truly vulgar picture. Thankfully that particular tradition had been dropped! But all the adult guests would have had to think very carefully about how much they would be giving. It was no easy matter, with so many points to be considered: how closely connected they were to the family of the bride or groom; how much it was probably costing the bride's parents for each guest's presence on the day; how generous the bride's family had been in the past for similar events when they had been guests; how much others were likely to give, as it might come out at a future date that a certain person had been particularly kind or miserly; and so on. It came down to family and community politics.

But those with the flimsiest of family ties would merely have bought a material gift, hoping that it would be still be well appreciated, once back in England.

For most of the short journey Giulia kept herself to herself. Nobody seemed to mind though; everyone knew or knew about Giulia. Armed with book and pen, which she quickly slid out of her ample leather shoulder bag, she scrawled down notes about how she felt and about everything she was able to pick out along the way. Of course she delighted in the sunny, marine atmosphere that surrounded them; who wouldn't have been moved to happiness? But she also had to deal with those deep-down churnings in the pit of her stomach, as she was returning to a geographical home she didn't really know, (that powerful word HOME again) but that had shaped generations of her family, possibly over thousands of years and a home which still secretly resided deep inside her, like an indelible mark. How strange it had been that it was her own father of all those people to break that invisible yet golden line. She felt a primeval urge to cry out to the souls of past, yet unspoken of, family members and let the gentle sea breeze carry her message to them: *Hello I'm here, I've come back, I'm with you now.*

So many invasions, so many takeovers by the Greeks, Romans, Normans, Spanish and so on, her Samnite Hirpini ancestors, subjugated by a variety of tribes and royal households; repeatedly moulded and coloured by different cultures.

At a later date, she wrote up this version of the boat trip in another treasured notebook.

Gouged out of pitiless rock I saw at once clusters of tiny village structures, painted across the palette of Neapolitan ice cream colours (the English version), structures which proudly clung to the rocks, distance perfect. The boat glided noisily on a dark turquoise sea, as the view of the coast road to my right-side evolved bit by bit. I made out an irregular line which could be traced on top of the upper rocks, creating a kind of second horizon from that of land and sea; between rock and sky. For a few fleeting seconds, though it seemed much longer, I felt a million miles away from the other guests as they babbled and joked amongst themselves. I was totally at one with the earth; the sky; the sea, lost in the extreme and poignant beauty around me. I knew I belonged there. But soon I could bear it no more; it was all too beautiful; totally alien and yet totally mine. The present and the distant past.

The village clusters, some lower, some higher, projected even more clearly from the rock now. Some of the rock was bare, other parts offering up a scant covering of shady green. We sailed by remnants of old forts, medieval castle-like structures, forming towers still upright. I then made out the shape of a bus halfway up the rocky coastline, making a parallel journey by road with that of our boat. And below this, the majestic and prehistoric rocks, eternally exposed to the wear and tear of the unforgiving elements. Much further below, terraces appeared upon which grew lemon and orange trees, and there were grapevines too. Lower still, rectangular and arched caves beckoned; each one different from the last; each offering up a differently dark promise. And taking one more look up higher again, I spotted a solitary metal cross planted on a pointed pinnacle of rock, a glorious yet brutal presence.

The perfect way of seeing the world from a safe, far-off place, like an astronaut looking back at all the life-enhancing possibilities of our blue planet; like God seeing everything from upon high; a pastel haze erasing all those wasted opportunities and violent struggles; like a once beautiful woman, trying desperately to catch hold of everything life was pushing her way before it became completely out of reach.

Giulia was sad all this seemed to be lost on her fellow passengers but she was comforted by the thought that it also meant she had it all for herself! Yes the others would be totally aware they were in a beautiful part of the world and that their skin was being caressed by the morning sun and yet they were much more interested in commenting upon what other guests were wearing and engaging in conversations about the day's festivities, speculating on the choice of a Sicilian bride and how many courses would be on offer at the wedding breakfast, all followed by a verbal sharing of past small or extravagant weddings they had attended; even commenting on their own. Giulia would re-join them soon.

If only John had been able to get away.

What nobody knew or had spotted on such an auspicious day was that there had been an elderly gentleman weaving his way in and out of the wedding party, especially when events continued out of doors. He would appear and disappear at will, blending in effortlessly with the guests and locals, though only ever stopping to speak to the latter. With his olive skin and Mediterranean features, a dull ochre lightweight suit, elegant in its cut and simplicity, and eyes covered permanently with sunglasses, he drew absolutely no attention to himself!

Each guest was far too locked into their own share of the day's proceedings and even Giulia had long deposited her pen and notebook, having also become fully immersed in the unfolding delights. A mental note had been made by her, however, to revisit the exquisite Duomo in the days to come.

She had spotted its shape and splendour whilst still on the boat. And the more clearly it came into view, topped by its bell-tower and tiled jade-green cupola, the more she became hypnotised by it as it brought together the worlds of east and west, north and south, with its Moorish Mediterranean style and deep Christian tradition. She was later to discover that its site had been chosen for having previously been a place of pagan worship. And that this was the case for the building of so many Christian churches and cathedrals throughout Europe over the past thousand years. It marked a continuity of spiritual need and a desire for people of all backgrounds to come together in the public celebration of their beliefs.

The horizontally striped marble and stone exterior, together with the lace-effect arches, served up a visual feast. On disembarking, Giulia raised her eyes to the vast Cathedral open-air staircase, with its dozens of steps, which would sweep the bride (and a substitute father) up to the altar where the happy couple would exchange their vows. The ceremony would be presided over by an Italian priest nobody seemed to know, and in front of a huge sun-kissed crowd of well-wishers. It seemed as if all the residents of the once prestigious, now tiny, marine republic had poured out of their homes, together with any stray visitors to the town, to lend their support, as well as feed their curiosity.

How privileged Lorenzo and Serafina were to begin their married life in such a place, surrounded by so much earthly and spiritual beauty, the thoughts Giulia was able to read etched on the silent faces of everyone she encountered that day.

Chapter 13
Moving

It only took James a few hours in fact to decide that Father John's eccentric plan for him was actually feasible; its most attractive feature being the 'no strings attached'. There would be no papers to sign, no solicitors to involve and if no longer happy with the arrangement, either side could make their position known as soon as possible. He did feel somewhat embarrassed, however, that he had changed his mind quite so quickly and therefore decided to keep the priest waiting a few days before telling him of his revised decision.

Such an outcome came as no surprise whatsoever to Father John.

For the past year, James had been living in a fine period town house, only a mile away; part of an elegant terrace that he had bought and redecorated with some of his inheritance money. It looked out onto a rectangular-shaped green. He had never made contact with his neighbours (not even those who lived either side), other than to exchange a quick nod of the head or low grunt should they see one another leaving or arriving at their respective homes. He had no idea of what they thought of him and neither did he care. They were likewise of no interest to him.

Structure, had explained John, was the key. It was jointly agreed then that James would move into Star House and stay there for a couple of weeks, after which he would then be 'free' to return home, in order to catch up with post, bills etc. He could also on such occasions give his house a proper airing. A Mrs T. would continue to clean there twice a week; after all she had her own key. Father John would remain 'on call' but no more dates had been set for formal meetings.

Within a very short period of time, James therefore moved into Casa Stella, having been offered a small suite of rooms on the top floor, which included an airy sitting-room and tiny kitchen. He had taken with him just enough clothes to last the couple of weeks and a pile of books he had randomly packed into his suitcase. Domenico and Carmela (or Menicuccio and Carmeli as they referred to each other) told him that he was very welcome to join them for meals in their kitchen whenever he felt thus inclined and said that they ate at 1pm and again at 6, cooking nearly always 'in the Italian way'! He thanked them politely but knew he had absolutely no intention, at least for the time being, of taking them up on their kind offer; he also found it very difficult to follow exactly what they were saying.

And then at last he met Giulia herself.

James would never forget his first brush with Giulia, which took place about a week after he'd moved in. It was a brief encounter to say the least, which began with the two shaking hands, he giving his name even remembering to make eye-contact to which she replied, eyes flashing, half serious; possibly half smiling, "How could I ever have agreed to opening our doors to someone called Giacomo Casanova?" leaving a bewildered James awkward and speechless in the hallway, as she swept out of the front door, leaving behind only the peachy-sweet trail of her perfume.

By now Lorenzo, who was in the very slow process of moving out of Casa Stella, had grown into a self-assured young man, unless he happened to find himself amongst a group of academics say, which was of course rare. When out and about, he habitually walked at a fast pace with his head held erect and was more than aware that women of all ages found him attractive, due no doubt to his distinctive Mediterranean looks: very dark hair with its short crisp curls, coal black eyes, cupid lips which helped create a semi-snarling expression, and that permanent air of self-confidence.

He wasn't the kind of person to reflect upon the passing day's events or on the state of the world at large. And he certainly didn't go in for examining his conscience. But he made sure he always knew as much as he needed for any given situation. As much as he admired Giulia, he wasn't at all interested in her world; the art galleries, classical music, theatre, literature festivals etc. Neither did he have specific goals nor a career path as such in mind other than to work hard and do whatever it was well. It was more a fulfilling of parental expectations, never overtly expressed but understood all the same, which appeared to coincide with his own needs, and so always meeting his and their approval.

He enjoyed his life as an airline Passenger Handling agent, its flexible shift work, the frequent sightings of celebrities more often than not from the world of show-business and then helping his father run the delicatessen on his days off. Lorenzo felt a high level of satisfaction from the vast range of people he would encounter during a typical week, especially the young and attractive women. Moreover, in just a short time, he would be eligible for his first free airline ticket for a European destination, having worked for the airline company for almost a year. And after that would follow as many 10 % concessionary tickets as was possible to take advantage of. He would be using the very first ticket for his wedding trip to Italy.

He had probably 'chosen' Serafina due to a combination of her lack of worldly experience, her apparent gentleness (or passivity) and, of course, for her beautiful face and figure. He would be the envy of his work colleagues for sure. And although he was still very young, he was aware of the status he would gain from his community (family and work) by becoming a married man, and certainly very soon after that, a father. He had always been brought up with the notion that if a bride didn't become pregnant during the first year of marriage, there was alas definitely something wrong '*ahime, qualcosa che non va!*' Not of a reflective disposition, he would have just assumed that their future children would arrive punctually and be handsome and healthy. His life would go on much the same as before, but even better. He liked the structure of family tradition and even went to church 5 or 6 times a year for important feast days or to celebrate the Sacraments, for family Baptisms, First Holy Communions, confirmations and marriages. Lorenzo liked to look the part and play each part perfectly!

James, on the other hand, had by now started to consider quite deeply many aspects of his life and life in general; something, like Lorenzo, he didn't ever remember doing before. Would he miss his house, his home; was it even a home for him; could it become one; what were Giulia and the family really like? What was their motivation in allowing him, a mere stranger, to share part of Star House with them? Could there be ulterior motives? Was Father John as good a man as he appeared? Just who had his own parents been? And so on. Yet rather than feel alarmed by a possible neurosis setting in, James felt relief; he was now experiencing emotion and was on the brink of beginning to understand, for the first time in his life, how it felt to be engaged in the act of living!

Within the first week, he had had one or two brief conversations with Domenico and Carmela, as he chose to refer to them, had on a couple of occasions exchanged a few platitudes with Lorenzo and spent a good half an hour in the company of Tina, the De Martino's youngest daughter. He liked her straightaway. Appearing to lack Lorenzo's vanity and hurried "I'm just a bit too busy at the moment to stop and speak to you" charm, Tina, decided James, was straightforward, relaxed and put people at their ease. At 21, she came across as a mature and intelligent young woman. She had just completed her final year at university, where she had read History, and having already broken up for the summer, he imagined he would be seeing her quite a bit around the place. James hadn't yet encountered the two older sisters.

It was Tina in fact who'd first suggested to Giulia that it might be an idea to ask James if he knew anything about gardening. The reason for this was because Tina still harboured (and treasured) a wealth of happy memories about the jungle garden of her latter childhood when of course it seemed even more vast and wild. Now, as an adult, she had come to the conclusion that it was crying out for love of a different kind; as when Giulia first took over the house, it too needed to be resurrected and made beautiful. Her Aunt had in fact agreed with her: "You are absolutely right, Tina; I had also been thinking along those lines. I've always devoted so much love and attention to the house, as you know, and never really got round to the garden. I do remember the nuns' rose garden at school, which was a real delight, all our visitors said so, every June a haze of flowers, a raised carpet of pink and burgundy but I don't have any expertise and I don't even have any idea as to how I'd like it to look. And there's one more thing I know it sounds odd, but I wouldn't want just anyone working out there even if they did call themselves professionals. And that's why things have never got started.

"But your idea about James we could ask him I suppose. He might reveal a creative streak. He might even enjoy having a project to sink his teeth into while he's here?"

Lorenzo was spending much of his free time moving into his new house further down the lane. Domenico, his papà was allowing him to spend a bit less time in their family-run shop in order to get things sorted before his bride was due to arrive. He was rapidly leaving Casa Stella behind, both physically and mentally. He admired Giulia, but it had always remained her house, even though she had generously given up a good part of it to his family. There were signs of her everywhere. And so for the first time in his life he was looking forward to having a home that was his alone and he wanted to make it as different as possible, which under the circumstances, wasn't going to be too difficult.

He and some friends had recently hung some striped wallpaper in the upstairs bedrooms; a new bathroom had been fitted and the front garden tidied up. The rest of the house could then be redecorated a bit at a time, after the newly married couple had moved in together. His mother and sisters had also been busy, helping with the cleaning in particular, and all anxiously excited for him and his future life. And as for Carmela, she was already planning to take round a variety of Lorenzo's favourite meals, such as spinach cannelloni or her famous, multi-layered parmigiana (and other such homemade delicacies), even after the two were married. She presumed Serafina wouldn't have had much in the way of culinary experience and didn't want her son to suffer any unnecessary hardship. But she hadn't really given her new daughter-in-law much thought at all; it was her son whom she so adored, whom she would continue to pamper and protect at all costs.

Chapter 14
Serafina by James

Serafina fell into my life like a poem, but a poem you had never been inclined to read.

I'd had absolutely no interest whatsoever in meeting Lorenzo's new wife. Exhausted by the constant before (and after) wedding clutter and chatter, I wallowed in a well-earned break while the wedding party was away. During the weeks leading up to their departure, I had patiently listened to each trivial detail and superficial snippet of nuptial news. On their return it went on, relentlessly. I was forced to suffer comments about the billowing dress, the bridal bouquet, the jasmine in her hair, the towering Duomo, the equally towering cake, the speeches, the saucy jokes and hoaxes, the exquisite food described across each of its ten courses, the music (complete with local brass band), the brief Summer shower, the repeated explanation of the adage '*Sposa bagnata sposa fortunata,*' the toasts of '*Cent'anni*!' and repeated demands for another '*bacio, bacio, bacio*' and all to be re-lived once the oversized wedding photograph album took up pride of place on a coffee table in England.

Of course I had to play my part, giving the impression I was adequately curious, laughing in all the right places, asking pertinent questions, making a huge effort never to let the light in my eyes grow dim. A tiny hypocritical act. Hypocrisy with its poor reputation but oh so necessary in the upkeep of civilisation. I am learning so fast. It was a very small price to pay; this family was little by little saving me; saving me from myself; had opened me up to the world, well to their world at least; and without their even realising it, which made my recovery all the more authentic and more acceptable: no quasi-professional advice; no medical jargon; no well-meaning chatter. Never forgetting the saintly instigator of all this, Father John. And now they had brought me Serafina.

It was a Friday evening. Within seconds she lodged in my heart, a non-removable bullet.

The only things I had been told about her, other than wedding day gossip, was that she was 19 years of age, had lived her whole life with two dotty but devoted aunts and had never left Sicily until her wedding. And it didn't dawn on me for quite some time, that her beautiful name actually had an angelic link with the Seraph, highest order of six-winged angels, who were associated, the New Oxford Dictionary informed me, with 'purity, light and energy'.

For three days before the newlyweds were due to return from their honeymoon (an extended stay in Italy), there had been much activity passing between Star House and Lorenzo's new property, which he had bought about a year beforehand with the help of his family, the two houses being separated only by a row of shiny front doors. I was quickly aware of the constant flitting backwards and forwards by the female component of the family. They were like busy yet demented butterflies. Every detail of the nuptial bedroom and bedcover had to be perfect; unwritten rules having passed down the female lines for generations; each daughter or niece, growing up with such knowledge and perfectly able to put it into practice when the day came around. The fine quality bedlinen had been lovingly rewashed and ironed; the shiny coins collected; the sugared almonds scattered; the design of the bedcover pattern finally chosen.

They told me that double bed in Italian is 'letto matrimoniale' and I do remember wondering, together with this grand ritual of bed decoration, (hoping to keep any resulting smiles well-hidden), whether tradition also had it for the newly wedded couple to make passionate love on top of the coins (and other paraphernalia) or whether everything just got swept onto the floor in the heat of the moment but I naturally kept such mind-bending thoughts to myself! I must admit I was beginning to find some of this newly received and totally bizarre knowledge quite interesting in an anthropological sort of way. But it did beg the question: had anything actually changed in their world since the Middle Ages? I thought my world, or the western world in general, was enjoying a social revolution and here was I witnessing, even participating in, something akin to fertility rites! Not to mention the promotion of the idea that women in marriage remained male property, being passed over from their fathers to their husbands, in a matter of seconds as they stood in front of the altar.

I had also made my contribution, on a practical level, by managing to prise open the old padlock (no key to be found) of the vast metal chest, which had recently arrived from Syracuse, having for years been keeping safe the priceless bounty, a vast collection of items for her 'corredo da sposa', which would have been started and then continuously added to from the time of Serafina's birth. And apparently the numbers of sheets, towels etc. would have revealed the financial status of the family, 40 items of each, indicating considerable economic ease and so on. It was also usual for a female member of the wider family to take an on-going responsibility for the trousseau, someone who understood the importance and quality of each chosen item. I had no idea in this case of the numbers but there seemed to be quite a vast collection. So many oohs and aahs had greeted each offering wrapped in reams of tissue paper, as it was reverently removed from the chest, laid bare and then commented upon. It was pointed out to me that all the sheet, pillowcase and towel edgings had been hand embroidered in a range of pastel colours, each including what was probably a family crest, beautiful, delicate workmanship in what looked like twisty vine leaves, a shield of some kind and a rampant lion. Lorenzo's family had decided early on not to recreate in sugared almonds (confetti) the crest motif on the bedcover, as Serafina had now become a De Martino.

Everything not needed for the nuptial bed was removed, aired and then eventually refolded and put away in the bedroom furniture Lorenzo had chosen for the square-shaped, now anachronistic bedroom.

Not able to enter into the frenetic family chatter, due to my lack of Italian, I hovered at one end of the sitting room, giving the impression that I was there, if needed, to help carry suitcases, answer the phone or even make a pot of tea or an instant coffee, which they referred to as an English coffee (or even 'acqua sporca', dirty water, when feeling less than magnanimous towards the English and their appalling tastes and habits!). Giulia was yet to teach me how to create the perfect espresso in her precious yet slightly battered 'macchinetta'! A skill she confessed she had ironically picked up in the South of France!

But blending in with the surroundings is not always a bad thing and for me it was a golden opportunity not only to observe the lovely bride but also pick up on her mannerisms, study her body language, listen to her low husky voice, watch her interact with her brand-new family. All in all, I was learning fast, a language which often revealed far more than words. She happened to be everyone's focus of attention that evening in what was a fairly jokey atmosphere probably a temporary situation, I assumed, once family expectations had kicked in and life became normalised.

Unusually for Lorenzo, he didn't have much to say for himself but was clearly enjoying all the fuss being shown him and his wife, his beautiful new *'mogliettina'*, and surely couldn't have asked for a warmer welcome home. Carmela had proudly set out a variety of different colour liqueurs on the top of the sideboard, which I later discovered included the likes of Strega, Millefiori, Centerbe and Amaretto; varying shades of yellow, green and gold, a line of sturdy bottles standing equally proud amid an army of small sherry type glasses. There were also dishes of hand-made nutty cantuccini and sticky piles of honey-coated strufoli, only usually served at Christmas and Easter. And this was after Carmela had tried to persuade everyone that 'due spaghetti' were in order as the returning couple couldn't have had much to eat while travelling all that way. After about ten minutes of pleading, she passively accepted defeat and moved their attention over to the sweet treats on display.

It also struck me as never before, and Tina had in fact already alerted me to this, that when the De Martinos gathered together, about three languages were on the go. Domenico and Carmela spoke in the dialect of their childhood; the children spoke to their parents by and large in English, often having to repeat themselves more slowly and if that didn't do the trick, they'd have a stab at their parents' rendition of Avellinese. This was also mixed up with the Italian they had picked up from Italian school, which they'd been forced to attend two evenings a week for what seemed like years and years. The opportunities for misunderstanding were therefore enormous, which always brought a sense of potential comedy, farce even, to the proceedings. So it often appeared to take a huge amount of time for relatively trivial or simple verbal transactions to be effectively communicated. Giulia, of course, spoke in the standard form of Italian, having involuntarily or deliberately, left behind any traces of dialect years beforehand. And now with Serafina among them, conversation was likely to become even more intricate. Now did she only speak a dialect from Syracuse, or was she, like Giulia, versed only in standard Italian? I would have to wait and see! It was more than likely that speakers of the two distinct dialects would not have understood one another at all!

As for me, I was picking up fragments of Italian, no doubt standard and dialect, on a daily basis, especially the short regularly repeated expressions such as: *Vieni qui*! (Come here), *Ma dai*! (Oh come off it), *Tutti a tavola*! (Time to eat).

Back to Serafina, wedged somewhere between girlhood and womanhood, what was she really making of all of this? Was it all quite similar to her life back home or as Tina had recently explained for most Italians the links with their region (and there are 20 altogether) were even tighter than their sense of belonging to one nation, and that in many ways these regions were starkly different and distinguishable from one another in their local language, history, geography, customs and of course in their cooking. Even more thought-provoking for me and something my mind often returned to ponder upon was the fact that in Domenico and Carmela's childhood village, people could identify the specific provenance of visitors from the five closest villages, since each had a slightly different take on the prevailing dialect not merely a matter of accent but also a whole collection of individual words, sayings and phrases. So if that were the case, was Serafina feeling foreign twice over?

Of course it was far too early to tell. She was now married and having to cope with all that entailed. She had just starred in a summer wedding fit for a fairy princess. She had only just returned from a honeymoon, so I have been told a million times, in one of the most beautiful corners of God's earth.

But as far as I was aware, neither Lorenzo nor his family had any plans to return to Italy for good.

Chapter 15
Lastborn

Tina was the youngest member of the De Martino family and probably the most intelligent, if rated academically. However, her name didn't exactly start out as Tina at all. It was only one of about four ongoing variations but used exclusively when at home with the family. And it is of interest to note that this anomalous situation also appeared to have sealed her fate, paving the way for a life of secrets and different identities. Just like Wilde's Ernest; the Prince and the Pauper; even The Scarlet Pimpernel.

In this case twenty or so years beforehand Tina had actually been baptised Immacolata De Martino, having been granted the honour of carrying on the name of a paternal grandmother, a very religious name, which points directly to the Immaculate Conception itself, to the Virgin Mary's having been born without sin. This tradition of passing down the same names every other generation kept the beloved relative alive in the hearts and minds of those who still remembered them, and who would from time to time pass on anecdotes about that person to their offspring. It maintained a sacred line of continuity. Like the Popes' direct line back to St. Peter, the Apostle handed the Keys of the Kingdom by Jesus himself. It also kept the harsh divide between life and death more hazy.

To those interested Tina would explain it something like this:

In English we tend to shorten names when creating nicknames, which makes good practical sense, giving friends and family members very short, easily recognisable labels, and which often entails chopping off the last few letters. And so in most cases, it's quite straightforward guessing the original name. This is not necessarily the case in Italian. Nicknames tend to grow in size and then having become ridiculously overblown often shrink back. The added letters have meanings linked to concepts such as little, sweet, cute, young, and so on to give some of the more agreeable. Such additions always happen at the end of the given name so function as suffixes such as for Antonio, which might become Antoniuccio (sweet little/young Anthony) and there is often a vast range of variations.

The trail from Immacolata to Tina went accordingly: Immacolata became Immacolatina (sweet little Immacolata) and then having been judged far too long, containing all of six syllables, was soon shortened to Tina, the last four letters of her childhood nickname, but leaving behind all recognisable signs of the original name, like a snake sloughing its skin. So she could really have been named: Martina, Clementina, Valentina, Costantina, or even just plain Tina and so on; it was anyone's guess!

And so the name Immacolata was discarded, side-lined to officialdom and the excruciatingly dull world of form-filling.

To her friends, peers, teachers, and more recently to university staff, she had always been known as Immy. Her very first school teachers had probably instigated this, having not been able to read, let alone pronounce, her full name with any level of confidence and Tina, never wanting to create an unnecessary fuss, just went along with the alteration and actually ended up quite liking it: even building a new life for herself around it! Tina at home, Immy when out in the big wide world. Tina, when Italian and tied; Immy, when English and free!

Years later, when she first met Nicholas, introducing herself to him as Immy, he thought she must originally have been called Imogen after the sweet and affectionate character from Shakespeare's Cymbeline. He even decided that it suited her perfectly and continued to use it. Thus even more confusion! (Or opportunity!)

They had been secret lovers for about three months, and she had been living on a soft, floaty, pink cloud of happiness ever since meeting him. Ordinary life continued in parallel as something vaguely remote, which she was able to look down on from a great height life, coated like a pill, from its hitherto knocks or difficulties.

Why change anything when life was already perfect? Why muddy crystalline waters by involving others? They were both overwhelmingly happy with the inward-looking world they had so rapidly and effortlessly created.

Having previously made Lorenzo her life-time work, Giulia, whom incidentally no one had ever addressed as Giulietta, had been stupidly blind to Tina's future promise. It was true that she hadn't been a particularly attractive child, regarding looks or character, and on reaching adolescence, nature had once again been unkind to her as it repeatedly attacked her face with myriad spots of varying sizes and shades of pink and red, not to mention the all too visible blackheads around her nose. Her dark hair was wild and seemed permanently greasy at the roots. And all in all she gave the impression of a girl who neglected her appearance out of laziness. Giulia had also noticed on many an occasion just how clumsy and ungainly she appeared as she worked her way around the house. Although always polite and respectful towards Giulia, she had, unlike the others, never felt inclined to ask her for help or support, advice or information. But Tina was probably only too well aware that for the time being at least she couldn't compete with her brother, having quickly picked up on the adoration Giulia manifested towards him, even though her aunt knew that she had a good brain and was naturally curious about the world around her, traits so close to Giulia's heart.

However, it was only ever going to be a matter of time. As Giulia was begrudgingly having to let go of her dreams for Lorenzo, she was being quietly compensated by an acknowledgement, very faint to begin with, that Tina also existed; what's more the spots had more or less disappeared, her features had softened and regular visits to a local salon (now that the daughter of one of her mother's friends had started to work there) had worked wonders on the wild mop of tangled dark hair.

Reports from her school, which only recently Giulia had taken to reading, were full of promise to the extent that the latest had referred to a 'very bright academic future', which awaited her. And as a result Giulia experienced sentiments of deep shame and deep admiration, both equally balanced, and she had to swallow yet one more of life's bitter pills in that Tina had achieved this all by herself! Only the long hours she had spent shut away in her room had witnessed this ongoing transformation and the sheer hard work undertaken within those four walls in order for her to achieve such excellent results.

Giulia so intelligent, or so it was thought, so sensitive a being, so in touch with events happening around her, so keen to support academic success, had unlike the teachers at school, been desperately slow at recognising Tina's potential and she had concluded from this, after much self-examination, that it all could be traced back to an overwhelming urge she had always felt towards people (and things) she considered visually beautiful. Lorenzo had been the beautiful demi-man, ripe for seizing and nurturing under her maternal wing and this awful weakness of character had blinded her to the fact that he, though not unintelligent, had never displayed any of the qualities required for the pursuit of so-called higher things.

The seeds of a new and affectionate relationship had thenceforth begun to bear fruit between the two women, primarily as a result of Giulia's humility and self-knowledge, of a character weakness she wanted to guard against breaking out again in the future. She didn't take that final step of closure and apologise directly to Tina perhaps due to a lingering trace of inculcated wisdom which advises us never to show deference to a younger person and in her defence, she hadn't deliberately harmed the girl in any way. But from now on she made sure that Tina would always be aware of the warmth and admiration that she, Giulia, felt towards her.

Tina had eventually been awarded a place reading History at a university in the north of England, an opportunity she was determined not to forgo. Such an unimaginable decision had been especially difficult for her parents to accept in all sorts of ways and this drawn out heartache stopped them ever being able to feel proud of their daughter's achievements. Decent girls ('*ragazze serie*') always stayed at home with their parents until marriage. Why did a girl and in this case their own daughter need to get a degree anyway? Why had she chosen to study so far away? She would be lost to the wider world; would never be the same again and they could hardly allow their thoughts to linger on what dubious people she would meet along the way and how they would try to deceive and exploit her. Their three older children had not behaved in this way so why was it happening to the family now?

It was thanks to Giulia's ongoing encouragement and a lengthy meeting which took place at the school with Tina's headmistress, that Domenico and Carmela finally agreed, albeit without conviction, to let their daughter follow her academic dreams…

And they really had no need to worry. Whatever Tina got up to when out of parental sight, she dutifully returned home on a regular basis, always staying the agreed number of days or weeks, and even spending a fair amount of each summer in Italy with the other De Martinos, as part of the family's annual exodus south. She also rang home at least once a week. There was no unwanted pregnancy, no signs of nicotine, no evidence of alcoholism or illegal drug use! In fact the rest of her family had even admitted amongst themselves that their once eccentric ugly duckling was growing into a very attractive, affable and self-assured young woman though there were still the lingering doubts as to what it was all leading up to; where exactly it was all going to end.

Giulia was naturally very happy with the situation and she too often wondered what the future had in store for this unusual girl, who had shown such determination and resilience in her battle for self-realisation.

Tina had met Nicholas, when she was visiting a teaching college not far from home, as she had been considering a PGCE course and a possible career as a Secondary School teacher. He had been lecturing there for a good few years and was a member of the Music Department. They had met in very banal circumstances, while queuing in the refectory for a coffee in fact. It happened to be crowded that day, also very hot and sticky, and it ended up with them having to share a tiny rickety table. Tina found herself having to sit much closer to him than she would normally have liked in the company of a total stranger. Only that on this occasion she did actually enjoy this physical closeness; she liked his face, his smell, his warmth and how he smiled; and she especially liked his voice. He did of course seem a little older than men she had known at university. He was also wearing a wedding ring but each of these observations made speaking to him all the more fascinating another step into the unknown.

Tina had also made quite an impact on him. He found her Mediterranean looks exotic and appealing: the dark eyes and dark wavy hair. But there was also something else about her. Something from a past age, he decided later, as he was not able to process everything in his somewhat befuddled head, while still in her presence. Yes, that was it; she reminded him of certain paintings he had come across on his studies and travels, those depicting young females in pastoral settings, genuine milkmaids or fashionable, young, eighteenth-century women in the guise of milkmaids or servants and it fast dawned on him, for probably the first time, that these were the physical traits, a combination of youth, pink-tinged cheeks, curves, a sun-tinged freshness, countryside naturalness, that he was most drawn to in a woman.

Chapter 16

A Bolt out of the Blue

"Mamma, Papà, there's someone to speak to you!"

Carmela made her way quickly from the tiny living room to the front door only to be faced with an elegant woman she had never seen before. The two young girls stayed glued to her throughout; Domenico didn't budge from his kitchen stool and continued to watch the television.

"Come in, come in," Carmela beckoned the woman to follow them, as she led the way, trying to plump cushions and remove bits and pieces of everyday life from chairs and surfaces. "Sit, sit down; here, here!" By now it became clear that her spoken English manifested a strong, almost guttural Italian accent.

It had been a difficult journey for Giulia to make even though it was a mere 15 miles away. She had passed her driving test a few years beforehand but only chose to use the car in the immediate vicinity of her home, always avoiding motorways, and other unfamiliar roads, whenever possible. In fact, learning to drive had been one of the most difficult things she had ever endeavoured to master and had never quite managed to work out why this was. Why was she always so different from the rest? Today she had once again decided to take the train. She needed to keep a clear head and keep her emotions completely under control. She could hardly believe this meeting would be happening in the first place.

The unknown woman dressed in turquoise spoke quite quickly and the two girls shuffled uncomfortably on a lumpy armchair they were sharing, not quite knowing when to interrupt, in a polite manner of course, to let this important-looking lady know that their mother didn't really understand English very well. Fortunately, at about the same time it also dawned on their guest that there could be a communication problem, and she asked the family, in perfect Italian, if it would be better if she spoke to them in a language they were more familiar with.

The relief was tangible and Mr De Martino, 'Menicuccio', was also brought into the room to hear what she had to say. She even suggested that the girls should leave the room, as what she had to say was of a sensitive nature, but Domenico wanted them to remain saying that he would decide if and when they should go.

"First of all, I would like to thank you for welcoming me into your home. You must be wondering who I am and what information I can possibly have to communicate to you. I apologise for disturbing you, I only had an address. I originally thought it best to write to you, but somehow under the circumstances, I changed my mind and decided to speak to you face to face, hoping, of course, to find you at home."

Even the two girls had noticed that the woman's eyes had been fixed primarily on their mother rather than anyone or anything else and that although she seemed so sophisticated, not someone from their world, she was also trembling slightly as she spoke.

Carmela, at the prod from her husband, jumped up all of a sudden and said that she would be right back, obviously rushing to the kitchen to make the obligatory coffee and serve some biscuits. From then on, the atmosphere became slightly more relaxed, the woman graciously accepting the coffee and a biscuit she was repeatedly urged to take but hadn't really wanted.

"So I gather you are both from Southern Italy as I am myself, well originally. My name is Giulia. Would you allow me to ask you, it's Carmela, isn't it, if you were ever told if you had any brothers or sisters? I know I am being intrusive but please trust me, I promise you it is for a very good reason."

"I don't think much about those times," Carmela wistfully replied, "but I think I did once have a little sister, only I can't really remember now if I dreamed it or made it up, you know what children are like. It was probably to make me feel less lonely only that I thought I once overheard my mother say something," her voice trailed off. "But it's so vague now, so hazy I can't remember any words; it's more of a feeling."

There was a sound of voices and general bustle at the back door, which easily made its way to the sitting-room. A young lad had just been dropped off. He was wearing a football kit and sporting two very muddy knees above his shin pads.

"This is our son, Lorenzo, say hello, son, to our guest!" Lorenzo did so and then was quickly shunted out of the room, football boots in his hands, to get cleaned up and changed.

Giulia slowly rose to her feet.

"Look I don't want to waylay you any further. I will leave you a card with all my contact details; please, Carmela, think back to your childhood years and try to remember if there's anything at all that springs to mind regarding your family and wider family. Any photographs you might come across, they could be useful. Perhaps you could help her Domenico, it is Domenico isn't it? And if in the meantime you would like me to return, then that will be fine. I am almost sure you have a sister or brother of course, and provided you are happy with the situation I will do my best to re-unite you but it is your decision at the end of the day. I hope this hasn't come as too big a shock for you. At least now you will have some time on your own to think about what you want to do. Thank you for the coffee, and the biscuit it was delicious, and thank you girls, it was lovely meeting you all."

"Oh yes, so this is Sandra and your younger sister, have I got that right, Patrizia or is it the other way round?"

"Such pretty girls, you can tell they are sisters, can't you?"

Giulia held out her right hand for each family member to shake, though having to stoop a little for the two girls. Lorenzo had not reappeared.

She remembered nothing about her twenty-minute dash back to the railway station, not even the fact that the light drizzle had been turning gradually into a much heavier downpour.

It is was only once on the train that she allowed herself the possibility of re-living that experience and trying very hard to hold onto every last detail of the house, the room, the girls (apparently there was an even younger daughter ill in bed), their parents and the surprise arrival of their sporty son. She could have handled it so much better; she had spoken too fast; had said too much or too little; she had been too tense and had found it hard to interpret what they were really thinking or feeling. They had definitely been suspicious of her in spite of the customary hospitality but then, of course they were; they could only see the stranger.

But it was the lack of reaction from her own 'sister', who looked nothing like her, as well as her obvious lack of enthusiasm regarding Giulia's precious news, that alarmed her most of all.

They clearly had little money or if they did, they were definitely not spending it on their home. Perhaps the house wasn't even theirs and they were only renting it. The children appeared healthy and came across as very polite; all in all, they presented a united front, not over-talkative, but there again she had given them very little opportunity to express themselves, she just couldn't stay any longer. She was at bursting point but grateful she hadn't broken down in front of them.

So this was Carmela, her life spread out for about half an hour in front of her, in the drab setting of the family sitting-room. But she was alright; she seemed healthy; she had a husband; 4 lovely children. These were true blessings. What did it matter that she didn't live in luxury and that there were few signs of her lavishing time and money on her appearance; that she was inevitably exhausted by the ongoing pressures of raising children, looking after a possibly demanding husband, keeping up with household chores.

She was alive and well!

Within a couple of days, Giulia made contact with the ever-busy Father John, imploring him to see her as soon as possible. He, the only person who had known about the meeting she had had with the De Martinos. And she desperately needed to speak to him about the outcome. Independent by nature, yet also fully aware that when life presented such profound scenarios, it was absolutely crucial to share them with a wise person, in order to retain some kind of clear head, or at least to keep that head above water.

And, of course, John didn't keep her waiting long. He invited her round to the presbytery and gave her the time she needed to pour out all the excitement of the circumstances but also all of the worries. What if they didn't make contact? What if they did, but only to tell her that there was no point raking up the ashes of the past? What if they just didn't like or trust her? She knew that they needed time to think. She had told them precisely that but several long days had dragged by, and still no call! Maybe they had lost her card, so easily done in a busy household so if this were the case when would it be best to make contact with them?

The priest was wary of ever giving precise answers. By allowing someone to speak without interruption, to pour out their woes, it often provided them with an opportunity to discover for themselves the best route forward without further intervention, spiritual or otherwise. John had also taught Giulia about a handy way of determining if something was really worth worrying about. Something she had never heard of before. Stinking thinking, as he referred to it, was when a person made themselves sick with worry about a situation they had absolutely no control over. That was obviously a complete waste of time and very damaging, as people tortured themselves for no practical reason. It also required a vast amount of negative energy. By letting go of such situations, one would then be free to tackle problems that could genuinely be sorted. Giulia tried to live within this relatively simple framework but often had to remind herself of it when approaching turbulent waters. It was always this example that sprang to mind: "Now I can't change my age, so no point worrying about that but I do have the power of getting rid of two kilos in weight," she would say out loud. In that, way she could recalibrate her thinking to the latest quandary.

However, this time it was better she involved John directly.

Chapter 17
The World of Nicholas Lydiard

A few streets down from Father John's church could be found a neat and leafy avenue, which on closer inspection, turned out to be lined with two rows of lime trees. And these sticky-leafed trees part-shielded from view the two rows of houses either side, which had all been constructed in the late Victorian or Edwardian age. Most were semi-detached or terraced properties. And likewise most of the avenue's residents fell into one of two categories: the comfortably off elderly or the comfortably off thirty and forty somethings. This latter group, having enjoyed a range of modest privileges for most of their lives, were now permitted access to a life of ease and opportunities, in which to bring up their own families. They had probably been helped by family inheritances or occasional acts of parental generosity in order to acquire these houses in the first place, houses which were not big or showy, but were nevertheless located in a desirable residential area.

Such families consisted nearly always of a husband and wife, with no more than two or three children. Living in this part of the world brought with it a choice of highly reputed infant and junior schools (crucial for those parents whose financial ease didn't quite match the fees and extras for acquiring a more prestigious private education.) And later on the all-important Secondary Schools some of which, here at least, having retained their Grammar status, basked in the glow of year on year academic success; gained through a careful selection of the most able students at the tender age of 11. However, as entry into these rare oases of excellence was becoming more desirable, it was also making the careful sifting process even trickier. And the curriculum provided in these hitherto sound primary schools was no longer deemed adequate to fulfil the rigours of guaranteed entrance to the Grammars. Comprehensive education was by now fully entrenched nationwide and certain parents, who lived further afield and in places with no grammars, also had their eyes fixed on a Grammar school education for their own children, regardless of distance. Competition for places was thus becoming very stiff indeed!

All this gave way to a flurry of activity in order for parents to find, at the very least, a local tutor, who would be fully conversant with the 11-plus entry system; yet also in all probability a piano teacher for each of their children in order to broaden their cultural heritage and horizons. They likewise put money aside for regular trips to the theatre; elocution lessons to remove the influence of the lively argot of the working classes; tennis coaching in the warmer months; cricket and horse-riding lessons, even French conversation.

Nearly every aspect of these families' lives was geared to giving their offspring the very best of life chances, richer in culture and even more varied than their own. Some parents even started attending church, as a church school could be a significant back-up should a Grammar school place not be possible. On a social level, it was also important that the choice of their children's friends was regularly monitored and as much as possible that it matched the desired criteria with little left to chance. Council estates were all around with all the chaos and deprivation their name suggested. Of course there was a wide range of emphasis. Not every parent who lived in this road was totally obsessed by such refined social engineering but there was enough dedication to spread over all the children growing up there and in the streets which ran parallel to it. Some of the more astute, middle-class parents knew that God-given intelligence was (thankfully) not linked to social status but they still felt compelled and fully justified to broker the best possible deal for their own children with all the tools at their disposal.

This was the avenue where Nicholas Lydiard lived with his family, which also consisted of a thin, efficient wife and two lovely children. And much of what has just been described, also applied to the Lydiard lifestyle. They had moved here about three years earlier with a specific set of expectations and so far had experienced no regrets.

"Dad, Dad, come on, you promised," whined voice number one.

"Yes, you did, you really did promise," echoed the second speaker, as both children jumped onto the bed where Nicholas was fighting the losing battle of clinging on to the last dregs of a weekend lie-in.

"Dad, come on it's Saturday, and you said on Saturday you were going to take us…to the farm," each burst of language corresponding to the bursts of energy between jumps, and coming mainly from the first speaker.

At about their fifteenth jump, he willingly conceded defeat, promising them that if they went downstairs straightaway, he would follow them in about ten minutes.

The two little angels disappeared as if by magic and Nicholas began to think about the day ahead: yes, farm with the children (while Jane went to the hairdresser's); a couple of private violin lessons in the spare room; piano practice with his own children Miranda and Daniel and much later, after supper, drinks at their friends' house along the road.

It turned out to be a cold and bright morning and provided one was well wrapped up and prepared to keep on the move, it was possible to enjoy it without suffering from frostbite.

Nicholas looked on at his son and daughter, two blond heads bobbing up and down, one slightly higher than the other, above royal blue coats and little legs, half-concealed by shiny red wellies, as they ran off ahead to greet their Saturday world of treats and precious time spent out and about with their father, whom they idolised.

He was so glad it was the urban farm they had chosen as it meant only a short drive; there was also decent parking on site and even better, entry was still free to visitors. He had recently spent more than intended on yet more musical equipment, and it was vital for the family budget, for the time being at least, that he found ways to tighten his belt. Only a huge metal milk churn, strategically placed, had pricked his conscience in the past that on leaving by the same gate, he should perhaps make a modest donation towards the always popular farm experience.

On this occasion the farm visit had also allowed him a good twenty minutes on his own, indulging in delicious fantasies about Imogen and the semi-rural scene which surrounded him was perfect for doing just that. She somehow seemed to belong more to the outdoors and fresh air than in a stuffy sitting-room; with her long, slightly wild hair; her beautiful curves; her darkly brooding eyes. A true Nature and Fertility goddess, a picture of how women should be, before they are inevitably made to feel insecure by the so-called beauty industry regarding their physical attributes. Imogen didn't manifest such lack of confidence, well not yet anyway. He acknowledged, however, that these were very much his opinions and he kept them very much to himself having probably arisen in the first place from his love of art and definitely not from a childhood growing up alongside nubile peasant girls. Apart from four years at university, he had spent all his life living in the local area.

After the pigs and rabbits, the ducks and donkeys, the play area and café', Nicholas, fully awake and by now in particularly good spirits, suggested they might pop in to see their cousins on the way home!

While at his brother's, he was able to disappear for ten minutes to call Imogen from a public telephone box; after all the cousins got on very well and it was only a flying visit! His irresistible lover had said she would be at home that morning.

And Immy managed to be first to get to the 'phone, making sure not to be overheard by anyone who might be around. She quietly shut the nearest doors off the hallway and kept her voice low in case anyone was trying to eavesdrop from upstairs. It was Giulia she most feared finding out about Nicholas and ironically it was more likely to be Giulia, rather than her own parents, who would become suspicious. There was something of the all-knowing about her…

"I love you too, my darling, *mon amour*, oh I think I hear someone coming, a thousand kisses. Yes, Tuesday, I'll be there, be safe, love you love you love you, *je t'aime*."

"So first we'll do times tables 7 times 2, Miranda; good okay 5 times 3; okay but a bit faster now: 4 times 9; 11 times 6; 3 times 12, good girl zero times one million no, it's zero! Remember anything multiplied by zero is zero, even a million!"

Times tables were followed by European capital cities and then proverbs he started, which she then had to complete: "A stitch in time… too many cooks… a bird in the hand… imitation is… yes, I know that's a difficult one, how about a rolling stone? Next week we will work on what they actually mean."

After ten long dragging minutes of conversation from which Daniel felt he had been deliberately excluded, he started to interrupt by making silly squeaks and then coughing noises and this of course was the obvious signal for Nicholas to switch his attention to his little son instead, asking him what he had enjoyed about the farm, what he had learned there and it all ended up with them playing a quick game of I-spy, made complicated by the fact that often the chosen objects were no longer visible as he drove the car back towards their home.

Jane got back a few minutes later and there was soon a family lunch set out on top of the stripped pine kitchen table, complete with brightly coloured paper napkins, some quiche, a range of cheeses, salad, French bread and smoked mackerel pâté. They normally had a hot meal in the evening on a Saturday.

After lunch, which also included a well-awaited glass of dry white wine, Nicholas made his way up to the spare room, (or now more properly referred to as his music room), where he could spend about twenty minutes in peace as he gathered his teaching thoughts, while lovingly polishing the beautiful violin his parents had given him. It made him think of them as he gently removed it from its ancient case and then of Imogen, for its rounded sides, its glossy sheen and ages old yet timeless appeal. He slid the taut bow's horsehair rapidly backwards and forwards over the small block of amber-coloured rosin, complete with central dent where it had worn down. He then proceeded to tune the violin itself and to practise scales and arpeggios before the arrival of his first pupil of the afternoon. The quietly spoken girl seemed very nice but was clearly under a lot of pressure from doting parents, who had discovered a great and rare musical talent in their only child, a talent which alas hadn't after about 18 months of trying ever surfaced in Nicholas' music room!

Nicholas vehemently disliked the system of Grade Exams, he felt it killed stone-dead any joy to be had from a life dedicated to music. If he had had his way he would concentrate first on developing a love for music; encouraging free expression, even if it did mean the student leaping round the room; stoking an interest in the life and times of the various composers and then gradually he would introduce his students to the instrument itself. But what the parents, his clients, wanted more than anything else was exam results. Very few gave him free reign.

The 14-year-old boy who came after possessed a wealth of natural talent, a talent he seemed totally unaware of; never seeing the need to give up precious free time in order to practise despite his teacher's patient imploring. Nicholas knew from experience that finding the right talent and personality combination was a very rare phenomenon if a true musician was to be born.

But all that now paled into insignificance; in Imogen he had discovered life's cure; the antidote to all its disappointment, pain, tedium.

Chapter 18

"Every Savage Can Dance"

One balmy summer night, James simply couldn't get off to sleep. He felt hot and sticky, almost feverish, and his brain was on overload with a swirl of thoughts. He just couldn't seem to fix on any one of them in particular and ultimately decided it was best to get up and face the situation from a vertical perspective. After refilling his glass with the water he kept in a bottle in the fridge, he made his way out onto the welcoming balcony; why force sleep if it wasn't ready to descend? Much better to look up and out into space; into the black depths of the universe; to empty oneself of all the nonsense of the day; to wait and see what would happen next. The moon loomed bright and large but was not quite a full moon. The surrounding clear black sky offered up more and more stars, the longer one was prepared to stare out and grasp them. Within a few minutes James was already feeling much calmer and accepting of his sleepless state. Unlike the majority of people, he could always catch up if necessary later that day.

Paradoxically, he enjoyed the fact that he was reminded (and whenever he looked out into the nightscape) just how small and insignificant he was; his life was. And all this meant in turn that many of the problems of mankind were likewise far more trivial and therefore more resolvable than we were usually prepared to accept. He rapidly reached the verdict that problems man experienced in the post-industrial world were the product of a combination of immaturity, vanity, greed, selfishness and man's obsession with the individual; multi-repetitions of past mistakes we have never properly learned from. Problems that would have been ridiculed by our wiser, tougher, distant and not so distant ancestors, for whom each day was a battle for survival against hunger, thirst, disease, cold, heat, attack. Neuroses, anxiety, panic attacks just what would they have made of such nonsense? Yet another 20th century luxury indulgence, no doubt! But surely all pointing to the fact that we were all doomed to suffer, regardless of individual situations. In other words, one didn't have to be a war veteran to have a first-hand understanding of PAIN, in all its forms.

The figure of the lunatic looking up at the oversized moon against the night sky.

All of a sudden, James' free-flowing torrent of thoughts was halted by some kind of activity going on in a garden to his right. From his lofty position on the top balcony (as if he were at the theatre), he had an excellent view not just of the Casa Stella rear garden but also, in part, of the gardens of the next four houses, which were invariably much smaller and narrower.

He made out a tiny figure, the ghostly figure of a girl.

For heaven's sake, it looked like Serafina; it WAS Serafina. James looked down at his watch, a past present from Harriet, and it was by now nearly 3.30 in the morning. What on earth could she be doing outside at this time, draped in what seemed like a longish white and floaty nightdress? She started leaping around, and every so often disappeared from his view, only to reappear, her movements each time gaining in strength and momentum. In fact James soon came to the conclusion it wasn't really leaping at all. That gave the impression of steps random and infantile.

No, it was actually a kind of dance. With his untrained eye, it wasn't easy to make much sense of such a dance, if that's what it was, but this didn't stop him from straining to follow the graceful yet deliberate movements of her arms, her legs, the circular sweep of her body movements. Could she have been dancing in response to a piece of music in her head? Why was she out there at all? Where was Lorenzo? Did he know about this? Was it something she did on a regular basis or as a reaction to something that had just happened? Was it a dance of joy, of rapture? Or was it an unburdening of all her frustrations? Surely it had nothing to do with an ancient Sicilian fertility rite?

After what seemed like a substantial but unguessable length of time during which James had remained as immobile as a lump of marble, entirely transfixed against the balcony edge, he eventually realised that she had gone, that the enigmatic performance had come to an end. He didn't know whether to be happy or sad though he was aware of a huge wave of tenderness directed towards her, surging out from a deep well of something unknown inside of him.

He felt very sleepy now, emotionally drained in fact. Yes, he would think about what it all meant later.

The following afternoon, he took the opportunity of broaching, in an informal and light-hearted way, the subject of dance with Tina, who was always willing to share her knowledge and the odd joke. She told James that she herself had never taken up ballet or tap, being she laughed "clumsy and ungraceful" and in any case found it almost impossible to learn the steps but did enjoy watching the experts or bopping around with friends at the university discos. It gave her a kind of 'release' she explained. She loved music anyway, and more recently was even becoming more interested in classical music…

James then went on to ask her about any kind of traditional dances she was aware of from Southern Italy. "Well, I don't know much about their dances but now I come to think about it there is one which apparently originates from a place not too far from where my parents were born but in a different region. It's commonly known as the 'Pizzica', a kind of tarantella, but I think it's only performed locally, like in village squares etc. I don't know if anyone from other regions knows anything about it. The word 'pizzica' in Italian means a kind of pinch or sting, like the bite you might get from an insect."

"I saw it performed once on one of our summer trips and it was really quite exciting. There were these two women, but we were told that it can also be a man and a woman, who danced accompanied by some musicians; yes, that's right, one played a huge tambourine I remember and then I think there was someone playing a piano accordion, yes, and a guitarist! The music is really loud and important in accentuating the extreme emotions of the woman. Well, it's all based on an ancient story of a woman who gets bitten by a poisonous spider, you know a tarantula and in order to defend herself against the poison, she starts to move in a wild and frenzied way, which gains more and more momentum. It's a kind of liberation ritual, which I believe was created by the village women hundreds of years ago and obviously despised by the Church. In fact originally it had much more to do with the women finding an extreme remedy for the oppressive, male-dominated society that they felt was crushing them. And the spider bit was just an excuse. I think it's thought of as pretty harmless these days, as it's lost a lot of its bite haha no pun intended and it's performed mainly at celebrations or for tourists."

"Oh that's so interesting but what is the actual dance, like tell me about the leaping around?"

"Well, what I do remember is that the women wear long dresses, which they grab and sweep from side to side, not in a vulgar way, but sort of becoming part of the dance and makes it all the more dramatic and sensual. It's very fast and gets faster and faster, lots of circular movements, quite primitive really, sorry I don't know that much about it. I can't remember but the woman in her frenzy comes across as powerful and indestructible."

After a short while, Tina got up and apologised for having to go out; she was in fact already running late and James was once again left with only his thoughts. Maybe there was a similar dance performed in the Syracuse area or perhaps Serafina had just felt compelled on one particular hot and sticky night to whirl around the garden. Just why had he been so moved, so affected by the scene?

He then began to reflect upon the whole concept of dance, a subject about which he knew precious little; about how and why it started in the first place. Did all human beings once possess natural rhythm and if that were the case, it seemed that many had lost or had relinquished it at some point to the cosy closet of inhibition. Just who were the first human dancers and did they merely stumble upon it? Did it arise from the convulsive movements made by someone very sick, which were then copied? Was it only another way of keeping warm? Or did it all start in a humorous way, with strange dance-like steps being made to entertain one's neighbours? Was it the result of a powerful, unfathomable joy or pain, which led the person to move in such a way as to escape an overwhelmingly powerful experience? Did it start out as an attempt to imitate the trees as the wind moved their branches? Were they lulled into the rhythms of the tides? Or maybe all these explanations were right It appeared to be a universal phenomenon; each ancient culture with its own dancing traditions and rituals, right down through to the present day. He was reminded of the words of a disdainful and superior Mr Darcy, commenting upon the dancing taking place at the Hertfordshire Assembly Rooms that: "Every savage can dance."

What he clearly didn't comprehend was that for some people, the urge to dance came from deep within, having very little to do with learned steps or social occasions; it was an urgent call and just as vital as giving birth. He dreamed of Isadora Duncan.

Chapter 19

Towards the Light

Mrs Judy Mogden was taking her first bold steps towards a life of church attendance and Christian belief, in the hope that by adding a spiritual dimension to her humdrum lifestyle, she would be able to make better sense of the world and her position in it; to lead the life she had been served up, but in a radically new way. There had to be more than what it had offered her up till now. She had got to know Giulia; Carmela and Domenico, and through them, Father John. Of course they too had their problems like everyone else but their lives somehow seemed more real, more colourful; more dynamic; more firmly anchored; more authentically lived out. They gave her a tiny glimpse into how her life could be and what did they all have in common? A religious faith. The question of money, she concluded, didn't come into it.

She had begun to meet with John, who surprisingly didn't appear to be any rush to claim her as a Catholic. He persuaded her that it would be preferable for her to take her time, reflect at length upon her past, find out who she was and work out why at this stage in her life she was showing an interest in Christianity. And he in turn would teach her about the Gospels and support her and together they would journey towards some kind of agreed destination.

Just the thought of looking back over one's life and scrutinising each remembered detail can be sickening in itself, particularly if it's for the very first time. So many painful and embarrassing memories, buried like Pompeii under years of dusty protective layers, but often destined to be uncovered, like most hidden goings on. And not merely individual incidents but whole chunks of one's life, which when examined, reveal a shocking lack of courage, honour and dignity: cowardly actions, the running away from tough decisions, the repeated fooling of oneself, the lies and excuses, the pride, the laziness, the lack of respect towards others; an interminable list of awfulness, which was to be faced head on.

Father John had suggested that she didn't try to tackle it all at once. It was not supposed to be the journey of a flagellant but more a fact-finding mission, heralding the first steps towards the light: merely a means to an end. She should not feel overburdened by past behaviour which didn't meet her present standards. Everyone had miserable life debris, including himself. Much better for her to consider her childhood to begin with, up to the age of about 10 or 11, to remember and rummage through the various experiences; rediscover her life with her parents, brothers and sisters, if she had any, to work out what kind of people they were, their attitudes to work and society, what they valued and how they transmitted those values to the rest of the family. And then the next time she and John were due to meet, she could share with him anything she chose for him to comment on.

So the journey back into her past life was underway; something she had never undertaken before, not even superficially. For her the past was dead; done and dusted. Now she realised that it was necessary to go back before she could go forward; she now felt ready to delve into the shadows of her early life, even though she expected to find it awkward (without quite knowing why!) What kept her on track was the belief that she would find out much more about what really made her tick, where she had come from, and that at a certain moment, she would finally be able to turn her back on that past and start living in a totally new way.

And Scrooge-like, she began to float (though unaccompanied in her case) back to her girlhood years.

She couldn't remember much about her life before the age of 4 or 5. But what was quite a disturbing discovery was that her first specific memories all seemed to be negative ones: the first two being linked to the classroom. There was the time when she had accidentally dropped all the drinking straws, which spilled out from the collapsed bottom of the soft cardboard carton, during the first week she had been appointed milk monitor. Even though she was pretty certain nice Mrs Carter had not shouted or reprimanded her in any way, she rediscovered her younger self inconsolable, bursting into a flood of tears and then doubly wounded by the humiliating public display she herself was putting on for the dumbfounded audience of classmates and teacher. How would she ever live it down? She re-experienced the feel of the flushed, red face; the jerky, uncontrollable sobs; those feelings of unbearable stupidity and ultimately failure.

There was also the unhappy episode when another child had accused her of something she hadn't done though details of the incident remained stubbornly vague. What was brutally clear, however, was that when the girl started calling her a 'beast', in such a hateful way, it made her feel that life had once again become too painful to bear. And not one of her so-called friends had spoken out in her defence. A double devastation. Fortunately from both these events Judy, the young child, had bounced back very quickly and within a few hours they had apparently become insignificant memories, unlikely to ever be trespassed on again. She now understood that in all likelihood and at that tender age, she wouldn't have spoken out either to support a friend or defend the truth. Our old survival instincts never far from the surface!

And then there were those early memories of harrowing pains in her lower abdomen and how these were being interpreted by her parents as an ongoing attempt, by their headstrong daughter, to stay off school.

This, Judy now realised, could possibly be explained by the fact that neither her mother nor father had enjoyed school, weren't successful academically, didn't value education and because of their own negative experiences defended themselves, as adults, by declaring on a fairly regular basis, that most teachers were stupid anyway. They both held that their sort of people didn't need fancy qualifications just a propensity to work hard and use the common sense they had been born with. And this was the family philosophy continuously imbibed by their three children. Judy was aware of the fact that both of her parents were semi-literate and she had often been summoned to help them with form-filling or read aloud letters from the bank to her father. This practice was never discussed or referred to in any way at home.

However, they did eventually listen to their ailing child, the matter going on for far longer than they would ever have played out to their own parents, and so they took her, albeit without conviction, to their family doctor, upon which she was quickly diagnosed with appendicitis. The past pains and frustration connected to not being believed, especially when it was by one's own parents, surged up in her again. She had been unfairly penalised by missing out on much of her education that year and had possibly harboured a deep resentment towards the two people she referred to as her parents.

She remembered receiving, while still in hospital, a beautifully handmade card from her teacher and all her classmates, a lovely, rediscovered thought; something she now wished had been kept. She also found herself delighting in memories of a hospital diet of jelly and ice cream.

Judy's parents both grew up on the same housing development, and appeared to be content to go on living in the same part of the world for the rest of their lives. They had married young and didn't waste any time starting a family. Her father worked for the railways, which allowed him to be the sole breadwinner, and her mother stayed at home, as did so many others then, responsible for the housekeeping and bringing up their three children. Never an easy life but a straightforward one. He would ritually hand over a portion of his wage every Saturday morning and each week she would endeavour to spend it wisely. Any money left over would be placed in one of a range of glass jars, which were kept in a kitchen cupboard for extra bills and for rare family treats and outings. They were proud people; lived frugal and modest lives and they kept their children adequately fed, bathed and suitably dressed. Their lives could have been symbolised by the front door step, which was kept clean and polished at all times, including the strip of glinting brass which covered it and Judy was reminded of one of her mother's favourite sayings, that cleanliness was next to Godliness. It was not a church-going family.

However, more recently even before her meetings with Father John Judy had started to think in a more objective way about her parents, something that had never really surfaced before. Yes of course she loved them; grateful that they were not heavy drinkers and that her father had rarely been out of work, unlike the parents of some of her contemporaries. But in terms of aspirations or creativity even, they were total non-starters. She and her brother and sister had never been encouraged to follow their dreams or discuss possible career paths. The unwritten rule that everything should just go on being as it was. That was how it was and it wasn't for the likes of them to upset the social applecart.

And although Judy hadn't achieved success at school, she had always clung on to the idea that had she been part of another kind of family, things might have been different. She had learned to read early, so early in fact that she couldn't remember not being able to do it. Primary School pupils weren't given homework as such in those days but were encouraged, during school holidays, to work on a range of projects. Her classroom imagination was always fired up and she would get quite excited by the many ideas which invaded her brain.

Yet once she got home, the enthusiasm inevitably waned, a mental laziness always set in, and nothing was ever pursued or achieved. She knew it was down to her; for in spite of her parents' views on the subject of education, they would never have stopped her getting on with a school project or two. In the classroom she was likewise responsible for underachievement, as she turned out to be an incurable daydreamer, and even when she promised herself, if only because she liked her teacher, that she would really try to follow the lesson being taught or the story being read aloud, within minutes and sometimes lulled by the teacher's tone of voice, she was staring out onto the scant grassy verges which surrounded the school building her thoughts carried away on a magic carpet to a faraway land.

She was also beginning to pick up on the fact that there were two types of pupils in her class, which in most cases, not only coincided with how clever or not they were and that had to do with the way they spoke and therefore the type of family they came from.

Judy could never stay serious for long and her mind wandered on to her school successes and achievements. She remembered being first in the class to learn to do the Splits and was Sevensies Champion for a good while, a competitive game which involved throwing a tennis ball against an outside wall in a range of different ways but didn't quite know how she would explain the splits to Father John, in the case he had never heard of it before and asked for a demonstration!

She burst out laughing at the thought and that brought to a close her first ever session of self-examination.

Chapter 20

Eden

The first proper conversation which took place between Giulia and James was long and intense. He had been inclined to bring up her 'lack of trust' comment from their first fleeting encounter but he quickly decided against it on two counts: firstly, that it would have shown that it had affected him in some way (it had certainly intrigued him) and secondly, that it would have appeared rude, seeing that Giulia had opened up her house to him (whispers of a new lifestyle?) with no questions asked. Sessions with Fr. John were already making their mark!

She had almost started to confide in him, laying bare certain thoughts she had been toying with over the weeks and months, regarding the state of the garden, an untended expanse that lay behind Casa Stella. Giulia had explained to him that in the early years she hadn't considered it at all as a place to do something with or for her to ever enjoy as such. It had always catered for visiting children, where, regardless of age or personality traits, they had all played out a tiny part of their childhood. It was a place where they had taken part in a range of different exploits hide and seek; treasure hunts; tree climbing; wall clambering; the building of dens; the putting on of plays; the creation of every type of adventure. It had promoted friendship, teamwork, laughter and breathlessness. The children of Judy Mogden, the children of Giulia's friends from Fielding House; her younger pupils during the warmer Summer months; the two brothers; even for a while the children of Domenico and Carmela.

It was partly laid to lawn and before Domenico had taken up residence, Giulia had always depended upon a series of her pupils' fathers, who would give up a few hours whenever needed, to keep the grass at a manageable level...Yes she could easily have hired a gardener, even a team of gardeners, but for some hidden reason, unknown even to her, she was loathe to do this. She herself had never been blessed with high levels of energy or much in the way of physical strength and despite a deep love of nature, she knew next to nothing about planting or sewing.

It had been solely the inside space of her house that had inspired her and had kept her brain buzzing with ideas, some bearing fruit and others proving far too wacky or inappropriate for such an elegant building. She was neither interested in current fashions nor in the glossy magazines whose photos captured images of 'perfect' interiors.

However, over recent weeks, Giulia had begun to install herself, for short bursts of time, in the small garden area at the front of the house, where the fig tree continued to thrive. At such times she humorously thought of herself as one of Harper Lee's Maycomb, Alabama old biddies "like soft tea-cakes with frostings of sweat and sweet talcum" as they sat on their rocking chairs of an evening on the veranda. She herself would sit peacock-proud upon a beautifully curved and ornate rattan chair, from which she looked out onto the natural world around her, trying to make sense of the birdsong which flooded the skies and the birds' desperate courting rituals. From now on the chair was always at the ready to be moved outside from its more familiar spot in the entrance hall.

It was during one of these 'Maycomb' sessions that a new idea began to take root, quite slowly to begin with, when her eyes and mind were opened up to connecting images, facts and events which had been there all along, only they'd remained separate and therefore insignificant. This had happened many times before to Giulia regarding her deep interest in words; she had often come across a brand new word, only to find it being used by different people in subsequent days, which strongly hinted that the word had been 'around' her all the time and yet also hidden from consciousness. Even more alarmingly, she would discover it then in a favourite book, a book she thought she knew particularly well yet unaware she had ever cast eyes on the word in question. So much to learn; so much already there and we just don't see it.

She had around that time stumbled upon a book she concluded that she must have purchased, but had no memory of doing so. It was a hefty, square-shaped publication with a once shiny cover, and described Renaissance gardens from all over Italy in words and pictures. She left it out and open around the house in convenient places, and whenever she had a few minutes to spare, would leaf through three or four more of its pages, buoyed up by man's timeless ability (and compulsion) to carve and shape the natural world into works of Art; a beautiful domination of little patches of our planet yet her mind always clinging on to the knowledge that the Nature Goddess would be back with a vengeance, rendering the neat straggly and turning the verdant brown. And in order for Man to keep intact the beauty he created, he in turn must become her slave and work indefatigably all year round to fight back against the excess growth, the frosts, the burning sun, the monsoons, the bugs, the fungal diseases. The goddess wins if the garden is worked; she also wins if the garden is left to its own jungle ways.

It was at this point that Giulia made the long belated link between the images in the book and the fact that for many years the well-proportioned garden space at the back of Star House had been totally neglected and unloved, more or less abandoned to its own devices. She could have created a place of beauty and wonder long ago. And as for the children who once used it, she still could have left wild a sizeable portion of it fit for their adventures. From her own reading adventures, she suddenly remembered Lucy Honeychurch telling her fiancé, the pompous Cecil Vyse, how she considered his natural setting to be in a room; how neither he seemed to belong to the world outside of rooms and elegant buildings. Was this really true of her? Why had she not thought of it, she who thought about everything? She who had often dreamt of the rose garden at her Convent School:

'Down the passage which we did not take

Towards the door we never opened

Into the rose-garden.'

What had caused her mind to block out even the possibility of creating something similar? Giulia vaguely remembered that visitors to the house had in fact sometimes asked her about what plans she had for it but in answer she would merely shrug her shoulders and casually change the subject.

However, once the first spark had been kindled, Giulia's brain was once again in overdrive.

Inspired by the book's images and the arrival of a torrent of thoughts in their wake, the first features for her new garden that were materialising in her brain were of statues of Venus and Cupid, and then little nymphs or cherubs which would peep out of half-hidden places, to surprise and delight the casual visitor and these she would be able to move around at leisure. Then she would get hold of vast Roman terracotta pots and fill them with miniature olive trees. Would olives actually grow in England? Rose bushes definitely. And then, of course, she would introduce water to her garden.

Yet once her imagination had stretched far and thin over the awaiting garden space having someone create a folly or two: a half-built bridge; an unfinished

Gothic arch – there was already an unstoppable ivy (one plant she could actually name) clambering most of the garden walls – she realised that perhaps her thoughts, like the ivy, had run away with themselves and what was needed was a cool head. She was not living on the Mediterranean amongst lemon and orange groves and it would be far more sensible to check out what kinds of plants and trees were suited to the local soils and the mild southern English climate. And then and only then inject a few subtle touches of colour to give the garden a warm Italian feel, in which she felt totally justified, she then identifying herself as last in one of the lines of an ancient tribe, which over the generations had helped people Southern Europe.

She delved back in time, into the maze of past thoughts and images, not with the help of history books, at least not to begin with. She merely wanted to dredge up from her own knowledge and education all that she knew about gardens from past epochs. First believing she knew very little at all on the subject, she was surprised by what emerged. A golden chain of names and facts emerged: the nearby Botanical Gardens at Kew, the Hanging Gardens of Babylon, one of the Seven Wonders of the ancient world, and yet not a trace of its terraces remained so what had they really been like? One could only imagine just like the Garden of Eden itself, there from the very start of human history. An earthly reflection of Paradise, offering up everything we could possibly need, seat of the Tree of Knowledge, of good and evil. And then of course the most poignant garden of them all where Christ spent those long and lonely hours among the wisdom of olive trees, leading up to Calvary, the scene of His crucifixion: the Garden of Gethsamane.

Trees she had always loved, but apart from her beloved fig tree, she could name or identify very few individual species. Years beforehand she remembered having accompanied a friend to a nearby town who had a job interview that day. It was a hot, balmy day and rather than wait for her in a local café' or even in the building itself, Giulia arranged to meet her afterwards in the nearby park. It wasn't long before she found herself lying under a giant tree - who knows what it was, probably an oak – totally entranced by the overhanging spread of its massive leaf-packed branches, which allowed tiny glimpses of the sky as a gentle breeze puffed and passed, offering up hundreds of moving pieces of blue mosaic; tiny windows onto a distantly cool blue world, softened by fluffy clouds. She couldn't remember after all these years, whether her friend was offered the position or not, but she had never forgotten those twenty minutes or so lying under the canopy of that proud plant. Her closeness to the ground and the tree trunk itself re-established in a moment; the collapsed bond between sophisticated, civilised man and the natural world, an authentic and powerful force, so subtle and far too poignant to put into words. The damp leafy smells of earth and growth.

Literature, she mused, was also full of magical secret gardens, sacred lakes, moonlit fountains and curative pools; all places of green comfort, the legend of the Green Man, possibly still on the move.

Which all took her back to another occasion when she had enjoyed a long conversation in a train carriage with a charming woman, the mother of a cluster of children, who had explained to her the importance of looking out onto the colour green and why in the days of those old-fashioned prams (perambulators), the inside of the pram's hood and of its fringed canopy (a baby's earliest view of the external world) were always green.

Chapter 21
An Unlikely Gardener

With eyes wide awake, James was falling into a state of semi-trance as he listened to this woman's spoken thoughts, as they drifted to and fro into past, present and future time. The workings of her eyes, her frown, her smile, her animated hands, all adding to the present moment, which caused the normal flow of time to be suspended. He listened patiently, her sentences almost without stops, her innermost thoughts translating into words whose echoes rippled endlessly outwards. He too had something to add to their conversation but he was holding onto it, holding back, wanting to surprise her to return just a little of the pleasure she was transmitting to him. It was a warm afternoon, not sunny but clammy and perfectly still.

At a certain point, he did take up the thread of conversation, quite effortlessly in fact, and started to tell her a little bit about his time at university, about how he'd had the opportunity during his second year to study the literature of the early eighteenth century something at the time he felt he knew very little about. The course was taken by a crotchety and snappy, seemingly ancient then, Miss Kylie. Had he been of a different, less awkward disposition, he would have allowed himself, like the majority of his fellow students, to sign up there and then to a lifelong love of this newly revealed, London-centric world. He did, however, admit at the time that she was the best teacher he had ever encountered when it came to her specialist knowledge and the hard passion she exuded for this literary period; its personalities, its architecture, its accomplishments, an age of Satire rooted within the emerging age of Enlightenment.

And now all this was catching up with him again. On the morning he left his house, he'd grabbed a pile of books to read while at Casa Stella, unopened since his late teens or early twenties, and it turned out to include some books from that Age of Satire course, which he found himself unpacking in his new surroundings.

He would notice in the days to come that Giulia also possessed some of the same titles. His present collection included: Joseph Andrews and Tom Jones; two hilarious late Restoration plays by George Farquhar; a book on the life of the lexicographer Samuel Johnson and the fiercely perceptive and satirical poetry of Alexander Pope. And at least two of those writers had lived in the local area! Having started to read them afresh, he quickly found himself making up for lost time; Miss Kylie's shared passion had reached James too, only for it to spill out years later in these very unlikely circumstances.

And he was reminded that from out of this brittle, spiteful yet uniquely colourful world, an age of masks and show, was also emerging an eighteenth-century taste for gardens.

James told Giulia that the City of London back then covered a much smaller area, more or less confined to the inside of the old city walls. Amongst the privileged and fortunate few, who inhabited the fashionable circles of the day, it was in vogue to have grand country houses built, in many cases along the banks of the Thames. Although not far from the city centre by our understanding today, these houses would provide an escape from the chaos, stench and dirt of the town and even more importantly, were places where one could impress one's friends. And such grand houses needed grand gardens (parks). He explained that even though he didn't have any specialist knowledge as such, he was aware that at that time in England, there was a move away from the geometric garden layouts 'de rigueur' on the continent, to a more natural landscape. It was the age of the influence of the sixteenth century Venetian architect, Andrea Palladio, and would launch to fame the very English 'Capability' Brown, with his external vision of vast sweeps of parkland, dotted for interest with Palladian pavilions, meandering lakes and pathways, bridges, temples, grottos, glasshouses and shrubberies. All in all a return to a distant classical age, which was to flourish during the reigns of the two later Georges.

He then went on to describe the pleasure gardens, another phenomenon of the age. Unlike the country estates, these were public places; Vauxhall and Ranelagh, being the names of two he remembered, which were located just outside of the city, and here was an opportunity for the different social classes to share in a similar experience. They were affordable and popular and offered a vast variety of entertainment: fireworks, concerts, balls and so on.

They also attracted a wide range of characters from the criminal underworld as pickings were rich.

Giulia listened in silence, fascinated by the unexpectedly fluid delivery of words. They had found a kind of mental meeting place and were both aware of it. She was now ready to bite the bullet:

"So how about you, James, helping me create a proper garden?"

"What? You mean me? But I know nothing about gardening. I've never even planted a… I don't even know what I should have planted as a child. The only thing I remember digging for in our garden at home was pirate treasure, even though we lived nowhere near the coast haha! I don't want to appear rude, but why don't you hire a professional designer and a few proper gardeners, why don't you just do that?"

"But anyone in my position could do that; don't you see this could be an adventure; a step into the unknown; I don't really know why you are here with us and I don't want or need to know but it might help you in some way."

There was an awkward silence and their fizzy meeting of minds went suddenly flat.

And James suddenly looking down at his watch declared: "Well, actually I have to go now. I said I'd give Father John a lift while his car is being fixed. Okay, so I will give it some thought but I think you've picked the wrong person, bye, Giulia."

Giulia didn't see James for the next couple of weeks at least. He had left a note for her on the kitchen table, which stated that he had to return home for a few days and that Father John was aware of the situation.

"Well, you know what this might mean, don't you, James? Have you considered the possibility that you felt uneasy about helping Giulia because you saw it as a kind of commitment? Let's make that your 'homework' this week. Think about times in your life when you've made a commitment to something or someone. Why did you make it? How did it make you feel? What was the outcome?"

"Will do, John, absolutely, it will be interesting if nothing else!"

A voice from deep within was also making itself heard. Was it a fear of the garden or failure, a fear of Giulia or even of himself that had caused James to withdraw so rapidly from Casa Stella? Both James and John were struck by very similar thought processes.

Giulia hadn't been overly affected by James' sudden change of heart. Yes, of course, it had taken her slightly aback but she had other matters on her mind, even more immediate than gardens or James. Her heart was heavy with secrets, some old, some more recently inherited, and she sensed there was more to come. It was a horrible situation, especially for someone like Giulia. A horrid clash of principles: honour, vows, family loyalty, personal morality, history, Christian teaching and even the law of the land.

For as many years as Domenico and Carmela had been living with their children at Casa Stella, they had been aware that Giulia would sometimes disappear for a few days at a time, usually just before the weekend and then return at the start of a new week, ready to take up her tuition commitments. These trips were never referred to other than Giulia letting them know how long she would be away. They came to know she had friends from her school days whom she liked to meet up with from time to time; they even came to stay with her and that sometimes she would visit places like Stratford upon Avon or go to literary festivals. Understandably, they had concluded quite early on that she had to have a lover; a mystery man, who for some tall dark reason, could not be part of her everyday life. And that meant just one thing that he had to be married. Strange though that she was so close to Father John, couldn't he as a friend and priest do anything about it? And why was someone as intelligent as Giulia wasting her time with a man she couldn't marry or at least introduce to the outside world? It would soon be too late for her to have children, but she could still be in with a chance and was in any case so good with them; they had seen that for themselves. How sad for a woman never to have known the joy of having children, not even one child. It just didn't add up.

Judy Mogden had also thought along the same lines as the De Martinos but they all made absolutely sure nothing was said while Giulia was 'in residence' and neither did they ever allow themselves to share a smirk, joke or giggle at her expense; they were all genuinely interested in her well-being, but it is also fair to say that such a mystery did arouse their individual curiosities.

Chapter 22

Journey Back in Time

"Buongiorno, Gennaro, come stai, e Nunzia?"

Giulia was met by a short, late middle-aged man on arrival at the train station. To Giulia it was a God-forsaken spot, that any visitor might also have labelled the middle of nowhere; somewhere in deepest, darkest England. As on a couple of previous occasions, once having made the sign of the cross, the man took her by car on a twenty-minute journey towards a house, even bigger and more palatial than Casa Stella. It was reached by a sweeping gravel drive, which continuously crunched under the impact of the car's wheels. Their conversation continued in Italian, Gennaro speaking a mixture of dialect and standard Italian, with dialect ultimately winning out. She understood most of what he was saying, as she had heard the same platitudes delivered up on numerous occasions, to such an extent, she now believed that she understood completely the mentality of those of his gender and generation from a shared region back in Italy and she probably would have been able to predict word for word the rest of their verbal exchange.

The journey had already consisted of three trains and had hitherto taken about four and a half hours. Giulia was understandably quite tired by the end of it. On this particular occasion, she had found herself dozing off in the knowledge that a pleasant young man in the carriage of the last train had promised to wake her, should she have fallen asleep by the time they were approaching her station. She would have to return home on Monday morning and therefore hadn't needed to take much in the way of clothing. But she did have with her a bottle of grappa and some Cuban cigars, both impressively boxed, items she had purchased at the airport from her last trip abroad. There was nothing her host would actually have needed but she had long been inculcated with the knowledge that one could never arrive empty handed when making any kind of visit.

At the house there was an invitingly huge sunken bath, in a room next to 'hers' on the ground floor, in which she would enjoy a long hot soak at some point after her arrival. And from within the rose-perfumed water, she would be able to look out onto the house's emerald green and velvet surroundings. Once again she wondered how the visit would pan out this time; what new information she would be privy to; what would be asked of her. She loved him intensely; she also hated him, only a fine line dividing the two extremes.

They were due to meet for a late lunch once her host, with the help of Gennaro, had cleared the day of its tedious business meetings and 'phone calls, and could then fully devote himself to a leisurely meal and Giulia.

She thought he looked in better health than when they had last met and was touched by the fact that, as a man of few words, he had felt the need to apologise for not sending one of the luxury cars to pick her up, but that there were good reasons for this. And Giulia duly reminded him that she had little interest in such excesses. He spoke entirely in Italian, asking the usual questions about her journey and life at Casa Stella. However, he appeared somewhat perturbed when Giulia told him of James and how she and the others were trying to help him.

"No, Giulia, I don't like the sound of this at all! None of you know anything about him; he could murder you all in your beds; have you checked where he is from? I don't understand you at all! Have you all gone mad?"

"There are very good reasons for what I do!" she retaliated. "And one day I will explain it all to you. But for now I know it would be a total waste of time and in any case, it was Father John, who first asked me for help. I can't exactly refuse him now, can I? After all he's done for us and James is alright. No one has had anything to say against him well not that I know of."

"Yes, Nunzia, bring in the antipasto, what have you got for us today? Carciofini? Good, my favourite, oh and the prosciutto looks wonderful. Yes more melon I think and have you any of those olives we had the other day?"

Nunzia dutifully returned with a second dish of melon, perfectly sliced, and the requested green olives and promptly left the pair to continue their previously animated exchange.

However, the meal continued in silence for what seemed, to Giulia, an unbearably protracted amount of time until she could no longer stay put. Her body was suddenly engulfed by a huge wave of filial devotion and in response and despite her age, she leapt out of her chair and hugged him furiously, kissing him many times on the forehead.

"I'm just happy you look so much better than last time! I'm just so happy you are safe."

Giovanni appeared to make little of her impulsive actions, waving at her with a repeated gesture from his right hand to sit down and get on with the cannelloni Nunzia had made in her honour. But he was about to surprise her as well.

"Are you sure about the last time you saw me, Giulia, I thought I cut a very dashing figure that day?"

"What do you mean, Papà?"

"Oh, Giulia, you disappoint me. I had always considered you to be the observant type. Don't tell me you didn't notice a very elegant gentleman of a certain age wandering in and out of the festivities at Lorenzo's wedding? A man in a light ochre coloured suit, panama hat, wearing sunglasses?"

"Papà, I don't believe it! What do you mean? You were actually there? With us all on that wonderful day? Why didn't you tell me? I just can't believe it! You actually saw Carmela? To think you were there and I had no idea?"

And thus their conversation took off and progressed. Giovanni even managing to produce a polaroid photo of the wedding feast, revealing his distinguished self, just as he had described, only centimetres away from the bride and groom. For once even Giulia was lost for words, as she was catapulted, if only for a few seconds, body and soul, back to that magical day on the Costa Amalfitana.

She then made a heartfelt plea to her father, the same plea which surfaced during nearly every visit that he might finally consider letting Carmela know the identity of her father, that she actually had a father who was alive and well. The harsh reply was also one Giulia had heard before: that the time wasn't right; that it was impossible to miss someone she had never known; that Carmela wasn't the sentimental type anyway, not someone who fantasised about her past and how things might have turned out differently; that she was a practical woman with few *grilli per la testa*, doing her best to bring up her family; that he wanted Giulia to put a stop to this nonsense once and for all, that she should stop applying her way of seeing the world to other people. He reminded her, not because she needed reminding, but to bring the matter to a close, that he had always used all his power to safeguard the interests of both his daughters, and that his decision to be present at his grandson's wedding had put him at substantial personal risk.

The pair made their way into a sitting-room, Giulia refusing all the liqueurs she was offered. Giovanni, on the other hand, took firm hold of a bottle of Fernet Branca, and was closely followed by a diligent Nunzia with a silver tray containing drinking glasses. Deeply sighing, Giulia sank back into a brown leather, Chesterfield type armchair, and her father chose the one opposite, so he could properly study his wilful daughter from a close distance. The room had huge rectangular windows, each flanked by wine red velvet curtains, which were tied with cords ending in hefty gold tassels. The dark oil paintings which covered the walls, each in an ornate gilt frame, were all of the same type: a mixture of romanticised scenes of Vesuvius, narrow and winding Neapolitan streets, still life, harbour scenes and seascapes all of which added to the gravitas of the room. Their feet had walked on marble floors, scattered here and there with an assortment of rugs.

The house apparently belonged to an old friend of her father's, who was happy to rent it out to him a couple of times a year, partly in order to see Giulia and partly for business purposes. He preferred this house to stays at a busy English hotel.

Funnily enough, it had only now dawned on Giulia as she once again took in her surroundings, that it was exactly the same style of furnishings that she encountered in each Italian home she entered, whether in England or in Italy, even those of far less grand interiors and far more modest dimensions.

Giovanni watched his daughter as her gaze wandered around the room. He wished she could shake off its intensity. She thought too hard and too deeply about absolutely everything, never allowing herself some time off, time to relax and escape into a world of trivial pastimes and pleasures, which he was clearly able to do; these she would surely have considered a waste of precious time. But there again he had to admit to himself that since he only saw her a few times a year, perhaps she was merely displaying a kind of bottled behaviour she kept exclusively for when in his company. He would never allow himself to consider the possibility of her taking lovers. That would have been unbearable. She was now about 40, still beautiful with those dramatic looks, though still a mere child, if judged by her outward behaviour towards him; the classic father-daughter dynamic. It was also true of him; he still felt the need to protect her from the world and she still needed to worship at his feet.

"So, Giulia, I will get Nunzia to call you with the dates of your next visit but don't let's waste the time we have now. How about a game or two of 'scopa' or draughts if you prefer? We can still talk and you can tell me about Lorenzo and his new bride. I won't be available tomorrow morning; Gennaro has planned something for you in the village but I hope to be back in the afternoon, at least in time for dinner."

"Don't worry, Papà, you know how independent I am. I have some reading to catch up with and if it's okay, I'd like to take a leisurely walk around the grounds. It's reassuring you look so well. I spotted a new twinkle in your eye as soon as I arrived and yes I have noticed you are growing your sideburns quite long. Don't tell me there's a woman waiting in the wings, oh, Papà, what's going on?" Giulia's words being delivered with a quiet mock disapproval.

"What nonsense, Figlia Mia, you know there is no room in my heart for anyone else but you!"

Chapter 23

Serafina's News

"Giulia, when you have a moment, could I talk to you about something?"

"Yes, of course, what is it, Serafina? Is everything alright? I tell you what, give me a few minutes and I'm all yours. Shall I meet you at your house or would you rather stay here?"

"Come to mine, oh that would be lovely and I've been making cannoli, well a kind of cannoli – I can't get all the right ingredients here. I'll see you soon then!"

Serafina left Casa Stella that day looking much happier than when she'd first arrived. All at once Giulia realised that perhaps she should have checked on her a little more often or at least invited her to her own suite of rooms, during her first few weeks in England. She comforted herself, however, with the thought that it was probably better that she had kept her distance; Carmela, she knew, popped to her son's new house at least three or four times every day surely leaving her new young daughter-in-law very little time to herself and her new surroundings.

Giulia arrived at Lorenzo's house within the hour, apologising for the delay. She was aware Carmela was out for the afternoon and that Lorenzo was at work so it was highly unlikely they would be disturbed.

The house looked clean and tidy with little touches here and there showing that, although far away from her sunny Sicilian world, she was trying to turn this alien English house into a home, as much for herself as for Lorenzo. They sat in the sparsely furnished kitchen, which smelled of sweet ricotta. There was, on the table, a little vase of brightly coloured flowers Serafina had picked earlier from those she had found in the front garden, and Giulia noticed since her last brief visit, that each of the four kitchen chairs had been covered with a padded material, a blue and white gingham, which added to the sense of homely cosiness.

The first part of their conversation was marked by mutual smiles and expressions of politeness. And Giulia was reminded just how young and lovely she was, made all the more attractive by the dusting of flour which part covered her forehead, and how gracefully she moved around the room. She tried to remember if she herself had once been so fetching in her youth but it was an impossible question and totally ridiculous. She was now fast approaching middle age.

The two women eventually made an arrangement that twice a week Giulia would give her lessons in English, provided Serafina made every possible effort to do homework and practise her spoken English whenever possible with Lorenzo, and whenever out and about. Giulia knew that so many people got excited about the idea of learning a foreign language but were hardly ever prepared for the huge commitment needed and conscious as to how lonely it could be, applying grammatical rules to awkwardly invented sentences and pouring over never-ending lists of vocabulary. She remembered declaring to one of her past students that if she had been able to drill a hole into his head and pour in the desired language then of course she would do so, but while that was still beyond the realm of possibility, he would have to do the work himself. She as teacher could explain, give examples and teach the pronunciation; he as student would have to learn, continuously revise and practise! As for Serafina, she at least had the distinct advantage of living in England and not confined to the artificiality of a distant classroom. She had also seemed keen to tell her guest that she had already made a start by making friends with the Englishwoman who lived next door and was already exchanging pleasantries with her.

It was becoming ever clearer to Giulia that she was in the company of a bright young woman (much more than the trophy bride, whom Lorenzo was planning to show off at a forthcoming airline party); she had nice manners and all in all was proving to be far more talented and competent than what might have been expected from a simple country girl from a remote Sicilian village. Was Lorenzo even aware of this? She wondered what he would have to offer her, other than material security, in the years to come once passion had paled.

This was a girl, who in spite of her hitherto limited opportunities and a life spent entirely with two maiden aunts, was able to speak beautifully and articulately on albeit a narrow range of topics, and had even read Giulia's own favourite Italian novel *Il Gattopardo* (loosely translated in English as The Leopard). If nothing had completely sealed their friendship up till then, this wonderful book served to mark a new start in both their lives. On mere mention of the literary masterpiece, Serafina leapt up from her chair, almost spilling the cup of lemon tea in front of her, only to return seconds later with a well-worn copy of the same title, explaining that her aunts had given it to her a couple of years ago and that she always kept it close by. She also found the courage to admit to Giulia that she didn't understand it completely, but that only added to the magic and joy of reading a text so beautifully written. She even remembered from her schooldays that most of her friends were eventually put off reading classic works because of words and phrases they encountered that made no sense to them, often belonging to a distant age. For her it was the opposite: it was those very words and phrases which filled her with a desire to read more and more, in the hope that one day she would be able to unlock their secrets.

For Giulia it was like meeting her former self.

After a few moments of silence, when each woman was locked into her own set of swirling thoughts, they both came to, remembering where they were; that they were not alone, and both began commenting in turn on the more mundane aspects of their everyday lives. They also went on to exchange examples of their particular likes and dislikes, keeping the tone jokey and light-hearted, neither yet wanting to divulge the more intimate details of their lives, but knowing that with time, they had each found the perfect person with whom to do just that, in spite of differences in age and life experience.

"I'd almost forgotten," laughed Serafina a couple of hours later, "the reason I asked you here in the first place. I wanted to tell you before anyone else, and I'm not even quite sure myself why that is, but I wanted to tell you, Giulia, that I think I'm pregnant, I'm going to be a mother."

"What? Are you sure, Serafina? Oh that's come as a bit of a shock oh gosh, are you alright; are you happy about it? That's all that matters, I suppose but perhaps the first thing we need to do is find out for sure; yes, of course, I will come with you, but I think it's best we keep quiet about it for now; Carmela might feel a bit left out of the picture and rightly so. Oh my goodness, that's the last thing I was expecting you to come out with. It's wonderful news, let me give you a hug!"

The two women then parted company for the time being, Serafina just a little uncertain about the effect her news had had on Giulia, the woman who had just become, albeit in a tiny way, a possible replacement for her beloved aunts; not that Serafina had even begun to think along those lines yet.

Along that very short walk back to Casa Stella, Giulia felt the proverbial weight of the world on her shoulders and didn't really understand why. The news that Serafina, her new young friend, would be losing her already limited independence and sense of identity at an appallingly young age only weeks after getting married was certainly part of it, and of course it answered her earlier question as to what Lorenzo might have to give her in the years to come; he would give her babies, who would in turn take up their place in the world, and continue the family line. And a devoted Serafina would look after them, especially when needy and helpless, pouring into them every last drop of love and herself and many years later, they would one day look after her; for the wellbeing and continuity of the species.

Carmela had already returned and the two sisters spent a while chatting, sweeping floors and folding sheets together in the main downstairs kitchen. Carmela also wanted to begin dusting the vast collection of bonbonniere (many still with uneaten sugared almonds attached) and other knick-knacks she kept in a curved-legged glass cabinet, proud witness to the many weddings and other special occasions she had attended. And Giulia knew her sister would never trust another cleaner with such treasures and so always undertook the dusting process herself.

Giulia had her own smaller kitchen upstairs but didn't spend much time in it; it was more a convenience, while she was in her rooms on the first floor. In spite of her own loss of personal freedom, she was clearly happy she had invited Carmela and her family to come live with her all those years ago. It helped keep her life on an even, normal path; it had taught her so much about human nature and family dynamics. She enjoyed the role of aunt and it gave her a deeply rooted satisfaction she had been able to reward a hardworking couple, a couple with blood links, whose previous lives had known only hardship. She had done it for them and for her father; she had done it for herself, having got back a sizeable part of hitherto unknown family. There was no such thing as a purely altruistic gesture; each came with its own exquisite or token reward but what did that matter when good was the outcome?

Carmela seemed a little more light-hearted on this occasion; perhaps she already had an inkling that Serafina might be pregnant or perhaps she was daydreaming of a time when she and Menicuccio would become grandparents. Their son would never have to suffer poverty's relentless bite as they had done for so many years. They already had a house; Lorenzo would bring home money and Serafina would cook, clean, look after the house, support her hardworking husband in every way and one day give birth, which in Italian is literally translated as a poetic 'giving to the light' to his children. There was nothing that could give a woman more happiness; a man more pride. And even though her husband Domenico would never talk about such things, by now she could read his heart and knew that he felt exactly the same.

Carmela was so happy they had eventually put aside their pride and suspicions, had made that leap of faith and had agreed to Giulia's offer of sharing a home with her. Even though there were still many aspects of her sister's life and character she didn't begin to understand, she loved her unconditionally. Giulia had never made her feel inferior or reminded her of the huge sacrifice she herself had made. This woman had also grown to love her nephew and nieces in spite of the long, dark adolescent moods and inevitable stark differences of opinion. And even the hard-headed Domenico had come to admire and respect her.

Chapter 24

Locked Doors, Drawn Curtains

Later that evening, Serafina was left dreaming of a future son, a son she would call Fabrizio. Just how would it change her? Her mind, her body, her life, which had already changed beyond all recognition, in a matter of a few weeks. Her mind was definitely in a maelstrom; a tight knot of whirling thoughts and impulses. Now she was also in a race to learn English. Her son would have Italian blood but would grow up as an English boy. She needed to be part of all of that, or else face exclusion. Oh but then, it could be a girl…

Past conversations surfaced, ancient chatter that had taken place in her silent presence, in that ludicrous way adults behave, fooling themselves that mere children were immune from so-called adult topics. Yes, they may not fully understand what they hear, but that's exactly what makes such conversations memorable; resurfacing every now and then in the child's mind, as they grow and develop, until the emerging young adult can complete the picture.

She remembered her aunts whispering on various occasions about births they had been present at or assisted in, at a time and place when birth was a much more public matter, a community event. Husbands or men in general were kept out, kept away always being informed of any outcome after the event. If the child was a male child, there would be celebrations; if the baby turned out to be a girl, verbal congratulations were much more muted in tone. There would also be no rush on the part of the baby's father to go visit his wife and daughter. If she was a third, fourth, or fifth daughter, commiserations were the order of the day. A case of never minds and better luck next time. It was also believed in their world that it was the woman's body that determined the sex of the child.

With time, however, a father's deep love for his daughters would often develop and it was accepted that each parent would have a favourite child, which eventually became common knowledge.

Over the years her aunts would also comment on the length of the various village births they had witnessed, the bravery (or not) of the mother in question, the mother's screams from pain to ultimate joy. There was also a popular saying which maintained that the more a woman suffered in childbirth, the more she would love that child.

It was traditional for the first-born son to take on the name of his paternal grandfather (even if he already had many cousins of exactly that name.) It was expected; a fundamental sign of respect for one's family. It would cause lasting problems for families, who for whatever reason, did not follow these strict unwritten codes of practice; some children more highly favoured than others, especially by their grandparents, all because of a name they had been given, or not given. A first-born baby girl would likewise take on the name of her paternal grandmother. Fortunately, for subsequent children, there was a bit more freedom in the choosing of names. Middle names, whether for boys or girls, were still rare.

If this were the case, it was highly unlikely that Lorenzo would consent to calling his son Fabrizio and he probably didn't have any interest whatsoever in the character of the Prince in *The Leopard* (even though paradoxically they had quite a few things in common!). In spite of his youth, Lorenzo had already shown her that he believed in the old way of doing things; that if people got rid of past traditions, we would be left with a meaningless, grey and empty world. It was down to each new generation to pass on such treasures, to keep the family story alive!

In reality her son would be called Domenico or Dominic in English. But she would do whatever she could to ensure that no one ever referred to him as Menicuccio, or even worse, Menicu.

Serafina then came to. How silly she had been, letting such thoughts run away with themselves, like young and naive wild horses. Her pregnancy had not even been confirmed yet she laughed aloud at her sheer stupidity. And was subsequently filled with a kind of warm relief. She had worked herself into quite a state. But was now calming down. One day at a time. And as for that particular day, all she really had to think about, now all the housework was out of the way, was that her new husband would soon be home and that they would once again be spending a long, sultry night in each other's arms.

What no one would ever know though about Serafina (except for the three others, directly involved), not Lorenzo, not Father John, not even Giulia, was that she had already known and loved a young man in Sicily. He had been her secret, summer-afternoon lover, visiting her while her two aunts, both heavy sleepers, enjoyed their daily siesta on the other side of the house. He would arrive and leave in silence, but they spent the time in between loving and listening to the songs of Franco Battiato (her favourite) and Vasco Rossi (his.) Fortunately for them, she lived in a fairly secluded spot, far from the prying eyes of gossip-starved villagers. The long, light and gauzy curtains would rhythmically dance to and fro in the gentle afternoon breeze but had anyone actually been passing, they would have merely heard the music, blasting out of the room; sometimes plaintive, sometimes rock. It had been her one and only love story. She and her lover were young and idealistic so, of course, the relationship hinged heavily on physicality, but also on wild promises and impossible shared dreams for the future.

Doomed from their first encounter, this heavenly interlude was brought to an abrupt end by her Aunt Maddalena, who one fateful evening, had seen a near-naked Davide running off across the fields. Serafina was in floods of tears, uncontrollable in fact, for many hours but by the following morning, she had fully composed herself, resigned to the fact that she would never see her lover again for her own good of course. Her aunts would take care of every aspect of the situation. It was time for them to act swiftly on behalf of their darling niece; a marriage had to be arranged, in order to save their wayward Serafina. They blamed themselves. They had left things too long and of course they even knew why. A marriage would mean separation; they would inevitably lose her and even though they had, years ago, begun a genuine local search for a serious-minded young lad, someone truly worthy of her, they hadn't alas found a suitable match.

By sheer coincidence and within a short period of time, they had discovered, through the family and village grapevine, that a young man was going to be arriving shortly in Syracuse province itself, from a country called England and accompanied by an older family friend, with a view to finding him a young bride. Ideally, she would be a village girl, who like him still believed in traditional values, in a rapidly changing world. So after background checks and research had been carried out, confirming that no handicaps, mental or physical ran in her family, a meeting was arranged at the aunts' house, where Lorenzo and Serafina might meet and get to know each other.

Serafina was pleasantly surprised, that on seeing him for the first time, it became apparent fate was being far from cruel: Lorenzo came across as physically pleasing; well-mannered and confident in his own brand of worldliness; someone who in spite of his youth, exuded a sense of maturity and responsibility well beyond his years. And he in turn was immediately charmed by her beauty and composure. He had been allowed to carry in his wallet a small black and white photograph of her which clearly didn't do her justice and had been reminded on more than one occasion that if the couple decided not to go ahead with a marriage, he would have to return it; it was merely on loan. '*Brave ragazze*' (good girls) from good families never distributed images of themselves. Serafina had thus never given a photo of herself to her former lover! Did she still love him? She knew it was futile to harbour lingering thoughts. So in an instant he had been felled out of her heart and mind with a single swipe of the knife.

Lorenzo's trip to Sicily had not therefore been in vain. Life was proving good; he loved his work at the bustling international airport; he was devoted to his family; he had now in all probability found the perfect young wife.

And things proceeded well. The couple spent, under the circumstances, a considerable amount of time together, with Serafina's aunts inevitably hovering in the background, whether inside or outside of the house. Her chaperones had an even more important role than before. It was planned that the couple would go ahead and get married, not in Syracuse, but across the sea, on the mainland where Lorenzo's family originated. This came across as a generous gesture on behalf of the Sicilian contingent but of course it also allowed Serafina and her aunts to avoid the humiliating custom of the bride having to expose the wedding sheet complete with bloodstain from an upper balcony, on the morning after the wedding, as evidence of her hitherto virginal state. And in this way the aunts wouldn't have had to go to the bother of creating such a stain from an alternative source!

They were in truth both devastated but had nobly continued to play out to the world the roles of two women full of proud satisfaction; a happy ending to their years of dedication. They had no idea if they would ever see Serafina again and were, in truth, shell-shocked and heart-broken, the centre of their universe about to be ripped out and smashed to smithereens. But if self-sacrifice were called for...and they each knew a lot about that – that was the course they would follow. One comforted the other in turns by reminding her that it was always going to happen; they had fulfilled their life's work alas, their sister's child would one day be leaving them!

But why, oh why did she have to be going so far away?

As for Giulia, she had become aware of her own niece Tina's uncharacteristic behaviour of late, nothing she could lay the proverbial finger on, and certainly nothing she had deliberately looked for but there was definitely something amiss! She had never wanted to play the role of the invasive aunt so just relied upon her experience of life, which had taught her that if it was significant, it would eventually come to light.

And her own life was on the brink of a possible new episode also with the arrival of Casa Stella's latest member: James Newhouse. He presented the kind of enigma she was happy and ready to unravel, though bit at a time, in the opposite way from how detectives operate. She would never demean herself by using methods which would cause her to spy, stalk or even make enquiries. She would never actively intervene. He would either quietly dissolve out of her life…or become a greater part of it. She shuddered and fizzed with excited anticipation, not knowing if he was ever going to consider a return to her beloved Star House.

Chapter 25
Around the Table

It was a normal Sunday at Star House; no birthdays to celebrate or church feast days to consider. Yet to any visitor, the huge kitchen would still have presented a busy and festive scene, infused with rich cooking smells and loud voices of the many people coming in and out. Carmela had begun to create the all-important ragu' the previous evening, making sure on the Sunday, it continued to simmer on a low heat and was religiously stirred at 15-minute intervals. And Domenico had remembered as always to bring back from the family delicatessen the necessary salamis, cheeses and a range of interesting looking jars, each containing vegetable layers, individually arranged 'sott'olio', such as sliced aubergine, artichoke hearts, sundried tomatoes and zucchini; all to play their part in an abundant antipasto. Had thirty guests turned up unexpectedly there still would have been plenty to eat.

Giulia, when home on a Sunday, always took it upon herself to lay and decorate the long kitchen table. She couldn't quite accept the fact that her sister, who cooked so beautifully and with so much skill and care, would have been quite happy at the end of her efforts to merely hand out plates and dishes, as people were taking up their places, and then deposit with an ugly clatter, a vast number of uncounted knives, forks and spoons somewhere in the middle of the table. No for Giulia, and especially on a Sunday (even if it were just the family present), it was important to make the table look as appealing as possible: sometimes with flowers or candles; always with gleaming cutlery perfectly positioned and neatly folded linen napkins placed in glasses. These were examples of the tiny elegant touches, which allowed Giulia to savour every moment of life rather than merely survive it. It was rare that anyone inside the family would comment on how pretty or colourful or interesting it all looked, whereas there would inevitably follow a whole stream of compliments for

Carmela about the ingredients, the flavours, the preparation process of the meal itself. Giulia knew one 'couldn't eat the table'; something her sister had once retorted, but she remained stubbornly happy in the carrying out of these superfluous tasks, if only for her own pleasure.

That day she laid for nine people; there would be no James – he still hadn't returned and no Father John, it being the busiest day of his week. However, Lorenzo and Serafina would be joining them, as they did every Sunday (and even Serafina on her own, when Lorenzo was working.) Today they would finally encounter Sandra's new boyfriend, who had yet to meet the De Martino family. Everyone was aware that for her slightly older sister, Patrizia, it would be a difficult few hours, as she had never had a boyfriend herself (Sandra now onto her third) and she knew the pressure was on. And in the same way as for previous occasions, Sandra would now be fully committed to this new relationship, yet also conscious of the fact that if it were to lead to marriage, it would highlight to the outside world, that is to the traditional Italian working-class world, that the eldest De Martino daughter had practically been left on the shelf and so, in a sense, defective.

The sisters were 23 and 22 years of age.

For Patrizia it would also mean that going out, in a social sense, would now be next to impossible; no longer would she get her father's blessing to go out of an evening with friends, as Sandra would want to be on her own with Gary (or for as long as she could get away with) and she had already had to get used to the situation, that a now married Lorenzo would no longer be inclined to accompany his older sister of an evening to a disco or to go see a film. The fact that she had reached adulthood held no sway whatsoever in this household even had she been much older; while she lived under her parents' roof, she had to abide by their rules, which included being back home by 11 pm. She hadn't given up completely, however, on the hope that one day, a 'Principe Azzurro', a knight in shining armour would burst into the delicatessen, where she worked alongside her father, and carry her away.

She who laughs last, laughs longest after all.

It was almost time for everyone to take up their seats around the table; Gary had already arrived, having been momentarily whisked away by Sandra into one of the side rooms, no doubt for a last-minute briefing on what to say or more importantly what not say in the presence of her family. Serafina had turned up an hour beforehand to help with the cleaning and clearing away of the cooking utensils; Lorenzo was now on the doorstep carrying a couple of bottles of red wine, much to his father's displeasure. "What have you brought that rubbish here for?" Domenico maintaining that the only wine worth drinking with meals was home-made and totally free of additives. On that minor matter Lorenzo was no longer in agreement with his father, having rapidly come under the influence of what he saw and heard at the airport. His work colleagues, although coming from a wide range of social backgrounds, all seemed to enjoy or at least aspire to a sophisticated life-style, as a consequence no doubt of what they had experienced during each of their concessionary travels, and even the workplace offered up the daily reminder of Duty Free shops, which sold goods of the highest quality; glamorous objects of desire.

Tina during all this was playing the buffoon by striding round the whole house banging a dented copper pan with a wooden spoon repeatedly screeching: "*A mangiare, a mangiare, tutti a tavola!*"

Goodness knows what was going through poor unsuspecting Gary's head at that moment in time But he was happy that, after witnessing the wild gesticulations slicing the air between Lorenzo and his father, his own bottle of what turned out to be a very cheap white wine had been forgotten in all the chaos, as it stood shamefully within the plastic shopping bag wound round it, on a little table in the hallway.

Domenico entered the kitchen last of all. He seated himself as was customary at the far end of the table, 'a capo tavola'. Carmela was seated closest to the pans, dishes and oven. "Bread, where's the bread?" he exclaimed. "You can't call this a meal, without bread on the table!"

"Oops, my mistake!" broke in Giulia, "It's all sliced. Now where did I put it? Oh yes, here behind me; it was when the telephone rang…"

The meal began in relative silence. Domenico didn't believe in table-chat while eating; he said it could cause you to choke on the very food which brought you together to table in the first place. It might also have doubled as a convenient excuse for him though, as he wasn't a natural conversationalist at any time of day; it was enough for him that people knew how to behave when in his company. However, Giulia had found his own manners quite rough and rude, to say the least, at the beginning. It was quite some time later she learned that he was not without kindness and did after all possess a deep, dry sense of humour. However, he preferred to keep these qualities hidden, she being the only one able to charm him or soften him into a change of heart, provided that it never appeared to the outside world that he was becoming weak. She had also come to realise that he was a loyal husband to Carmela, and that they both lived exclusively, for what they truly believed was the well-being of their family.

Once the 'primo piatto' had been served: massive portions of home-made gnocchi, complete with the necessary engravings, as they had each been fork-rolled by Carmela and her two eldest daughters, generously smothered in the bright red ragù sauce, Domenico broke with De Martino tradition and in very broken English began to engage Gary in conversation. "So what do you think of the gnocchi? My wife makes the best gnocchi in the world, don't you think?"

"Oh yes, it's really nice, thank you. And thank you for inviting me," came the shaky reply.

"Well if you are going to be part of the family…so what does your father do for a living? Your mother doesn't go out to work, does she? And here began an interrogation on Gary's family; his own prospects and intentions."

"Papà, stop it! You are embarrassing him, and in front of everyone," blurted out Sandra.

"Just making sure that Gary understands our ways, he's English after all! A 'fidanzato' (boyfriend) in the house is a serious matter. It means he has responsibilities; he's not here to play around with my daughter's feelings or even worse." And in spite of a very poor grasp of English and his heavy Italian accent, he managed to make his point quite clear to everyone present.

Giulia had fortunately interrupted Domenico's stream of vocal concern for his daughter's welfare, smoothing out any misunderstandings arising from the harshness of her brother-in law's words, as much as for Sandra as for Gary himself. She had also stopped Sandra from getting up to run out of the room by placing a firm hand over her niece's left knee under the table. And the meal continued in an awkward atmosphere yet free from further threats or accusations.

Several hours after Gary had left for home and a heartbroken Sandra had finally put a stop to the torrent of tears and soulful sobs, which could be easily heard by anyone who happened to be passing her room, she managed to convince herself that there could still be a chance that he would not abandon her. She headed for Giulia's rooms, praying her aunt was still at home.

"Giulia, Oh thank God you are here. Please help me, please promise you'll help me get Gary back."

"But why? Has he left you? He seemed to cope with the situation better than…"

"He went home early and hasn't tried to ring me oh please Giulia. You are the only one who can help. I did nothing wrong I think Papà does it on purpose."

"Okay, come in, of course I will help you. I'll explain to him how your father was only trying to protect you and that he didn't mean to be rude; it's his way; it's to do with where he comes from. But Sandra, listen carefully and not because I think this will happen. You seemed far more upset than he did. But if Gary decides he doesn't want any more to do with this family or with you, it shows his love for you isn't strong enough, in a way we can treat it like a test. If this is the case, you must find the strength to accept the consequences. But I have told you all this before."

"Yes, of course, oh thank you, Giulia, what would I, or any of us come to that, do without you?"

Chapter.26

Ocean

Earlier in the year, Father John had taken one of his habitual trips home; home being the west coast of Ireland. And inexplicably, each trip took on a surprising flavour of its own. An ongoing collection of bittersweet joys and old experiences re-lived: weather permitting long hours spent looking out onto the vast ocean from a weather-beaten old deck-chair; long, windy walks along the bay; random encounters with locals and sometimes with strangers, people whose memories could travel way back in time and furnish him with bits of quirky folklore about him as a child, his family, the local area. He was always humbled; couldn't believe after all these visits, he was still being fed intriguing historic morsels of which he had no prior memory or knowledge.

However it was the ocean itself which primarily fed his imagination – you just couldn't get enough of it, he remembered once telling his English parishioners; it was unfathomable, enigmatically powerful, overwhelmingly beautiful, a watery wilderness, in all its hourly changes. And then the comfort of making out the little islands always there, greenly welcoming; providing a frontline against the limitless grey-blue world stretching out west and south; stepping stones to a historic and ongoing escape route.

But surely nobody really wants to leave behind the place of their childhood; it's too ingrained; it can't just simply be chopped away from everything else: family, friends, home, school, place of worship. And even if the child's life appears to the outside world as a mosaic of poverty and suffering, any pieces of joy actually laid down become all the more significant, taking on an almost sacred status. It's not after all a top layer of life but one that quickly gets buried deep down, like sediment. And such images… buildings, rooms, weather and landscape are likewise welded onto both the mind and the spirit at a very young age.

For Father John, though, it was the outspread arms of the ocean that bound the detail of that earlier life together. When reclining in the rickety deck chair of faded cloth, pushed into position for the best possible view, he often allowed his mind to wander back to a time when it was commonly believed that the Earth was flat, a bit like a tea-tray his history teacher had taught him, and it was thought that if you sailed far enough across the Ocean, you would eventually fall off the edge but she never went on to explain, what people then believed would happen to them after that falling, falling, falling; dying even, but then? Did it mean floating or landing or flying? Of course no one tipping over the side had been able to report back. What exactly did they expect to see when peering down into the abyss? A short cut to the flames of Hell?

Just like unbridled thought journeys which can also take you further than it's safe to go.

He would also wonder as to just how many people had left their homes, for good, along that rugged coastline over the last hundred and fifty years, on a tide of scant hope and overwhelming desperation. In his mind's eye he often thought he could visualise lines and lines of shuffling yet otherwise silent humanity bundled together along the pier, a continuous stream of pinched and pale faces, perched on top of hunched bodies, young faces as hauntingly wizened as those of their mothers and fathers, and no one allowing themselves the luxury of turning back their gaze to take in a final draught of home; fixing it instead on the expanse of ocean confronting them. All clad in dark hats or bonnets; shrouded in black shawls; humanity at all its stages boarding an alien craft, a phantom ship, cold and indifferent to their futures; creating all at once an impressionistic tableau of downtrodden mankind, first herded like cattle, and eventually all disappearing over the steely grey-blue horizon. Just how many of the young (or old) had made a secret departing promise that they would one day return, stronger and wealthy, with a view to helping those left behind in their dilapidated homesteads? But long before that, did anyone have any idea at all as to what might be in store for them on the other side of the world? A courageous leap of faith astride a vast ocean when one had so little to lose.

Whenever thoughts of famine, exodus and desperation became too much to bear, John would re-join his mother for a while in the ever familiar stone cottage, realising that with each new visit, her once generously proportioned frame was clearly shrinking, that she was becoming a tinier version of her former self and yet she was ever greater in wisdom and mental strength. She had, with her simple

132

faith, learned little by little how to cope with the lingering illness of her fisherman husband and then much later, how to face a future without him. Life had never been easy for her. John had only recently begun to appreciate, however, quite how dignified she had always been, how quietly she had managed her suffering and losses: her own father dying in an agonising fishing disaster caused by a terrible gale, when she was still a child; a father she only knew through two remaining photographs. These she now kept hidden in a drawer away from the light, which had been gradually fading his all-precious image. She had also lost at least three babies in miscarriage, a possible result of the menacing shadow of poverty, which hovered ever close to their village. Moreover the recent absence of a beloved son and three treasured grandchildren, who had taken the bold decision to live in Canada in a quest for a 'better life', probably never to return. John always tried to joke her out of any silent pangs of heartbreak that only he was able to detect, by reminding her that at least her wayward and lumbering firstborn kept returning to her, albeit like a bad penny.

On hearing such 'nonsense', as she would refer to it, the dark descending clouds would quickly disappear and she would forcibly push him out of the way together with a wry smile and a mocking laugh. He just couldn't stay away and he reminded her that she had to conserve all her remaining energy for him: he still needed her as a guiding light; for him she represented the quintessential mother: modest, dignified, generous; the culmination of a life lived in harshly wise simplicity. The mental image of her, which he always took back to England, was of a woman sitting alone in the kitchen of his childhood, after all the day's work had been done, head bowed over her apron and praying the rosary.

John liked to take walks during his stay and these would beckon him along the ruggedly magnificent bay. Sometimes his mother would join him, for part of the way at least, especially if her knees were "having a good day." And their voices were sometimes heard drifting high over the bay as they walked arm in arm singing one of her favourite hymns:

Hail, Queen of heaven, the ocean star,
Guide of the wanderer here below,
Thrown on life's surge, we claim thy care:
Save us from peril and from woe.
Mother of Christ, star of the sea,
Pray for the wanderer, pray for me.

It rained a lot in their part of the world but they were well accustomed to it; it would rarely interfere with the pleasure they took in being out and about together. And the rain somehow added to the misty beauty of their surroundings: outlines became blurred and colours merged; it made its own kind of music; it lent itself to each day's unfolding drama; it quenched the needy soul with poetry. On rainy days the ground itself gave up its boggy sweetness and secrets, even though very little in the way of plant life was able to grow there. As John walked and prayed and sang and recited bits of half-remembered poetry, he turned his gaze towards the low-lying land that surrounded him, and then further up to slightly undulating green fields and even further towards the lines of hills. But this wider landscape was never bleak to those who called this place home. It was an ancient land, whose prehistory still poked out at them in the remains of bits of wall and stones and tombs. He could sometimes make out the ruins of an old watchtower from one of the nearby islands, when the mist decided to lift its enigmatic veil. And remnants of its myths and legends lingered in the minds and on the tongues of local people who had taken it upon themselves to capture them and then pass them down from generation to generation.

His had been a heartily solid fishing community; in the main, mackerel fishing. There had never been much room for sentimentality, daydreaming or rampant individualism. Life was tough; hadn't it always been so? People had to cope with their struggles as best they could, not looking for praise or pity, and as much as possible, the locals would rally round, offering support for worthy causes and praying for God's blessings. His were not a perfect people: as is the case in many isolated villages; it too suffered from the poison of gossip; the herd mentality; the casting out of those who seemed different or those too fragile to ably manage life's troubles; there existed an insidious narrow-mindedness, in sheer contrast to the Christian message they exalted each morning at Mass.

John had sometimes wondered whether his proximity to the ocean had, in some manner, triggered what was to become his vocation to the priesthood. He had, much later of course, visited the Holy Land; had become well acquainted with the major holy sites, but in all honesty it was whenever that he travelled north to the Sea of Galilee (which is in truth a vast lake) he realised that this was where he felt closest to God the Father, to Jesus His son, to the Apostles and the early Christians. Those early approaches made to simple fishermen, the ubiquitous presence of water, the changing weather patterns reflected in the workings of the lake. It was by the banks of Galilee that the first disciples had instantly accepted Jesus' message to 'Come and See'! The links with this place and his own early life had been forged fast and furious. While his own father, like Jesus' first disciples, had earned a living from catching fish in often challenging circumstances, John O'Flaherty set out to be a fisher of men and women and children.

Chapter 27

In Search of Cameos

While Carmela was in Italy for her son Lorenzo's wedding, a tiny personal wish she had harboured for many a year was about to be fulfilled. She had never gone in for fairy-tale dreams as such and all her hopes for the future were to do with the health and well-being of her husband and children. Domenico had likewise never been of a romantic disposition and it would never have entered his head to buy his wife any kind of jewellery or trinket, even when life did become more economically viable.

At a certain point in their adult lives they had been blessed; their meeting with Giulia; the chance to live rent free at Casa Stella for the rest of their lives, if they so wished; and she had lent them money, interest free with no set repayment dates. This had enabled them to buy some premises nearby and transform them into what was to become a highly popular family run delicatessen. They had sensed that she would even have handed the money over as a gift, had they so requested but that in order for them to preserve their pride, their dignity, it was better she had decided, to call it a loan. They had worked very hard and very long hours; they had made a success of the business and in turn had shown their children the fruits of their dedicated labours, but all thanks to Giulia. She had accepted their thanks only the once telling them quite categorically that there was no need to refer to it again.

It was now quite a while ago that Giulia had first turned up on their doorstep. And although appearing a little distant and sceptical at the beginning – life had never taught them thus far, how to handle such an event – Carmela and Domenico had never once questioned her integrity. However, it took many visits and much discussion to bring their situation – to a happy conclusion. Neither had appeared to be interested in discovering more about possible relatives linking them to Giulia, something she had found completely baffling. In any case she got to know them and the children fairly well, and one by one they were each won over by her humanity, charm and persistence.

Within about six months, plans were afoot for the De Martinos to make the life-changing move to Casa Stella.

Carmela came across as the stereotypical southern Italian woman, who many years beforehand, had left her home and come to live in England. As a child she had received only a rudimentary education and had been exposed to a strictly limited range of lifestyle possibilities and ideas. By coming to England, yet never becoming fully integrated into this new community, her understanding of the world, passed down by older family members and villagers (and of course Domenico), had stood still. And she herself became aware of this, when to her surprise, on returning to Italy some years later, it was apparent that other women of her age had to a certain extent moved with the times, in spite of the fact that deep-rooted Italian traditions changed very slowly, and she seemed to have more in common with people from an older and more conservative generation. Even their shared dialect showed signs of change, sometimes causing smiles to manifest themselves on the mouths of her listeners, upon hearing such a quaint rendition of the local vernacular! The social revolution was truly on the move and leaving its first hazy marks in towns, and later villages, all over Italy.

Something she hadn't shared with women of her class and circumstances in both Italy and England, however, was the obsessive desire to possess gold: rings, earrings, chains, crucifixes, bracelets, brooches and so on. And the gold had to be 18 carat, not the cheap 9 carat gold widely available in the many jewellers' shops on English highstreets. Such women from simple or working-class backgrounds took a deep and ongoing pride in their mounting gold jewellery collections. Many of these items would have been given to them earlier in their lives by godmothers, sponsors and relatives on the days of their Baptisms, First Holy Communions and Confirmations. But the girls would have had to wait years in order to be allowed to wear them. They were bought so they might be worn in adulthood!

And there again there were those who boasted of gifts their husbands had given them, sometimes not bought but passed down from older family members. Talk of possession of such treasures also functioned on another more symbolic level: by saying something was left to you, it also implied you were that person's favourite. So the jewellery also spoke. Conversations among these women were dominated by food, the house, children and needless to say general gossip, but they also drifted easily in and out of the subject of jewellery: one of the women present might be wearing a new ring or bracelet; there would be questions and answers as to the story behind it; there would follow an excess of praise and effusion; of sighs and admiration (probably not all generously given.)

In such cases, and there were many of these occasions, Carmela had always stayed quiet. What did she have to say? Her wedding ring was the only gold she owned and therefore of little interest. However, by the time the family business was doing well and she could have asked Domenico what he thought about her buying herself a gold cross and chain for example, on their next trip to Italy, she now realised it was too late, there was no reason for it, how would she explain it away after all this time? It remained a secret satisfaction that at least they were now in a position to buy it! And that if she so desired; she could have out rivalled any of them. She continued to wear the little silver cross and chain her children had bought her for her fortieth birthday!

Perhaps also when we wait too long for something we have desired, it all of a sudden becomes irrelevant. It would also mean having to replace the dream.

But Carmela, the child, had in fact inherited (or had been given) something she had vowed to treasure for the rest of her days. The circumstances to this were, however, somewhat vague, though she thought she remembered someone once explaining something, as it was handed to her in a little red box. It was a cameo brooch and she thought she'd never seen anything quite so beautiful. She had kept it in a series of hidey holes over the years, and on certain days when all alone had got it out, turning it round and passing the index finger of her right hand once more over the perfectly formed white profile which rested proudly on a pinkish oval stone, smooth and bevelled.

She had no idea just why she performed this ritual in secret or why it fascinated her so much; neither did she have any idea as to how her female friends would react to it. She believed the image to be that of a real person, a beautiful lady whose admirer had commissioned the creation of a fine cameo in her honour.

However, once installed in Casa Stella, Carmela soon discovered to her horror that the cameo was nowhere to be found. Her one and only treasure (material and sentimental) now lost forever. She had eventually plucked up the courage to mention it to Giulia, hoping not to reveal just how upset she was, referring to it as if it wasn't much at all. But Giulia instantly read her heart and said that she would get in touch with the new occupiers of the house they had left behind, to see if they could throw any light on the cameo brooch. As one might expect the reply came hard and fast: no such trinket had been found there. And as a consequence and years later Giulia came up with the idea, that since the family would soon be leaving for Lorenzo's wedding, that would give them the perfect opportunity to go cameo hunting themselves. They would after all be in a part of the world where cameos were traditionally made and that if Carmela didn't like the idea of a brand new custom made brooch, they could instead do the rounds of little antique and jewellers' shops which lined the cobbled streets where she could choose one closest to the one she had lost. Of course if her own cameo were ever to show up, then even better, she should never give up hope.

To some extent at least Carmela was pacified and was once again reminded as to how little she knew about the world and just how much Giulia did. And her beloved sister remained nevertheless unfathomable.

So once the wedding was well and truly over Carmela and Giulia found themselves in that rare and beautiful position with nothing to do, but more importantly, a guilt-free nothing to do, as both sisters truly deserved a little time to switch off, to float back down to earth and reflect upon the many highlights of the last three or four days. They were each emotionally exhausted from the extended run up to the wedding, the day itself and the continued responsibility they felt towards each of their guests over the following days. Did each guest or family have the all-important 'bonbonniera'? Were there any problems at their hotels or 'pensioni'? Had they checked their airline tickets for their return flight details?

Promises exchanged, in most cases unrealistic, to meet up as soon as possible once back in England.

As a result the two sisters spent a lovely day, rarely unlinking arms as they wandered around the myriad of narrow streets crammed to bursting with tiny shops, which together with their colourfully decorated straw hats, sheltered them from the sweltering silvery-hot sun. And Carmela was introduced to her first taste of pavement café sophistication. Domenico, even to this day, would never have paid extra to sit down and be waited upon: he would have stood for no more than a minute or two at the bar inside such an establishment, downed his espresso after masterfully tapping the sachet of sugar against the side of the cup before tearing it apart, and proceeded on his way. Carmela on the other hand was learning about those more subtle, lingering and luxurious pleasures, which she had to admit, did cost scandalously more and it was the closest she had ever come to understanding the nature of hedonism or even decadence!

Later that day, they visited a cameo factory and each learned a vast amount about the history of cameo making in the little coastal town. One young man in particular was a mine of fascinating facts and information. And Carmela was for once blissfully happy; it all seemed to authenticate her secret, childhood instinct that the cameo was something to treasure, stretching back to Roman times; the stones and shells coming directly from the earth and sea. To create a cameo required expertise and love; each was unique; it was an art form; it was jewellery but somehow even more personal to the owner; its colours reflected the colours of the natural world: pinks, pale peaches, bluish greys, the ivory whiteness of the intricate carvings. And it had close links with the part of the world where the two women had been born.

Carmela neither understood nor would remember half of all they had been told that dreamy evening but she had at last chosen the cameo for her brooch, a cameo which had mysteriously spoken out to her, with no help whatsoever from Giulia.

Chapter 28
James' Return

"Oh, James, there you are! I suppose I should say Bentornato! No it's true; we've all missed you, it's been, well, different. I know I'm going to sound like Carmela but you look as if you could do with some fattening up, so you're certainly in the right place! Look I had wanted to say and then never got the chance I really hope it wasn't me who sent you running for the hills; you know the garden thing? But you are back with us now, that's all that matters."

He allowed her to wrap him up in her arms as if he were a pardoned child.

Father John had told her that James would be returning at some point during the week but she hadn't been prepared for quite such a prompt arrival. Nevertheless everything was in place and Mrs Mogden, quite taken by James, had taken extra pride in sorting out and spring-cleaning his rooms. James had been gone for over a month and all anyone knew was that John had continued to visit him, letting Giulia and the others know that it was only a matter of time until he would be back with them. It was merely a brief relapse.

But James sat at the kitchen table looking ill at ease and lethargic and only replying to Giulia's questions and comments with a nod or shrug or grunt or sigh or rolling eye movement. But a wide smile did eventually spread across his face, when she pretended to scold him for picking off grapes, one by one, from the bunch in the fruit bowl. "Have you forgotten everything you learned from us? When it comes to grapes, you break off a tiny sprig at a time look like this, and that way you don't ruin the display! Oh I despair of you Giacomo Casanova! Look I tell you what, do you feel up to going for a walk? I was going to do just that and I think the rain has now finally stopped."

"Yes, Giulia, I've really missed you all. There's nothing I would like to do more."

They grabbed their jackets and set out for the park.

Serafina meanwhile was not enjoying the early stages of her pregnancy, and once the initial euphoria had evaporated, she felt lonely and discarded; almost shocked at no longer being the centre of the busy family's attention. It was as if her life had been whittled down to that of a mere role, to be played out each and every day, always the same. She had become reduced; she was now just the carrier of the baby they all wanted, a first-born De Martino child for the next generation, the first grandchild. She felt permanently nauseous and missed her aunts more than ever, as annoying as they could be on occasion with all their fussing and flapping. Her life had been ripped apart, as had her world. She was no longer a girl; no longer felt young; no longer Serafina, but a hollow shell existing in a grey, rainy place far from home! No one here really cared about her how could they? They knew next to nothing about her. She was the new arrival; an appendage even; a means to an end, and no one bothered, after the first couple of weeks, to find out how she was really feeling or to see the human being behind the proud and smiling mask. Yes, Carmela was always pleasant but not exactly the kind of woman one could open up to and even Giulia, whom she really admired, just didn't seem to have time for her other than for their lessons (in which she came across as strict and always wanting more); and at other times it seemed that Giulia was often out or away, or just about to receive visitors.

Lorenzo's behaviour was also less than she had expected. Back in Italy he had been gallant and attentive, charming and complimentary but now it all seemed to have been some kind of act. Mission accomplished! He had accomplished everything he had set out to achieve, he had it all: freedom of movement, a job, a doting family, a pretty little wife waiting for him at home, at whatever time of day or night his shift happened to be over. And next year he would have his first child; maybe the first of many?

But then the doorbell rang, a short yet invasive buzz, which pierced through her lingering self-pity. She leapt up to answer it, straightening herself and practising facial expressions of natural happiness.

"Oh Giulia, James, oh what a surprise! Yes, do come in, oh watch the floor. I don't think that bit's dry yet; no, I don't mean I mind; I just don't want you to slip over."

"So how are you?" Giulia continued the conversation in English. "James and I have just been out for a short walk to blow away the cobwebs. Okay, I will explain that to you in our next lesson! So how are you? Perhaps you would like to come with us next time?"

At this point, James cut in and made his apologies; he really did have to get back to the house to sort out his things but that he would be catching up with her and Lorenzo soon. The door banged shut behind him, leaving the two women to their supposed domestic exchanges.

"You are looking a bit pale, are you sure you are alright? Look. You sit down; I'll make us both a tea."

Serafina let Giulia take over, at least as far as the tea was concerned, and wondered whether she should just pour out, like the tea, her heart and see what Giulia would make of her situation or merely stay quiet and laugh off her pallor. In a split second she found herself opting for the latter. "Oh I'm fine really. Maybe rushing around a bit too much, you know, haha! Lorenzo's home early today and there were certain things I wanted to get done."

"Just as well I've popped round to make you sit down then. Those 'certain things' can wait. I suppose you're having a bit of morning sickness; how many weeks are you now? Oh, well it will be over soon then. The textbooks say that from the fourth month, not only will you stop feeling sick but you will really start to bloom you know *'sbocciare'.*"

Ha what nonsense! What did she know? How many children did she have? What a nerve? She was getting a bit fed up with her endless simpering wisdom. Yes, she got it all from books; she'd just admitted it; she didn't actually live, she just read about the business of living! What a fake; what a joke!

"Yes, you are right of course, I'll be fine. I'm already feeling a bit better, thank you, Giulia."

Later that evening, when Serafina was genuinely feeling a little less nauseous, she deliberately returned to earlier thoughts and felt totally ashamed of herself. Yet she was still so relieved she hadn't begun to reveal to her new and older friend exactly how awful she was feeling, inside herself, and towards the world. Her aunts had brought her up to be kind and gracious in her dealings with others, and especially when, in the case of Giulia, she had only ever been supportive. She had to admit Giulia was a true role model, a force for good, witty and lovely and positive! She promised to become more positive herself in the days and weeks to follow, to think more about the baby she was carrying, and less about herself. And perhaps she had been just a little hard on her husband; he worked untiringly for the two (soon to be three) of them and never brought his problems home. Perhaps she should do something different with her appearance to get him to notice her a bit more though she wasn't going to be able to disguise the fact that her body was already undergoing a series of strange and rapid changes of its own.

Giulia had also been deep in thought that evening, not about transforming bodies, but about James' return. She could sense where things were heading. Only she could put a stop to proceedings, and if that's what she chose to do, now was the time to act. Yes, she wanted him; yes, she probably deserved to treat herself, it had been quite a while. She had been trying extra hard of late to be patient with Carmela and the others, with Mrs Mogden, with this year's students, who for some reason didn't seem to sparkle so much as those of the past, and it was fair to conclude she was winning this battle. She was also helping Serafina to learn English.

But what about Father John? Well, she could always go and make her confession to another priest?

And what of James himself? Her father was right; they knew so little about him. Nothing could come of it of course. It would be an indulgence; an irresponsible act; something she would have to live with for the rest of her life. It could also prove painful; it would only last a short while in any case. But who would tire first? Would he want to finish with her before she was ready?

But even if she tired first, it could still be painful watching the spurned lover fall apart in the least dignified of ways. She was the older of the two and therefore felt she had a certain responsibility towards him. She was in good health but he was recovering from some kind of deep-rooted trauma. If she followed her desires, would she be scandalously exploiting the situation, his vulnerability? But there again, it wasn't often she felt this way; that pure, carnal need and surely that very feeling gave the situation an authenticity, the rare chance of a beautiful green sea for them both to plunge into? She then burst out laughing at herself, even though she was all alone. Thinking about all those millions of consenting adults from all over the world, who don't think at all but just get on with it! What would they make of her manic musings?

Did she really want this, yes or no? So much to lose, but also much to carry forward. It wasn't as though she was taking him away from a wife and children but she didn't know exactly who he was – he could have ten children. OK, so that was highly unlikely. Her father's words were circling close again. She remembered James telling her about his studies; the early eighteenth century; talk of pleasure gardens. There had certainly been a meeting of minds already and it really did amuse her that his very name, translated as Giacomo Casanova also thrilled her in a spine-tingling kind of way.

Giulia heard a couple of tentative knocks at her door. "Yes?" she called out.

"It's me Giulia, may I come in a moment?"

"Yes of course. Is everything alright?"

"Giulia, I know I have absolutely no right to ask, but can I come to your room tonight?"

"Yes, I mean No I will come up to you – it will be a bit more well, private there. See you later then."

James placed his hands on her shoulders for a few seconds and placed a kiss on the top of her head. He then left the room in silence and a very radiant Giulia.

Chapter 29
The Rose Garden

In the end Giulia did get her rose garden and pergola and pond; at least the initial stages were underway for all three. It had been James who had raised the subject once more, shortly after his return, but even though she had had her doubts (obviously due to what had transpired a few weeks beforehand) James insisted that she knew it was what she wanted and that he also wanted to play his part in her far-reaching plans.

After much pacing around outside, checking on areas of light and shade at various times of day, and devising a shortlist of potential beds, from which the future rose bushes could both thrive and look their best, Giulia eventually made her decision. She also chose a spot for the long-awaited pond; adamant that she wanted no fish to inhabit it; a heron was often seen perched on top of a neighbour's roof, biding his time as he rested ever watchful between swoops. No, her pond would instead host a range of other creatures: frogs, water beetles and boatmen, pond skaters and would of course attract dragonflies. She made sure there were no trees close by, whose leaves, fruit or blossom might otherwise litter its surface.

But then came the news; that terrible news, which began to trickle, almost unnoticed at first, out of our television screens late one evening, long before the picture of devastation had been totally pieced together. There had been an earthquake in Southern Italy, in Irpinia, the area the family were from, and the place they had visited only a few months beforehand. 6.9, on the Richter scale, and of maximum Mercalli intensity. It was November 1980.

And amongst all this devastation there was a village or 'paese', which looked out onto the green-grey folds and peaks of the Appennini Mountains. There were also four or five other villages in the vicinity, each with its own customs and linguistic variations.

The village in question stood a good few hundred metres above sea level and its population over the centuries had continued in turn to rise and fall, fall and rise, but never superseding a couple of thousand souls. Many different tribes and peoples had lived there or ruled over its surrounding lands: Sanniti, Irpini (hence the name of the area), Romani, Longobardi, Borboni and so on (Giulia always thinking in the Italian version of their names, the ones she had absorbed in childhood).

The village had enjoyed many religious connections, including a monastery, and hundreds of pilgrims had passed across its boundaries over the years, on their way to nearby sacred shrines. And it was a strong Christian faith that had sustained the people, in the face of each visiting disaster and its fallout: earthquake, disease, war, emigration. A deep and bloody mark had been engraved upon the hearts and homes of those who had somehow managed to survive each catastrophe or ongoing struggle. They were therefore a resilient people, unsentimental, pragmatic, hardy; fatalistic and materialistic in equal measure. And this ran alongside their understanding and practice of Christianity. They were (and even up to the present day) an inward-looking community, lacking in trust of others; wary of, even if also drawn towards, the Foreign.

From early April to late October the days in the village were hot and sunny; the evenings soft and balmy, and winters were in the main bearably short in spite of the cover of a cold and menacing darkness. But alas this pleasant climate could do little to protect the timeless village from nature's repeated scourges.

A cruel pestilence had also once raged there, felling the population by nearly 600 and less than a century later, an earthquake had totally destroyed it, causing another 25 or so fatalities. Over time the depleted populace had once again found the strength, both mental and physical, to re-build their lives and the life of the village. As before, this centred round the church and surrounding piazza, and the clusters of two-storey buildings were constructed primarily out of the local 'tufo', a volcanic rock, silent witness to past disasters. These buildings, perched under their rust-red pantiles, made up the villagers' houses, all huddled together and all vying haphazardly for a ring-side seat.

Everyone knew everyone else and every morning the women made their way to Mass, dressed in black and making sure their heads were covered before entering the church.

Many of the women and girls, having reached a certain age wore black not so much to protect themselves against the sun's heat, as is commonly believed, but because they were in mourning; a very outward and rigid expression of human loss: a minimum of 2 years in black for a brother, 5 years for a son, 10 years for a husband? It was quite possible therefore for a young woman to spend the rest of her life dressed exclusively in black.

And each time a villager died, the church bell was rung and within an hour or so, each family would have learned the name of the deceased and be making plans to join the queue of mourners paying their last respects, as they filed in and out of the affected family's house. The body would be dressed by a loved one in his or her perfectly conserved Sunday best; and then laid out for the visitors on a bed in a room on the ground floor, with the head always facing the door, creating easy (if not explicit) access for the walk past, which would involve prayers, touching or even a kiss. There would be an ongoing stream of gasps and audible tears and the interminable praying of the rosary. (This custom also explained why, when arranging bedroom furniture in happier circumstances, it was crucial the bed should not be positioned thus). Children were never excluded from these ancient and regularly repeated rituals. Birth and death being inevitable points on life's repeated cycle. At least one priest would complete the scene.

The funeral would take place the very next day, after a night of litany and female wailing. The coffin would usually be carried directly to the church by a group of able-bodied men closely related to the bereaved family. Sometimes the boys from the nearby seminary would join the straggly procession, everyone reciting the rosary over and over again, in Latin (the language of the church), as they all wound their way to attend the funeral Mass.

Ave Maria, gratia plena,

Dominus tecum.

Benedicta tu in mulieribus,

Et benedictus fructus ventris tui,

Iesus…

It was not unusual to make out the loud, primeval cries of women, who might also feel compelled to bring on a faint or attempt, repeatedly, to throw themselves onto the coffin, unable to finally let go of their loved one, and it was down to their menfolk to drag them back to the land of the living. One villager told of the case of a mother, whose son had died at the age of 12, and who had in her grief shouted out in all seriousness, "He should never have died; he could already swear and smoke as well as any man in the village!"

So many deaths; so many stories.

More often than not the person's remains would be placed, not in the ground as with English burials, but above it within one of the wall tombs, which were arranged in rows, over three or more 'floors'. Tall ladders were always at the ready therefore for visitor access. But for those that could afford it, the body would be taken to a family vault or chapel, built within the walled cemetery which was always located at some distance from the houses (unlike English graveyards once positioned within the bounds of the local church), and which would be dutifully visited, especially on a Sunday: candles lighted; vases cleaned; old flowers replaced; photographs kissed; more prayers said. There was never a chance that the dead person would be forgotten. It is still the case today.

As the years flowed by, the dead would continue to be prayed for during daily and Sunday Masses, prayers imploring God, through intercessions, that the souls of their loved ones might enter Heaven as quickly as possible. There was no known timescale and for those who had died with no family members left to pray or mourn for them or tend their tombs, there would always be someone willing to take on these solemn duties as the result of a past promise or ongoing act of penance. The dead person could also expect to be talked about at length even if they had achieved very little during their lifetime; their death marking merely one kind of departure. Every life counted.

And there was no avoiding the subject of death or crossing to the other side of the road in order to avert one's eyes from someone in mourning.

At some point in the future, permission could be obtained for bones to be exhumed and cleaned with bottles of pure alcohol (spirito). Once again it was incumbent upon a senior family member with past experience to take on this responsibility, often with the help of the cemetery's warden.

News of this latest earthquake was by now arriving via our television screens, rapidly gaining momentum. The first footage of damaged roads and railways, helpless under a blanket of thick fog, was casting its grim shadow in the warmth and safety of our English kitchens and living rooms. It revealed the even more distressing news that it would probably take the rescue teams many days to reach all the affected villages, as so many roads had inevitably been blocked by falling rubble, trees and other debris. These were roads often difficult to access in any case, as they were typical mountain roads, narrow, winding and in the main, very steep. Fires had broken out; water supplies were disrupted; the nights were becoming ever colder. Villages and hamlets were completely cut off from one another and thus the rest of the world. And there were few guarantees that the supplies being dropped actually were reaching the people who needed them most.

Giulia lost no time at all in making plans to fly out to this part of Italy the very next morning, and help in whichever way she could. It was a purely gut reaction to the news breaking across her TV screen; she just wasn't able to sit and watch any more of the traumatic scenes unfolding a few feet in front of her. She left word of her plans with the family, and made a call to Father John. Everyone wanted to know how long she would be away but she replied that she had no idea! James was told of the situation by Mrs Mogden and he tried to keep well-hidden from the others any signs which might reveal the thick black cloud that had suddenly descended upon him as well. What was this madness? Just what was Giulia up to?

No one seemed to know anything what on earth was going on?

And once again the gate which was to open onto the Rose Garden had to remain closed.

Chapter 30

Suspended In Time

The lead-up to Christmas was devoid of its usual colourful bustle that year, with the De Martino family holding its breath that Giulia would be back in time to share in the festivities. She had already indicated that her 'mission' was almost at an end in Italy but that it would be continuing back home. What did she mean by this? She had already asked Father John to make an appeal to parishioners, over a series of weekends, for them to send donations to her in Italy for the 'terremotati', victims of the earthquake. But what more could she have in mind?

Each member of the household missed her, whether they voiced it or not, in a different way, and for different reasons, and couldn't wait for the moment when they might finally hear the turning of the key in the door, signalling her arrival.

James spent most of this time helping Father John in whatever way he could; catching up with his belated reading and even managed to get on with digging up some more of the garden in spite of the cold conditions. To his surprise (and embarrassment), the child that still lay submerged within him was also looking forward to Christmas, as he had to admit to himself he had definitely enjoyed helping set up the nativity scene in St. Raphael's Church, a scene which had to be kept under cover until the 24th. It all had the feel of an exotic fairy tale. He was both amused and touched by the fact that the three Kings were to be kept well away from the other iconic figures, as they would still be making their epic journey as they followed the star, and wouldn't be arriving at the inn (or cave) for another 12 days or so. And that someone at the church, Mrs Sullivan perhaps, would be responsible for moving them and their gift-laden camels a few steps closer each day until their arrival on the Feast of the Epiphany itself. Likewise the baby Jesus couldn't be placed in the manger until Christmas morning.

His own knowledge of the Gospels was very sketchy, to say the least.

He still had his own deity however, and comforted himself in his continued worship of Serafina, whose blossoming shape was now transforming her from budding girl goddess into quintessential Earth Mother. It was enough for him that she was there. He caught sight of her almost daily. Her hair and eyes shone out against the veil of late Autumn-grey drizzle; her beautifully curved belly, by now the shape of a giant Easter egg, carried the promise of another human life; and it seemed to him that her smile alone also fed and clothed the world.

He quickly put to one side the thought, that he needed Giulia just as much as before her rushed departure, once the daily Serafina worship was over. He was not prepared to push things, but instead decided to wait and see what would happen. He resolved in any case that he would never be compelled to return to a life of paying for company whenever he felt the need. His life had moved on to a brave new place.

He sometimes allowed his past life to loom over him though, if only for a few moments, and he found it wasteful and squalid.

Domenico wouldn't have been conscious at all of missing Giulia, well, it was only a matter of time that she would once again cross the threshold and take up her position at the centre of the family. Neither did he bear any animosity towards her; it was after all her house and her life. He knew he could remain or move out whenever he wanted, and even though he considered that latter option once in a while, he always pushed it forward into the future yes we might go in a few years, who knows? His day-to-day life had, however, begun to show signs of Giulia's absence during the last few weeks. Even James had noticed. For example, whereas Domenico would normally meet up with his male friends (practically all Italian) in a back room at the delicatessen after work, for their thrice weekly card playing sessions, he was now inviting them round to Casa Stella, much to the annoyance of Carmela, who had the extra job of keeping a watchful eye over them and making sure that they were out of the house by midnight; they had a business to run, after all. Some of her husband's friends were younger and therefore to her mind immature and irresponsible and she didn't want him to be led astray at this time of life. The card playing sessions at the delicatessen had been out of her sight and therefore out of mind, provided Domenico was in a fit state to open up the shop on time each morning. And fortunately this had always been the case!

James had also picked up on the fact that the older men in the group, including Domenico, all grew the last fingernail of their right hand much longer than the rest and this really intrigued him, coming up with a whole range of ideas, some much wackier than others, as to what it all meant.

He was likewise intrigued by just how noisy and passionate these games would become, with the cards themselves creating a loud slapping noise, each time they were flung down onto the table, like a medieval throwing down of the gauntlet, sometimes a gesture of frustration and sometimes, one of triumph. He had even joined in with them once, though could hardly make out the suits or the instructions, being given in no particular order and in a mixture of Italian dialects, with some broken English thrown in. And the sound of their screams and shouts seemed to slice the very air. The evening would always end in some kind of row, as to who was ready to leave before time or who the overall winner was. The men would, however, turn up again and again. Any signs of mutual hatred had of course been misinterpreted; they were all in truth great friends and it would take more than a game of cards to separate them. James had even suggested to them, in his innocence, that perhaps it would be better to establish at the start of each game, what time it should end, so no one could be accused of wanting to go home too early with their winnings. But his advice fell on deaf ears and all at once he was surrounded by a sea of incredulous faces, which when fathomed were all saying: who was he to tell them what to do and what did he know about it anyway?

They used the traditional Neapolitan playing cards, which James had never seen or heard of before. He eventually managed to work out that there were 40 of them in each pack, physically smaller than the cards he was familiar with; more ornate and more brightly coloured. The suits in this case were clubs, swords, coins and cups. And there appeared to be no queens! They played games which they called Scopa, Scopone or Briscola. They played for money but rarely for high amounts and the games seemed to require a good memory, a good deal of luck, but then again backed up by innate cunning (and probably cheating). The room would quickly fill with a grey haze, carpet-thick, of cigarette smoke and their glasses quickly fill with the wine, various liqueurs or whisky Domenico would have spread out on the table. No one appeared to care that the cards became grimy and sticky and no one would ever bother to check at the start of the evening's gaming if there were any cards missing.

Carmela was definitely missing her sister. But decided to spend her time usefully, getting through more and more of the never-ending household tasks she would usually have passed on to Mrs Mogden. The spring-cleaning process was therefore well underway in darkest December. However, she had to admit, if only to herself, that there was a certain satisfaction to be had after each task had been accomplished, seeing the cupboards cleared and orderly, and the sparkling glassware wink back at her from behind the newly polished glass cabinet doors.

She did of course have a circle of friends from her own community and they would take it in turns to meet quite regularly in one another's homes. It was a very different experience from her time spent with Giulia. With her friends there was always an element of competition, sometimes overt, sometimes more subtle, but it was rare for any of them, including Carmela, to fully open their hearts to the rest. She had learned early on that if any of the 'friends' were missing from the group, they would inevitably get talked about, and not always in glowing terms. So why would it be any different if she, Carmela, had decided to stay at home? Female friendships would naturally wax and wane; some women would over time disappear completely. And very few of them wasted opportunities to comment ad infinitum upon their aches and pains and other medical issues. Carmela tried very hard not to gossip as such, if only because it would be letting down her sister in some way, and also Father John had often referred to gossip in his homilies, and how poisonous it could become.

Yet given the company, circumstances and her own deep-rooted (and passed down) opinions on a range of matters, it was very difficult not to let down one's guard and join in with the rest.

With Giulia it was different; she could speak her mind freely, unhampered by the presence of others. And she knew that these spoken thoughts would travel no further. Giulia also helped Carmela to see for herself why she was feeling a certain way, or when she hadn't thought about something at all and was merely passing on a point of view that had been handed down to her. There again, she didn't relish spending too long pondering such matters. She had no desire to turn into her sister no matter how proud of her she was. It was precisely that part of Giulia she didn't understand which made her sister all the greater, in her eyes at least; like the concealed part of the Moon or the submerged reality of an ice-berg. Her sister's life also scared her a little but she wasn't sure why this was.

Giulia did eventually turn up a couple of days before Christmas; her face pale and drawn; possibly also a little thinner. She was clearly relieved to be back but stoutly defended her decision to have taken off so quickly in the first place.

It was a good few hours before she had an opportunity to speak properly to James. It turned out to be an awkward meeting, Giulia's life having changed so radically in such a short space of time. And James realising this (if only in part) had no idea as to whether there would be any chance of resuming their prior liaison. Neither had they managed to speak freely on the telephone, while she was away.

Chapter 31
Christmas Day

Casa Stella had not been decorated in the usual extravagant way that Christmas. No one had felt it appropriate to buy a tree in the wake of the terrible earthquake, something Domenico usually organised through his friends. However, the two older daughters had said they would put together a nativity scene complete with crib, because it was still important to celebrate the birth of Gesu' Bambino, something they had been doing all their lives, at this time of year.

It was also the emptiest feast of the year for Immy, as she felt drained of any emotion these days outside of the rainbow world she inhabited with Nicholas. A time for families; a time for children and their infectious laughter; their sense of wonder, all apparent. He would be at home with his little ones, a mere walk away but it may as well have been the other side of the world. She would just have to content herself with the memory, that only a few days beforehand, they had spent a lovely day in a tiny countryside village, making the most of that day's every gift, of all nature's colours, of each other. No time wasted on the woes of the world they could do nothing about or trivial matters arising at work and home, instead a time devoted to stares, smiles, words, touch and to the dream world they continued to assemble.

Immy seemed unable to appreciate her own family; they bored her; they seemed irrelevant to her and even worse, a stumbling block. She had become wholly blind to her own selfishness and refused to accept that sooner or later, this profound dalliance would have to stop. It was bound to burn itself out at some stage in any case. If she'd allowed herself to contemplate the future, she would have discovered that even if Nicholas had offered her marriage, after agreeing to separation and divorce (though he'd never mentioned any of this) was that really what she would have wanted? And if he'd already learned how to betray one wife, how simple it would be to repeat the performance. No, she must have known in that dark and secret place, that she wasn't in search of domesticity, well not for a very long time. She had no desire to snatch him from under Jane's nose. How squalid and vulgar it all sounded. She liked and wanted just what they had: the here and now and its secrecy; the adventure; the concentration of heightened emotions; the total dedication to each other during the stolen hours they spent together.

For the musician and the would-be teacher, their passion had almost become an art form.

But in truth it was all a vain and egocentric escape from the grind of late twentieth century life. It kept pain and negative thoughts, as to the futility of life, at bay.

Their affair was somewhat easier for Nicholas to handle at this time: plenty of Christmas distraction and, as odd as it may sound, he was in truth, devoted to Miranda and Daniel, fully enjoying nearly every moment spent in their company.

In spite of Giulia's return, Father John was likewise a little more subdued than usual, possibly because it was such a busy time for him and that he had already said Mass twice that morning. He was making every effort to mask from the world, the effect on him the terrible reality that his mother was by now fading fast, and that he of all people should have been able to face such an inevitability with much more faith and fortitude. He was being put to the test again! To a confirmed Christian, death was not the end. It only marked the end of our transient earthly lives and the beginning for someone like his mother, who had never missed a Sunday Mass or Holy Day of Obligation, of an infinite and intimate life in the presence of God a future in Heaven. The only woman he had ever actually known whose life had truly mirrored that of Jesus' mother Mary.

As well as already having presided over hundreds of requiem masses and funerals, burials (and the reluctantly growing popularity amongst Catholics for cremation), John had had to deal with the death of his own father and that of close friends he had known a lifetime.

Perhaps the highest price he had to pay, in all of this, as regards his vocation, was the creeping realisation, especially when trying to offer comfort to those family members left to mourn, that he wouldn't be leaving behind any children of his own once his time had come; his own stem coming to a blunt end. And once both parents had died, he had to admit to himself, like many others at such times, that it definitely concentrated the mind that he would be next in the family 'firing line'!

157

Nevertheless bursts of Buon Natale, Merry Christmas, erupted from around the table as soon as Father John had said grace and little time was wasted before they all started ferociously tucking into their much-awaited antipasto: a huge and varied array of tasty offerings being passed around the table on oval platters, including wafer thin slices of prosciutto and mortadella, folded in pinkish curls; salsiccia, salami; different kinds of melon, artichoke hearts, zucchini, tomatoes, anchovies, olives and so on. To an inexperienced guest, it might have seemed next to impossible to contemplate eating anything else, but of course this was only the start – a homemade lasagne would soon, like every Christmas day, be making its spectacular appearance, complete with little meatballs and lashings of ricotta, a creamy bechamel sauce and a contrasting meaty sauce of bright red tomato, interspersed between the layers of lovingly handmade pasta, generous portions being the order of the day, with requests of 'only a little' never being heeded. Carmela and her daughters (including a somewhat lacklustre Tina) continuously bobbing up and down, busied themselves with the dishing up, collecting of used bowls and cutlery (which all clattered noisily) handing out replacement napkins, not to mention the endless washing up, so all could be ready for the next course, the next offering. Serafina had made a couple of brave attempts to join them but was quickly bustled back to her chair, being told she could help them next year.

Two courses later and roast turkey still to come, (though in Italy this would have been an impressive capon), it was agreed that they would give their digestive systems a bit of a rest, and so they spent a good few minutes pulling crackers, forcing paper hats upon one another's heads, reading out the all too predictable cracker jokes, regardless of the fact that no one was listening, and fiddling with the multifarious trinkets that had poured out at each cracker breakage. Even Domenico had a fixed semi-smile on his face, revealing how much he always enjoyed this special time of year!

More bottles of wine, red and white, were brought to the table once it had been cleared of cracker rubbish and jugs full of water were regularly replaced either end.

At the end of the meal when everyone was too full or too tired to move, Giulia suddenly made a surprise announcement; that she had come to an important decision she sincerely hoped everyone would support, especially as it was the 25th December (and that only hours ago they had all been present at Midnight Mass.) The reason she hadn't mentioned it till now was that it was something that had taken a lot of thought and planning. It was a decision she felt she had had to make alone as she would be wholly responsible for the outcome.

"Oh come on, spit it out," hastened a wine-filled and impatient Lorenzo, "just tell us what it is that's so important for us to know! Hell, Zia Giulia, you're getting worse the dramatic build-up, the silence and in falsetto tones: I just can't take any more," and he pretended to slip and swoon under the table!

Even Father John looked surprised as he turned his gaze towards Giulia who had by now stood up to speak; strange she hadn't previously confided in him.

The room was now silent and all heads were turned and chins tilted towards Giulia, as she looked down on them.

"I've arranged for two boys, Stefano and Matteo, two brothers in fact, to come and live here for the foreseeable future. Their father was killed in the earthquake and therefore their mother is now widowed and homeless. She's being looked after for the time being by her brother-in-law's family but things are very difficult in all sorts of ways. I offered to give the boys a home here, while life in their village gets back to some kind of normality. Gianna, their mother, needs to stay put. Here the boys can go to school, learn English and when the time is right, they will then return home, in a better position to face the future. They should be arriving in a couple of days. It's the least I could do in the circumstances. I have already spoken about this to Carmela and Domenico and about the horrors I witnessed and you've all been watching the news, reading the newspapers; the people are now at the mercy of the harsh weather conditions battering the country and of course totally dependent upon the future decisions of Government ministers, which let's face it, don't exactly inspire much confidence. We all know just how long everything takes over there. I hope you will all support me in this venture. Of course it won't be easy but these boys, who come from a village not too far from our own, and with both villages now razed to the ground, deserve a chance and there are other people who've gone out there doing so much more than me."

Giulia's voice eventually trailed off realising that a dark shadow of silence had filled the room as each person at table tried to make sense of what they had just heard. Christmas Day and all its fripperies had suddenly been pushed to one side.

It was in fact Lorenzo's voice which again shattered the silence. He had also been trying to keep Serafina abreast of all his Aunt was explaining, whenever she didn't understand a point. "And how old are these boys Zia?"

"Oh yes, didn't I say? They are 13 and 11. I'm really hoping we can, under the circumstances, try and get them places at St. Raphael's as soon as possible. Father John, perhaps I can rely on you to speak to the other school governors about the current waiting lists, I would hope them to show some compassion. I will see to their clothes and all their other day to day needs; get them registered at the GPs, the dentist's and so on; give them English tuition if that's what it takes and for you Carmela, it will just mean I'm afraid cooking for a greater number of people."

And thus Giulia continued, answering questions, giving more detail about the two brothers, praising her family, John and even James, for everyone's willingness to give it a go. She didn't feel a surge of breathless support coming from any of them, but to be fair, neither did anyone openly disapprove. To be sure, Giulia had surprised them once again.

But it was Immy, or Tina, should we now say who had surprisingly stayed the quietest. She was deep in her own whirling thoughts, far from the fate of earthquake victims, old or young or was she? In the blink of an eye, she found herself having made a decision, one just as great for her as it had been for Giulia, regarding the two brothers. Nicholas would no longer be part of her life. The liaison had run its course. They had each squeezed out of it all that was possible. They had been lucky, blessed even they had lived out an intense and secret adventure which would remain theirs forever. No one had found out; no one had got hurt; but it just couldn't continue. It would end at its best. She would speak to Nicholas as soon as possible. He was an intelligent person; he would of course understand. Their lives would continue along separate, maybe even parallel lines, enhanced forever by this beautiful yet illicit gift life had permitted them, which paradoxically could be put to a greater good.

There would be no going back; neither did she allow herself to dwell upon her own sense of loss or pain that Christmas Day.

Chapter 32

Vestiges

The evening Giulia had returned to Casa Stella, exhausted though she was, found her spending several hours with Carmela and Domenico (unusual in itself) in front of a large welcoming fire in the sitting room, spilling out her raw and recent experiences; so many things she had seen and heard; recurrent sounds and images of overwhelming suffering. Domenico had also been in touch with a distant relative who had first-hand knowledge of ongoing events, but telephone lines had also been affected by the devastation and so much of the news pouring out of the receiver was difficult to follow with strangled voices and intermittent interference. Now they could begin to piece together more of the actual scenes and subsequent chain of events, and Giulia was able, in part, to unburden herself, for the first time in many days.

However Carmela and Domenico had learned early on that the village of their birth – all they had seen and known in the world until their joint arrival in England stood no longer; obliterated after a thousand years of history, in a matter of minutes. Certain individuals were putting it down to an act of God; an act of revenge for lives badly lived. And this was because people no longer feared Him, were no longer in awe of Him and His beautiful Creation. Instead they were displaying a watered down, pick and mix attitude towards the Church's Sacraments, as a creeping materialism and chronic individualism had been fast taking root.

Giulia had encountered this line of thinking as well, during her brief stay, from the moment she had checked into a nearby hotel. Fortunately the hotel had not been brought down in the quake and was deemed safe for business but at the same time clearly revealed a few long, freshly made, vertical cracks, on some of the internal walls. She didn't really buy into the 'God's revenge' kind of chatter, but if it offered people a temporary explanation on which to fix their minds, then it surely served some kind of practical purpose, and an examination of one's own conscience was after all always to be commended.

So she found herself listening but rarely adding to the melange of local standpoints. Her own personal philosophy didn't go in for past golden ages, unless they referred to Art or Culture. How could one ever conclude that people behaved more badly today than in the past? Yes there might have been a semblance of greater obedience to God, but that was mainly due to a variety of other factors, which included ignorance, fear, lack of education and opportunity, habit, and of course prevailing double standards; the great divide between appearance and reality. The Church presented a perfect model for living and something lofty, which people could try to aspire to, but it seemed to have very little to do with man's true nature, (from which we just somehow can't manage to shift, she had long ago concluded), and thus from a Catholic perspective, we were surely doomed to fail and fail again ad infinitum with or without the warning signs of earthquakes.

She also concluded that in the technologically advanced twentieth century, we were still led, first and foremost, by our survival instincts whether individually or as a group; still felt the absolute need to reproduce ourselves; still wrestled mentally with the more negative of our human emotions (and even they surely still served some practical purpose); behaved in a civilised manner precisely because it was in our interest to do so, that is, as it guaranteed mutual safety and well-being. It was a hard pill to swallow but as Giulia (cynically) saw things she self-questioned how it was ever possible for any human being to perform a purely altruistic act of kindness, an example of pure love? There was always a reward, a real or metaphorical pat on the back before, during or after. But did this really matter? The outcome still counted. Good was good, regardless of the obvious or unconscious reasons behind the apparently noble action!

And it was for all of this she found it impossible to live up to her Church's impossibly perfect standards. Often she had felt that the harder she tried, the greater she was failing falling away.

She was in any case very clear (in her own head) as to why she herself often went out of her way to help those in need.

Though for all her education, sophisticated posturing and self-examination, she had to accept that many of the homespun explanations she had heard, as regards the true cause of this natural disaster, did return to whirl round her brain and she couldn't admit to dismissing any of them completely and all this was probably to do with her own watertight Catholic upbringing, in Italy and then in England.

She had been fed diverse accounts of events leading up to the recent disaster by people living in or close to her own birth village, and there so happened to be one story in particular that stood out from the rest, one that really stoked her imagination, especially since there did appear to be corroboration from yet another source, that events really did transpire as described.

About twenty years beforehand a family had decided to uproot itself from Giulia's village and go and live abroad. It was made up of a husband, wife and three teenage daughters. It had not been a decision lightly taken and there were valid reasons for the family's belief that a better life awaited them elsewhere, notwithstanding the fact that financially they was now doing fairly well. What was of particular interest, however, was the incident which had triggered the idea of their leaving in the first place and it all started with an ice cream. The couple's middle daughter had accepted the offer of an ice cream from a local lad, not much older than the girl herself. The incident had been witnessed by a certain resident, who took it upon himself to go tell the girls' parents straightaway, so they could decide whether or not to take action. It was not known if anyone else had seen the buying of the ice cream or exactly who had begun to sew the first seeds as to its probable implications. But as was the way of this village, (and which would have been the case for many others in that part of the world), salacious rumours, gathering freely in detail, colour and momentum, were about to make their ambush.

One only gave to receive something back; the giver now had power over the one who had accepted.

The girls' mother, herself the youngest of a family of about 13 children, (many of whom had since gone to live in New York, Chicago or Argentina), had been orphaned at a very young age. The onus was therefore upon her to carry around at all times a huge burden of shame; something she had dutifully undertaken, for as long as she could remember and it had to do with the life choices of two of her sisters. They had brought dishonour to the once well-respected family, a family whose ancient surname littered the two majestic cemeteries located on the outskirts of the village. And it was an ongoing dishonour; not merely the result of a single action, a heady moment of adolescent madness, which as a local news item might sooner or later have been overtaken having lost its former glamour; its novelty appeal; in all likelihood destined to be forgiven. These two sisters had willingly and openly led revolutionary lives amongst anarchic bandits, proclaiming the Communist cause against a backdrop of Mussolini's Fascist fist, had fled abroad with menfolk on horseback; had given birth to children out of wedlock; had blatantly flaunted and trailed their family name in the mud!

And even the woman's loyal and patient husband had been made to suffer over the years, having to cope with the stares, sniggers and obvious whispers as he went about his daily life. What kind of man would marry a woman from such a tainted family? It could only be a matter of time…

What made the situation even more poignant was that the girls' mother had never tried to find out more about her sisters' situation and had therefore never retaliated or spoken out in their defence. Could it all have been rooted in political ideals, self-sacrifice, a quest for freedom and the greater good for people like her own; a heartfelt desire for social equality or even compelled by true love? She was ignorant of all this and too afraid to know more than what the older villagers in particular delighted in telling her. Having been blessed (or cursed) with three daughters of her own, she had made it a personal crusade to ensure that they would each lead impeccable lives. There was little she could do about her sisters' immoral escapades, but she could certainly protect her own daughters' honour; their good name. The ice cream incident therefore had to be nipped in the bud.

As soon as was possible, once overseas contacts had been made, and all the paperwork finalised, the day arrived for the family's departure. Of course they each looked a little tense and pale as they began to board the bus, which would take them and their belongings to the railway station. And as was always the case when anyone was about to leave, many of the villagers would start to group themselves around the bus to watch the proceedings and wave goodbye, a phenomenon this village had become very familiar with.

But at that moment something finally snapped inside the mother; so many years of silence, of acceptance of her family's guilt, her head bowed low in the shame and the burden she carried wherever she went. She leapt down from the bus that crystal clear morning, raising her fist and shouting at the top of her voice: May this God-forsaken village be struck down for good and may the only thing remain standing be the statue of Our Lady.

She returned in silence to her seat in the bus and it swept the family away in a matter of seconds; the curse had been cast.

And it happened thus: twenty or so years later, (and rapidly noted by the more elderly survivors) that although the church, like the rest of the village buildings, had been razed to the ground, the much revered statue of Mother Mary was in her usual upright position, on top of her plinth in the niche on the left hand side, looking down on the devastation spread out before her.

For a good few days (and nights) in succession Giulia was unable to dislodge this story – no piece of real life – from her brain. She also wondered if any of that family had ever returned to the place of their birth…

But within a couple of weeks of being back in England, she again found peace and cure in the secret comfort of James Newhouse's embrace. A brand New Year was underway.

Chapter 33

Evacuees

In many ways, the sad events leading up to the death of Father John's mother, Norah, could also be interpreted as tiny blessings. As far as anyone could tell, and confirmed by the ongoing medical reports, she was not suffering any chronic pain; it was more a case of her drifting in and out of life, like a flickering candle, whose flame was still stubbornly clinging on to its final bit of wick. It wasn't going to be a sudden or dramatic relinquishment, more of a drowsy fading away. Resembling, John had imagined, when you find yourself one morning basking in a twilight world between sleep and wakefulness, when you are semi-aware of sunshine straining to get in through the window, but you don't yet possess the energy or desire to get up and greet the day, and neither do you have to, because it happens to be a treasured day off! Surely one of life's rare but simple indulgences.

The link between Death and early morning dreams.

Thus the blessings continued: John was able to be at his mother's bedside for the last few days and hours of her earthly life; he held her hand, reading into their shared touch a subtle meeting of minds; it was he who gave her the church's final Sacrament of Extreme Unction, which made up one of the "Last Rites." With each passing and flickering hour he saw her slip further away from life, and of course that meant out of his. He continued to pray and persuade himself, this was to be a good death, second only to dying in one's sleep overnight when it comes out of the blue, but no, maybe even better because when death isn't anticipated, it causes prolonged pain and trauma to loved ones, who haven't had the benefit of time in the coming to terms with their loss.

He was with her; she was in capable medical hands; she would die in her own home, her own bed (a matter so dear to so many, especially from that place and that generation). She was advanced in years; she had superseded the anticipated lifespan for a woman from that background and part of the world. She had loved and was loved still.

Any lingering heartache was going to be all his, he told himself; one brother soon to be flying back from Toronto; one sister busying herself with all the practical minutiae of the situation, wrenched away from her own family's needs for once. And the rest of his brothers and sisters sorting out their day to day lives, so that it might be possible to accommodate a family death and subsequent funeral. For many that was the problem the rest of life kept on spinning ahead, just as you needed to jump off its ride for a while, to stand still and gather your thoughts, to make sense of this inevitable, yet unfathomable event ultimately just to BE…for as long as it took.

Meanwhile back at Casa Stella, there was a totally different atmosphere: the two brothers from Irpinia had finally arrived and everyone was supporting Giulia with them as best they could, conscious of how seriously she was taking her new responsibilities. Mrs Mogden had prepared two separate yet adjoining rooms for them on the same floor as Giulia's large suite under strict instructions "to keep things simple" even though her employer would in truth have loved to create two luxury den-like spaces for them to enjoy. But she had thought the situation through very thoroughly and wanted to avoid setting herself up in direct competition with their own mother and what she was able to provide for them. Giulia reminded herself each morning that she had not taken on these boys for herself, but was merely giving them a place to stay, while things were sorted in Italy; probably then for no more than about six months. It would be unforgivable, she decided, if at the end of this time, they didn't want to return home because life was treating them so well in England. She had also made sure they started school as quickly as possible and had managed to squeeze into her busy schedule English lessons for them every evening; often with Serafina joining in. Every week and under her watchful eye, the boys each had to write a letter to their mother, letting her know how they were getting on and describing that week's events. As regards their suitably Spartan rooms, they had to keep them tidy and beds had to be made before school each morning. Everyone in the house, except for Carmela and Domenico as it would have been pointless, had to speak at all times in English to the boys, except in the case of an emergency.

Of course there had been quite a few teething problems. Over the first few days the two brothers often seemed dazed or lifeless; then all of a sudden would display bursts of energy and verbal aggression, the younger boy often being swayed by the behaviour of the older. They would start play fights, which regularly developed into more serious wrestling bouts. Stefano often couldn't get to sleep even though it got dark very early and he wasn't in the habit of reading in bed, which Giulia had tried to explain to them was the perfect way of dropping off.

Matteo, the younger boy had actually wet the bed on a couple of occasions, which of course she promised to keep quiet about, and she had once or twice found him bursting into tears as he hugged and hugged her while under the cover of night. But these were poignant, nocturnal incidents; during the day the two brothers turned out to be loud and boisterous, as was fitting with their ages. They loved the (unfinished) garden; they loved the kitchen, where Carmela often had little treats for them to try: dried figs, biscuits, tiny meatballs. And when they promised to behave themselves, she let them help her make gnocchi or pasta e fagioli (their absolute favourite). They regularly made fun of Domenico behind his back, as they practised ever improving impersonations of him, but were in fact quite fond of him because he reminded them so much of their own Nonno Franco in Italy. And once they were turfed out of the house to go to school, their former sleeping patterns were more or less restored though neither of them had relished the thought of abandoning the vast 'playhouse' that was Casa Stella, for a life at school which they already hated at home. They would no doubt hate it even more forcefully in England, as they couldn't communicate; would be objects of ridicule and curiosity; aliens dropped from the sky.

Tina was brilliant. It hadn't taken her aunt long to realise that whatever world she had been inhabiting over the last few months, her beloved niece was definitely 'back' with them now and Giulia had put it down, at least in part, to the arrival of the two brothers. Tina helped them with their homework, took them out at the weekends, sometimes to the local pool (the boys still hadn't learned to swim) and sometimes to the park or cinema. The brothers soon came to realise though that work of any kind had to be carried out before there could be any possibility of treats. Yes they would protest, moan, come up with heaps of reasons or excuses that they "would do it later", knew every trick in the proverbial book, as regards wearing down those in charge of them but Giulia and Tina managed, nearly always, to stand firm and united, winning that ongoing and mentally exhausting battle that only one day in the distant future, the boys would come to appreciate, as everything had been designed to help them grow and mature; an ongoing act of love!

Their life in Italy couldn't have been more different. Their mother loved them unconditionally, but this overpowering love had led her down the familiar yet exhausting path which, after lengthy verbal battles, let them off punishments, rarely following through threats, rewarding bad behaviour by giving them even more attention, shouting and screaming to such an extent that they no longer heard it. Their father had worked long hours and sometimes didn't even get to see his boys before they went to bed, but when he did, he often found himself playing out the role of the strict disciplinarian, the returning father, who had to sort out all the mounting domestic issues of the day, in the space of a few minutes. He rarely needed to use his loud and powerful voice, of which everyone was in awe, his brand of discipline hinging on a range of tactics: body language; a kind of continuous, spitting whisper, as his eyes growing ever rounder and bigger rolled in his head; dramatically designed attempts to remove the belt from his trousers or the shoe from his foot; getting the wooden spoon out of the kitchen drawer; a stare which seemed to burn holes through them in the confident knowledge that his sons would melt in his presence, even though he rarely used, or cared to implement, corporal punishment.

So in spite of the uphill struggle to keep these boys in check, most of the Casa Stella household eventually grew to be truly fond of them, emotions which went far beyond the fact that they were unfortunate victims of the earthquake; that they had lost their father to the falling rubble. And slowly the boys came round to appreciating the care they received, although never expressing their feelings through the spoken word. They might unexpectedly grab Carmela by the waist and give her a short but hearty hug. They might kiss Tina swiftly on the cheek or lose themselves in Giulia's turquoise eyes, as they competed over whom she loved the more never of course though if anyone else was around, especially the friends from school they had also started to invite home. Domenico had shown them how to make pineapple wine and taught them card games they had never heard of. They liked to shake his hand before and after each meeting with him. Stefano in particular admired Lorenzo, tall and imposing looking, who would sometimes give up 30 minutes out of his all-important day to kick a football or two around the garden with them. And just think he worked at the biggest, most famous airport in the world; he had seen Antonio Cabrini; he had actually spoken to Ornella Muti – so much to tell their mother each week.

A couple of days after his mother's funeral, Father John felt he now had to drag himself back to England and once more take up his parish duties. His bishop had shown great patience and compassion over his situation, and hadn't pressed him for an early return, but John himself knew that the longer he stayed in Galway, the more difficult it would be to wrench himself away from his childhood home. He was looking forward to seeing Giulia in any case and wondering just how she was coping with the two Italian brothers. He had also had some ideas about how they might help him with a few bits and pieces at the Presbytery.

Giovanni was also reflecting upon Giulia and what the future held for her.

She was his smart and elegant daughter, a woman who could light up any room, as Giulia the tiny baby had warmed his granite-cold heart many years beforehand. He prided himself on the fact that money spent on her and her education had been money well spent, a wise investment, and yet he was not so blind to the fact that she would have risen above the rest regardless of the circumstances in which she found herself. She carried his best genes and his rich blood flowed through her veins so it was both comfort and condemnation that she had no children of her own. It kept her safe; it broke his heart, the waste of the promise any son of hers would have fulfilled.

Chapter 34
Sunday's Child

Serafina had asked Giulia, earlier on in her pregnancy, to be with her in hospital when the time came to give birth to little Domenico or Carmela (not the Fabrizio or Valentina she would have preferred.) A strange choice of birth companion perhaps, considering the older woman's total lack of experience, but Lorenzo had already stated that the delivery room was no place for him (although the twentieth century was regularly throwing up ideas, such as the role of the 'New Man') and that he would definitely be seeing mother and child only AFTER the birth. This, Serafina had accepted quite readily, even though it surprised her in subsequent weeks that most of the other expectant mothers she encountered at the clinic, regularly spoke of how their husbands would be there to support them. But the thought of being on her own in an alien English hospital, as she suffered hours of surely the world's greatest agonies, simply terrified her and she once even found herself conjuring up words and images from the Book of Revelations:

"She was pregnant and cried out with pain because she was about to give birth. There was a giant red dragon there. The dragon had seven heads with a crown on each head. It also had ten horns. Its tail swept a third of the stars out of the sky and threw them down to earth. It stood in front of the woman who was ready to give birth to the baby. It wanted to eat the baby as soon as it was born."

As a child, she remembered eavesdropping, in and out of her aunts' conversations about how most of the villagers still believed that hospitals were places from which you rarely came out alive and that once they got you inside their four walls, they would perform experiments on you, in order to advance their scientific knowledge. And if you did survive, you only came out in a worse condition than when you went in. Of course Serafina had more faith in the medical profession than her medievally minded people, but it was also impossible to fully erase such terrifying images forged onto her erstwhile-developing brain.

Carmela had naturally agreed to look after the two brothers (while her sister would be fulfilling her latest act of charitable kindness) and to continue to 'hold the fort' at home. Giulia was at first thrilled at the thought of being present at the birth of the baby; such a privilege to have been asked! The latest De Martino, who would continue the bloodline of her ancestors. And yet this lofty feeling soon evolved into a nauseous well of fear and awe. She would now be playing a key role in the drama which heralded the painful and messy arrival of another human life.

And as the time drew near, she realised she was just as scared as Serafina, though equally determined never to show it – they would always be able to confess their fears and laugh about it all at a future date. She bought a textbook about childbirth, which she left on a shelf in the bathroom, and on each visit, leafed her way through the chapters. The stark black and white photographs, not to mention the ugly medical jargon often left her feeling queasy. But she forced herself to persevere with each new discovery: a remote female universe loomed, intimate and ancient! How strange to think as they approached the third millennium that there wasn't a more 'modern' or sophisticated way of bringing human life into the world, but also one without the need for technology, which appeared to her somewhat out of place. The secret act of childbirth had remained something that directly linked us to our stone-age sisters and of course the wider animal kingdom. Animals, our fellow mammals, who seemed to give birth so quietly and acceptingly and oh so regularly! And never once losing their dignity, as they played out Nature's role for them in a range of outdoor locations.

In that book, she also read something about how the baby, on its journey out into our world, turns and tries for a split second to return back into its own familiar universe.

Giving birth the ennoblement of women? Or something bestial? Or something merely to be expressed in medical jargon? Of course she knew she couldn't express her own thoughts on the matter in such a precious or mock-heroic manner to the people around her; it would only go to confirm yet again just how different she was from everyone else; how ridiculous her line of thinking. How frustratingly superior, since she felt the need to bring the cosmos or philosophy or poetry into simply everything.

The forty weeks had passed quickly to those looking on, but they of course had their own busy lives to manage. For Serafina the last three weeks in particular staggered by like an old man who had lost his way home. She knew that birth could come any day now, her baby being completely formed and able to survive on the outside. Each day appeared and disappeared but nothing. At least her fears of the actual labour were now subsiding a little; she just wanted her waters to break; the pain to start so that it could be all over. So that she could re-assemble her former self.

If only she had had an inkling of how James continued to worship her in secret, how she epitomised his perfect image of the quintessential earth goddess, serene in all her thoughts and movements, she would have collapsed in tears (of laughter too perhaps) knowing that she had failed miserably all along the way; all those fears and sometimes tinged with regret; her frequent pangs of maternal denial, as she fantasised on the life she could have had before Lorenzo and before England; her recurrent nightmares punctuated by the uncontrollable screams of a child who would simply not stop. By 41 weeks, however, she had got to the stage that she could hardly remember events at all before becoming pregnant; she had by now been pregnant all her life!

Days continued to crawl by and they told her at the hospital that if the baby hadn't arrived within a few days they would have to INDUCE her. Such a scary word it smacked of artificiality; drugs and invasive practises; brutality. Not what Nature had intended at all. But a first baby was usually late in any case; there was naturally nothing to worry about. It happened all the time; part and parcel of the hospital assembly line.

And thus is was. Domenico took the two women, each with her own little suitcase, to the now-familiar hospital, where Serafina had dutifully kept all her antenatal appointments: scans, checks, tests, guided tour of the labour and delivery rooms, the childcare class, the classes for baby craft, relaxation and the ones for breathing techniques during the various stages of labour. Giulia had already paid in advance for a little room for them to share until the time came for Serafina to give birth. She would sleep that night on a reclining armchair with a couple of spare pillows while Serafina would lie, perhaps in agony, on the hospital bed. Earlier talk about a possible home confinement or a baby emerging from the gentle waters of a birthing pool now seemed risible; this would be a highly technological event. If nothing else, Giulia was determined to stay by her side at all times, taking up her place amid the jungle of monitors, drips and wires.

24 hours passed and there was still no change, no sign of the baby wanting to make its way into the world. And who could blame it thought Giulia to herself. The two women were even granted "permission" to take a walk outside the hospital and make their way to a stretch of the river that bordered the hospital grounds. Perhaps the walk, her being upright, would get things moving. And if nothing else it might puncture the nauseating atmosphere of life inside the hospital building. But nothing came of it, which meant even more medical intervention.

At about 1am the following morning however, Serafina began calling out to Giulia in the darkness, alerting her that she was sure her womb had started to contract and that she was feeling quite uncomfortable. Her birthing partner not knowing whether this was real life or part of an unthinkable dream, instantly clambered to her feet and held out her by now well-rehearsed hand in the direction of the red button. They waited and waited. No one came, so she headed out along the linoleum-floored corridor which took her past some side offices and to the little reception counter. A nurse had spotted her and both swiftly made their way back to Serafina, with Giulia explaining on the way that her contractions had begun but didn't yet know how regularly (or how painfully) they were coming. She was by now fully awake; a tense ball of fear and expectation.

Fifteen hours later violent pains were ravaging the insides of James' Earth Goddess, now coming every five minutes, and as each new one arrived, she resolved to face her death, as she couldn't possibly take any more; death in fact seemed like a sweet release. She was now more than happy to let go of life's kite-string; no longer such a big deal. Oh if only a crazed killer would enter and blast her brains all over the lonely room! They took her temperature, measured her cervix, talking of 'still only 2 centimetres dilated' an alien language and that she needed to be '10 centimetres' before being allowed to start pushing still probably many hours away. Giulia pleaded for them to fetch pain relief, an epidural, as the gas and air Serafina had been clinging to, was no longer enough. A sorry sight as she looked out from within the shapeless spotted gown they had made her wear. The reply came that it would all be arranged shortly enough, but that no guarantee could be made as to how long it would take to find the anaesthetist (there were only two on duty who served the whole hospital, not merely the maternity wing) and it was coming up to changeover time which meant a new shift of midwives, thus even greater disruption. It also happened to be a very busy afternoon, with a couple of emergencies and a growing waiting list of patients' requests.

The epidural was administered five hours later, Giulia herself having spent so much of that time in masked desperation, crouched down by the side of the hospital bed, whispering words of praise and encouragement to the vulnerable young girl, enthusing that it would all be over eventually and describing the wonderful joy that awaited them.

And within the hour they came to break her waters.

By 10 the following morning, Serafina was 10 centimetres dilated but according to the midwife still not ready to push. The epidural had been topped up a couple of times, but this also meant that she would have to be told when to start pushing as she would not be able to feel nature's urges. No one would commit as to how much longer it was still likely to take but at least she had been drifting in and out of sleep over the last couple of hours.

When the time did come, Serafina took forty minutes to push out her little son, Giulia counting down from 10 to 1 for each push which rode each contraction. She saw the first appearance of the top of his head a tiny moon-sliver of head which appeared and disappeared during a series of pushes until finally the whole head appeared, followed swiftly by the rest of his little body, a head covered in a mop of dark hair.

It was a Sunday and Sunday's Child (or Dominic as he came to be called) arrived, weighing in at 3.5 kilos.

Giulia rejected the midwife's instant offer of cutting the baby's cord.

Chapter 35
The Recluse

Giovanni had long ago accepted the fact that he had to live in hiding for the rest of his life, no matter how long or short it was destined to be; a situation which over the years had certainly put his mettle to the test, psychologically, physically, emotionally. He had already lost nearly all those he had ever loved, many when he was still a young man; some through death, others through estrangement. But so it had to be. He neither complained about it nor allowed himself to sink into any pools of self-pity.

In fact in many ways he managed to live very well indeed, enjoying the very best commodities the world had to offer; was served by a husband and wife team whose total loyalty was testament to a closely connected past. His house was the kind of house he had dreamed of possessing when still a child. He had drawn it on scraps of paper over and over again. Now he would no longer have to endure the poverty (material and cultural) of his childhood yet neither could he ever be at peace obliged to be vigilant, day in day out. He was a powerful man and therefore paid the price of 'all-powerful' men; a man of granite; one with a legendary past (at least to those of his kind) and yet a man with one tremendous weakness that he had to conceal to that same world at all costs. Once sniffed out, it would only be a matter of time. And it would then not only be his life in danger.

His weakness came in the shape of Giulia Cristaldi.

Giovanni firmly believed he had done everything in his power, from the very beginning (that is from the day of his daughter's birth) to protect her from the ills of the world: poverty, ignorance, vengeance. She had also been aided by Nature, Time and Place. Nature had endowed her with good looks (not always a blessing in a woman, he had since concluded); an equally good brain and she had been born at a time and place in History which had heralded a new dawn, a new age of peace, together with numerous social opportunities for the ordinary citizen. It was now possible to break out of the social class of one's birth. Giovanni had accumulated great wealth; he could buy into these opportunities for her, including the privilege of a fine education. However, their relationship was always going to be flawed and one of conflict. Her love for him was inevitably strong, yet could also border on hatred. His love for her was total, even though his voice and manner came across as diamond hard; the voice of intransigence. Given the circumstances it was natural she still wanted to know so much more about him and his life, both past and present, but it was impossible for him to give her the answers she craved and when on the odd occasion she did manage to prise out of him some tiny morsel from his rarely opening shell, she felt mortified by what tumbled out.

And in the mirror, she often saw his face in hers.

His latest triumph had surely been that trip, incognito, to his grandson's wedding! The meticulous planning; a complex brotherhood of silent allegiance; a secret network of gossamer steel.

According to Giovanni every man and woman of a certain age had things to hide, be they habitual, tawdry goings on or isolated acts of shame, carried out in the dark of night, far from human eyes And he believed that the more highly regarded the person, the vaster the chest of 'schifezze', he tried to conceal from the rest of the world. This rather extreme point of view might have been the result of encounters he had invariably made with such people or perhaps the result of a subconscious desire to absolve himself (partially at least) of his own acts of wickedness. People who still occupied his life he moved around like chess pieces, whether they knew it or not; for their own good of course but always also for his.

As he sat at his cumbersome writing desk on that golden October morning, he suddenly remembered that Gennaro had arranged for a trusted doctor to be brought to the house, time for his twice yearly check-up, and he needed to decide very quickly whether or not to mention the two recent falls he had suffered. No one in the house had witnessed them, thank goodness, and he was able to hide the resulting bruises from Gennaro's busy eyes. He was almost certain it was nothing significant, merely a silly coincidence due to a lack of attention, but should he say something to his personal physician? It was bound to be made a great deal of, and followed up with a barrage of annoying questions and tedious tests.

Whereas that morning Giovanni wanted him out of the house as quickly as possible, his heightened need for privacy and solitude made all the more intense whenever matters concerning his health were on the agenda. He checked his watch once again and was able to conjure up in his mind's eye the scene of the two men, Gennaro having picked up a certain Dottor Masini, who would be ensconced on the back seat, with a carefully designed blindfold covering the upper part of his head upon which rested a pair of oversized sunglasses (for diverting the curiosity of anyone looking in) and his hands gripped together by handcuffs. It had been explained to the good doctor, very politely of course prior to his first ever visit, that it was predominantly in his interest to be thus treated in that way he would have no idea as to the roads covered, should anyone ever question him. Gennaro also took the added precaution of using different routes for each of the trips.

The falls, it was decided by his patient, would definitely not be referred to on this occasion!

Within a couple of hours, the doctor was about to make his departure, leaving just as he had arrived doctor and client shaking hands and exchanging, through gritted teeth, their superficial smiles and pleasantries, as Gennaro waited patiently from outside the car. They would see to it that the tall and distinguished looking doctor was generously rewarded for his troubles; the driver always in possession of thick wads of high denomination notes, which he kept rolled together, bound by rubber bands in a cloth purse attached to the inside of his trousers. In this way he was ready for any arising situation. As anticipated, the delighted recipient had wasted no time in placing his overblown fee in an awaiting wallet just before the mask and manacles once again made their bizarre appearance.

As for Giovanni, he decided that he would wait for Gennaro to return before having lunch that day; he'd already popped his head round the kitchen door, taunted by the wonderful combined smells of parsley and garlic, all finely chopped and sizzling in a film of olive oil, which were emanating from Nunzia's culinary lair. He had seen that she had also prepared a glass jug of red wine filled to the brim with chunky slices of peach, whose skin and flesh had become a suggestive shade of dark red after hours of wine absorption. Homemade food and heavenly wines such a modest, habitual, yet divine pleasure, he mused on his way back to the study, after having called out a greeting, a compliment or two as regards her expertise in the kitchen (he had even bedded her just the once many years beforehand) and letting her know the time he wanted to eat that day. Another two or three hours of business calls by which time Gennaro would be back and the three of them could eat and talk over a sublimely modest meal together in the kitchen before his late afternoon siesta.

It was getting late. He could put it off no longer. The moment had come. He felt the rush and Gennaro was ushered into his study; within minutes the brand-new file had been unsealed. Operation Lorenzo. It had been his two falls which had triggered the present venture. So many successes up to now but one had to think of the future, and not just his own. He and Gennaro were no longer in their prime. They had to accept the harsh truth that they would not be around for ever. And Death sometimes roams the world in her carpet slippers. The two men, same age, same birth village, one and the same mission; two men who had once allowed drops of their adolescent blood to mingle, discussed preliminaries for the setting up of a meeting that would soon be taking place between them and Giovanni's grandson.

After countless strategy options had been discussed and dismissed, there remained one which might just work.

They had sorted through all the tiny reports on Lorenzo, gathered and stored over the years and were about to collate and present them 'officially' in one main file. They had learned that he was vain, impatient and a pragmatist; not a great listener, and yet a man not without his own personalised code of conduct. There was plenty of corroborating evidence to show he was conservative by nature, believing in the status quo and the continued practice of old traditions. He was mature and responsible, loyal and dutiful (of sorts) towards his family. Although affable and good-humoured with work colleagues and passengers, he didn't go in for close friendships or go in for the habit of unburdening himself of worries, with others.

He had had many sexual encounters with women who worked alongside him at the airport, and before that with a couple of older women, customers he had served at his parents' delicatessen. Lorenzo had recently married a simple village girl from Sicily (an arranged marriage) and rumour had it she was already pregnant with their first child. Fortunately, she didn't appear to hanker after a career, which might conflict with her marital and domestic duties. But they needed further research to be carried out into her past life and family origins. Appearance and reality sometimes stood astride a wide chasm. Lorenzo was not an intellectual or part of Giulia's academic world; not prone to overthink or examine his conscience but neither was he a fool; his single-minded pragmatism had served him well at home and in the outside world.

Giulia herself had been considered and swiftly discounted for the role, many years beforehand.

However, her off-the-cuff remarks, made during spasmodic visits, had helped them enormously with their ongoing research. It filled in gaps; it confirmed other observations; or negated them, sometimes throwing things into temporary confusion. One example in particular was concerned with Lorenzo's reported reaction to a film (on video cassette) she had recently recorded, a black and white masterpiece, as Giulia had introduced it, called *Fontamara*. Lorenzo liked the cinema, his favourite films being spaghetti westerns, James Bond, and old family favourites: Italian films starring Toto' or Alberto Sordi. In the film, *Fontamara*, the name of a fictitious Italian village, the audience gets to see life from the point of view of a peasant community and how through years of isolation from the sophisticated world of cities the villagers' poignant simplicity (very few can read or write) they are continuously ridiculed, mistreated and exploited by those in powerful positions.

However, by the end of the film their inner-strength and tenacity is shown to win through.

According to Giulia, Lorenzo became very restless and even a bit bad-tempered during the viewing and yet couldn't quite manage to remove his eyes from the screen. She couldn't work out whether it was the ignorance of the villagers which had annoyed and embarrassed him or whether it was something else that perhaps he didn't fully understand and neither of them ever referred to it again!

But she did know that she had never seen him quite so clearly affected by anything else he had watched on screen or in real life.

Chapter 36

In the Confessional

"Bless me, Father, for I have sinned. My last confession was a month ago and these are my sins:

"I feel I'm losing my faith, Father, I keep going back to the thought that if I had been born at some other time or in another part of the world, I might not be Catholic at all and so I find it hard to accept that why should it be MY Religion, MY Faith which is the true one? I've also been thinking about evolution. If life on earth has always been evolving, what will become of human beings? Why should it stop with us? It can't just stop still but if we are told we are made in God's image? And why is it that we are taught that some parts of Scripture are to be taken literally whereas others have a more poetic or symbolic significance? How do we always know which is which? All these thoughts whirl round and round my head especially at night."

"I have taken part in nasty gossip.

"I have entertained impure thoughts about a gardener I have watched from the dormitory window.

"I have once or twice forgotten to pray to thank God for each new day.

"I have not paid attention during Mass or shown the necessary devotion towards the Blessed Sacrament.

"I have not cared sufficiently about those worse off than myself.

"I have cruelly made fun of one or two of the Sisters behind their backs.

"I have shown anger towards my father.

"That is all I can remember, Father."

The elderly priest, whose turn it was to visit the exclusive Girls Boarding School, had of course heard it all before, in one way or another, from so many other girlish hearts, but there was something about this young woman's intensity of feeling and genuine desire for the truth – she had even clearly written it all down beforehand, for fear of forgetting something. (He had heard the bit of paper being scrunched and crumpled, as she delivered her Confession through the grille.) He was clearly not able to deal with all her fears and questions now; that was not the point of the Sacrament with at least twenty others still queuing and shuffling along the Chapel pews. He said he would speak to the Sisters and suggest that they arrange some Spiritual Direction for her.

The Spiritual Direction was never forthcoming, however, as Giulia and her peers would be leaving Fielding House for good that very week.

A much later confession; same confessant, different priest, no queue. The light glowed green for GO. And, if scripted for a play, would have read something like this:

"Bless me, Father, for I have sinned. My last Confession was a month ago."

"I'm not expecting you to absolve me of my sins today, Father, but you are I'm afraid the only one I can share this with, only in the confessional. I may not even be able to express myself adequately, and if I find that the right words just don't exist to describe or explain, even slightly, the last three weeks (from that moment Giulia would always if only to herself... refer to that episode in her life as The Three Weeks) then I might have to break off so I'm letting you know from the outset."

"They were sun-filled days (and sin-filled, she thought to herself, but now wasn't the time for puns or humour so she dismissed any word-play) yet wanton, sinful in the eyes of the Church and yet it has been an awakening, a revelation (deciding perhaps best not to choose the word 'Epiphany'), well really on par with a religious experience something much greater than me, outside of me but also inside, where God, or Fate, arranged everything in such a way that I was wrapped up and transported to another world, a beautifully pure nether world, no, an overworld, rather than an underworld, a temporary place by its very nature and yet at the same time, our true home."

"I met a man a fellow seeker of the truth. For three weeks we were together every second every minute every hour every day. By day the sun shone down on our backs and by night we drank red wine, but never to excess. A pitch-black sky was drawn across us sequinned with multifarious stars. He played a guitar he carried everywhere and I danced in a way I never knew I could. If this is sounding like a cheap love affair or tacky holiday romance, I will stop talking now..."

The Priest's silence gave the go-ahead for her to continue. "There were no promises or embarrassing declarations, we just lived out every waking moment in total symbiosis. Neither of us wanted to be anywhere else or with anyone else. No power struggle, no black moods or objections a perfect balance; a joint yet silent commitment to the present moment. His hair was how Jesus' hair is depicted in western art…in fact he looked like Jesus. He joked that my eyes contained the whole of the Mediterranean Sea and that he was gladly drowning in it, in them."

"Each day we must have walked for miles without realising it; we paddled, we bathed we had become part of the natural world, a surreal and crazy twentieth century Adam and Eve."

"When our time came to an end, it was strangely bittersweet, but not painful as such. We both knew from the start we couldn't continue living in that exalted way or even go on seeing each other we had merely taken time out of the normal run of things to rediscover a place where human beings can be how they are meant to be I suppose. There was no desire to drag that relationship out into a trail of ugly regrets, broken vows or marital bitterness."

"Its short duration does not reflect the depth or immediacy of passion and freedom that the two of us lived out to the full, each of those days."

"Forgive me, Father, I don't know now how to bring this to an end I will never be sharing these words again so please indulge me just this once and let me continue for a moment or two more. I remember no, I'm reliving the sounds of the tides, as intoxicating as the sun's rays and the taste of the wine. He smelled of all three. We lived mainly outside, amongst the birds and the trees, the fields and beaches. We had moved in with nature's primitive rhythms and had joined them up with the primitive sounds he plucked, strummed and slapped out of his guitar."

"There was one morning I felt the need to scream. Have you ever felt that desire? I simply needed to release the weight of long years of silent compliance, let go of all the repeated nonsense that had been mounting up inside like molten lava or no, rubble, more like: the million early morning wake up calls; the nuns' stupid habits; the rules rammed into us; the never-ending assemblies; the prayers we spouted without actually praying; the umpteen Masses where our hearts and minds were just not present; the clanging school bells; the strict mealtimes; each and every day being brutally sliced into timed segments; the exams (even though I really enjoyed doing them) ha ha see how twisted I am? All those expectations that weren't coming from within; our precious virginity; the ghastly uniform designed to keep us bound and locked away from the world."

"And then, me, being wrenched away from my people, in the first place, by my father, when I was only ten years of age."

"All these things that early morning suddenly rose to the surface of my being all those things which had weighed me down without me ever realising it but when I actually tried to let out my scream one attempt would surely do it, if I tried long and hard enough the only thing that emerged was a pathetic sham of a scream, more of a low, rasping cackle! It took me about another 5 or 6 attempts to let out that solitary, primeval scream my body so craved and in the middle of nowhere. And finally it came loud and rumbling, trembling even, like thunder and then stronger and then even stronger; I let it power through me, heartfelt and necessary, like giving birth to my first precious child. And he looked on."

"It had been a scream of release, a scream of freedom, a scream of joy, a scream of discovery so great."

"So that is how we lived out those Three Weeks in our very own universe of blue and green, white and yellow, with untamed horses frolicking in the distance. A time of music and very few words."

This time the 'confession' had been made face to face, something by now positively encouraged by the Church. The priest in question was Father John and this was the very first time he had encountered a young woman, named Giulia Cristaldi. He instinctively felt a sudden rush of relief that he was soon to be leaving the Parish of St. Raphael's, where he had served for merely a year. But once he'd let reason return, which took him more than a clutch of seconds, (and he'd had no warning as to when her haunting story stream was about to end), he advised her quietly yet with authority, to go home and reflect at length about all she had told him, now she had taken that courageous step of putting into words all that had transpired. She was clearly an articulate and introspective young woman and that he was certain when she felt ready to confess any sins she believed she had committed, then he or any other priest (since he would soon be packing his bags for another part of the country) would be happy to absolve her of them.

In the time remaining, he told her not to be too hard on herself, as much of her experience had to do with hormones; the passion of youth, eroticism even and was therefore natural and understandable, but that he thought it would be helpful for her over the next few days to measure it all against the teachings of Jesus in the Gospels and see where her behaviour had been lacking, selfish or amoral, and why the Son of Man wouldn't have wanted that for us. It was not for him, a Parish Priest yet also a fellow human being, to judge her in any way; he said he trusted she would, in time, come to find the true path out of this breathlessly overwhelming yet misguided experience.

What Giulia never told Father John, however, was that The Three Weeks never did leave her, never did fade into the mists of long-ago memories; on the contrary, they continued to inspire and sustain her, providing her with an ongoing wellspring of beauty and truth to replenish her.

Life would never be the same again; could never be the same.

Chapter 37

Empty

"Aaaaaghaaaaagh! Where is he, where is he, *dov'e' il mio principino*? (Where is my little prince?) *Dov'e', dov'e?*"

Lorenzo's wife burst into the kitchen of Casa Stella, as she hastily threw a light-weight gown around her shoulders, partially covering the white cotton nightdress, which clung to her. Her hair was unexpectedly dishevelled, as even though she had just risen from her bed, she would normally have taken a few minutes to present herself in a more self-respecting manner. Her eyes looked wider and blacker than ever, and the image of Charlotte Brontë's Bertha, Mr. Rochester's first wife, suddenly surfaced within Giulia's somewhat overworked mind's eye.

"Giulia, have you got him, have you seen him? He's no longer in his cot. Where's Carmela? (Serafina still couldn't bring herself to call her 'Mamma', much to Lorenzo's continued annoyance, but she had explained to him on more than one occasion that she had never called anybody by that sacred name and that it was very difficult for her to start now.) Has she come down yet? I wish my mother-in-law wouldn't take him without letting me know. How come I didn't even hear her?"

"Oh, Domenico, there you are, have you seen Dominic? Has Carmela got him? Who else is in the house? I can't even remember O Santo Cielo," at which her father-in-law promptly disappeared again.

"For goodness' sake, Serafina, calm down! He's here somewhere, he can't walk; he can't even crawl or shuffle on his little bottom yet. There must be a rational explanation. Did you check under his cot? Yes, okay, of course, you did. Domenico's already gone to find Carmela. He must have heard you wailing from his room. Sit down, I insist, you're working yourself up into a frenzy. I'm going to make us both una camomilla."

Even Giulia was by now feeling very uneasy as regards this incomprehensible situation but once again, she was determined not to let down her guard, all in the cause of promoting the wellbeing of those around her. It had become second habit; her own pain she could and would always deal with, later.

Both Carmela and Domenico then padded into the kitchen, Domenico cracking his knuckles in his habitual manner, which always caused Giulia to shudder. "We've got the girls searching all over the house," burst out Carmela, in a poignantly heady mix of Italian and English. "No one's seen him; no one went to get him; we wouldn't do that without letting you know! *O Mio Dio,* where is our little angeletto?"

"Has anyone seen James?" demanded Domenico all of a sudden. "He was here last night, wasn't he? And what about Lorenzo? Don't tell me he got back earlier than planned and he came to collect his son while we were all asleep? Look I'm going round to their house."

At that thought, he grabbed a spare bunch of keys to Lorenzo's house, and slammed the front door shut behind him.

By now Serafina was a waxen lump, slumped heavily at the table with her arms and raven-black hair spread out insanely over the flowery plastic cloth. She was locked into a state of icy shock and although she needed to cry or even shout out, no sound came from her mouth, which was set wide-open, an eerie cavern. It seemed that one hundred hours had passed since her waking up, admittedly a little later than usual, and from her staring down in disbelief, at the cruel empty cradle. It just had to be an apocryphal nightmare, one that for some reason she couldn't yet force her way out of. As each minute crawled by, the sounds of the ticking clock became more and more unbearable. Why, oh why? Where was the little boy she now dedicated each beat of her young life to? The most beautiful little boy in the world, her Sunday's child and destined for such a golden future.

It had been a late night and the De Martinos had decided quite rightly that with Lorenzo away, on some kind of airline course, it would be much better that Serafina and Dominic stayed overnight with them. The family had been holding a little party earlier in the day for the two Italian brothers, (and some of their English school friends). The boys had seats booked on a flight leaving that same evening for Capodicchino Airport, from where they would once again take up the threads of their former lives but this time somewhere on the outskirts of their earthquake-ravaged village. They would re-connect with their real mother, the woman who had given them life. The memory of Giulia, Carmela, Tina, Mrs

Mogden and the others would eventually fade away, becoming mere names in an address or telephone book; dim faces in an ageing set of photographs in a rarely opened album.

With Lorenzo away, James had kindly offered to drive the boys to the airport and when he eventually returned, they all found themselves chatting nostalgically about their stay at Casa Stella, about how much the two brothers had blossomed after such a shaky start sharing previously told or untold stories about their escapades and misunderstandings; also laughing a lot about some of the more colourful incidents.

It had also been the case on previous occasions that the family had encouraged Serafina to stay overnight with them; it seemed the most logical thing to do. But why, oh why, had she gone along with it this time? (At Star House a little pale blue room had been lovingly set aside for just such a situation, complete with bed and cot, for mother and baby, together with a chest of drawers containing all the necessary baby baggage). Had she returned home last night, her precious baby, she reasoned somewhat illogically, would now be safely wrapped up in her arms.

She suddenly felt the tingle which heralded the readiness of her milk. He'd be getting hungry. She eventually screamed out of her silence. "Oh, where is my little boy? Who's taken him?"

Carmela, seated in the corner of the room, began to recite the rosary, after having silently slipped back to her room to pick up the well-used row of amber beads her own precious son had given her.

Ave, o Maria, piena di grazia, il Signore e' con te. Tu sei benedetta fra le donne e benedetto e' il frutto del tuo seno, Gesu'. Madre di Dio, prega per noi peccatori and so on, and this continued relentlessly for the next twenty minutes or so, her voice growing all the more low and husky.

Giulia had already been thinking about alerting Lorenzo, but knew that by now it was impossible to make contact as he would be on route for his home; they just had to wait for him to return. Her very next thought was the police; yes, if they hadn't found little Dominic within ten yes, ten minutes, she would have to ring them. Oh but surely it wouldn't come to that; no, of course, they would all be spouting tears of joy any minute now as soon as his whereabouts had come to light. It would become the latest family anecdote, to be passed on with all its twists and turns by each member, *Please could that moment come now! Please*

188

God, please God, I will do anything, ANYTHING you ask of me; please look after our precious little baby and bring him back to us!

And there was also one other person she knew she would have to contact, as soon as her presence would not be missed.

Just at that moment, James slipped shadow-like, into the kitchen, his face drained of all colour. Domenico had also just returned from his son's house, a wasted trip in any case, and James quickly whispered something to him, as he hovered by the door. Both men swiftly made their exit, without Serafina raising her gaze to pick up on their hasty retreat or overtly awkward body language. The other women, all looking in on one another, clenched their fists and gritted their teeth in preparation for what they would soon be hearing or seeing; something unimaginable; there could be no other explanation.

The body of a baby boy was floating face-down on the surface of the pond James had been helping to create; a perfectly proportioned little body, arranged as a fallen star, rolling gently to and fro alongside the lily pads; the glisteningly wet baby skin stroked by a quivering green haze of Capel Venere which nestled below long stems of papyrus, standing noble and erect, lending shelter; the baby's once dark wavy hair now made straight and even longer by the water, as it reached his pretty dimpled shoulders.

And James, who in the past few days, had often taken the opportunity to admire his pond and fountain handiwork from the balcony which wrapped around the upper rooms, had only a few moments ago looked down in dazed disbelief at the anomalous shape, which hovered marble-white, a fallen cupid on the water and wasted no time dashing downstairs and out into the garden to investigate.

It was without doubt the worst moment of his life.

Within twenty minutes, Casa Stella was swarming with uniformed police and diverse members of medical and forensic teams, each with their relevant paraphernalia and vehicles haphazardly parked outside. Serafina had been swiftly whisked off by ambulance to the hospital, while being farcically comforted by a totally distraught mother-law and an ashen-faced yet tearless Giulia. Carmela continued to recite prayers, always clutching the amber rosary, between sobs and gasps and her sister chose to use silence as the kinder remedy, never letting go of Serafina's left hand and shoulder, both of which she constantly rubbed.

She only knew the English version properly now so it would have been a futile task praying (or competing) alongside her sister.

Lorenzo had only recently arrived back from his trip and was being restrained at the house by a sombre James and a devastated Domenico. He was beside himself and ready to lash out physically and verbally (whatever it took) to the unwelcome invaders of their family home. They were total strangers, knew nothing about his family and what family meant to them. They were merely carrying out a role, detached and remote, farcically pretending to be caring and supportive, going through their professional motions, with their phoney advice and well-practised faces and empty phrases.

But, most of all, his vitriol was targeted at the by now absent Serafina. Why hadn't she protected his son; his only son? Why hadn't she returned to their marital home? Had all this got to do with some crazy Sicilian vendetta? Perhaps he should have checked her background and suitability a little more thoroughly? He had done everything to provide for his wife and son, and this was how she repaid him. Regardless of who the perpetrator of this terrible crime turned out to be, he would always hold HER responsible!

He was clearly inconsolable and in no mood to listen to reason. And as he poured out his pain, in fits of anger and bursts of verbal offence, Domenico and James also suffering, never left his side!

Chapter 38
Tableau

A Few Weeks Later

The former curate at St. Raphael's, but now assistant priest, Father Paul, turned up at Casa Stella shortly after Father John. It wasn't his first visit to Giulia's elegant house but that didn't stop him on this occasion from feeling particularly tense and somewhat superfluous. He thought back to the time he had first met Giulia and the others, introducing himself in the same jokey way he did with everyone: "Father Paul Wilby, the only priest whose surname appears in the (daily prayer). Our Father."

Today as he made his way up the path, he could see quite clearly through the ample downstairs windows, the family arranged as if for a Victorian photograph, the women motionless as they sat huddled together on the settee with Serafina's aunts squeezed either side of their beloved niece and either side of them, Carmela and Giulia. The nearby coffee table offered scant comfort: a box of tissues, some untouched glasses of water, and two or three scattered rosaries. A tiny well-worn prayer book sat unopened on Serafina's lap. Each of these women, except Giulia, wore over their heads a version of the traditional black lace mantilla, which kept out prying eyes, as well as signalling to the outside world, a stark show of gravitas and well-practised mourning. Giulia had instead chosen a pair of big dark sunglasses. All were dressed in black from head to toe; their black leather handbags piled up on a free armchair. And the younger De Martino women, dressed in black or dark grey, (though with heads uncovered), filled the remaining sofas and armchairs.

If anyone had spotted Father Paul, as they stared blankly downwards or out of the room, should they ever raise their heads in his direction, they certainly hadn't shown any signs of welcome or even recognition.

The men in that room had all chosen to remain standing at the ready to lend support, moral or physical, yet unsurprisingly quite unfit for the task. They wore the dark suits that also would have doubled for Midnight Mass and winter weddings. And each had chosen a plain black tie. Domenico and Lorenzo's shoes shone out of such a bleak morning, the result of Carmela's meticulous polishing as did quick flashes of their gold cufflinks, whenever they lifted their arms, making visible the white sleeves of their shirts.

There could be no mistaking the fact that Father John was their trusted family Priest, as he kept his big protective hand on Serafina's shoulder at all times and every so often bent down from his standing position behind the settee, to whisper wise words of comfort to a seemingly tiny and paralysed Serafina.

The day they had all been dreading had finally arrived and had somehow to be got through.

Father Paul saw no reason to enter the house at this point, even though the front door had been left wide open and he soon became aware of the hearse (followed by three or four equally formidable vehicles) creeping darkly and silently up to the house. It was not hard to make out the impossibly small white coffin, which he alone could have carried in his hands. The family wreaths and other floral tributes had been reverently propped up against the garden wall, and he watched the team of undertakers, each furnished with a suitably deadpan facial expression, as they placed each offering, with utmost care and respect, inside their untimely and abhorrent black motor car.

They appeared to know, perhaps by osmosis, that the little wreath covered in greenery and tiny star-like white flowers was to travel to St. Raphael's Church on top of Dominic's little coffin.

Chapter 39

Sandra and Patrizia;
Patrizia and Sandra

The two elder De Martino sisters had lived out a symbiotic existence, for as long as anyone could remember. Being close in age – only eleven months separating them – their lives had followed an almost identical course. They even looked alike, but with the younger girl just that bit taller, that bit prettier and that bit more successful in every way. This had never overly bothered Patrizia, however, provided Sandra was there at her side.

It was therefore interesting to muse upon what might have happened to the older sister, had Sandra not 'come along' when she did; would Patrizia have merely withered away finding the world too hostile or impossible to manoeuvre her way through or would it have been the making of her, rendering what Destiny might otherwise have devised for her? Had Sandra's supportive presence not done other than clip the wings of her older sister forever? Patrizia's early school years were punctuated by her feisty, yet also charming sister, digging her out of (usually tiny) holes, but holes nonetheless. And as a consequence life did eventually improve for her, as Sandra had made her early mark on the rest of the school population and Patrizia was therefore mercifully left alone. Two or three acts of public courage was all it had taken.

But those who knew the family well came to realise that Sandra also needed Patrizia, almost as much as Patrizia needed her; it was a much more subtle and complex exigency, that she herself probably had little idea about. The two sisters had always shared their life experiences; why should that ever change? As they grew into young women Sandra's boyfriends came and went, and as mildly annoying as Patrizia found these dalliances, their own relationship remained as solid as an ancient Roman wall.

And she would always have her sister to confide in and exchange gossip with. Young women stayed in the family home until they got married.

Something both sisters had long enjoyed, as they were on the brink of falling asleep, was to discuss the day's domestic events and exchange opinions, whispers which whistled to and fro from under warm bedclothes in the dead of night, as they each lay on their backs, with eyes wide open staring up at an invisible ceiling. This ritual had begun way back in their girlhood, even before the move to Casa Stella where they inevitably found so much more material to get their teeth into: who exactly was Zia Giulia? (an ongoing debate in itself); a joint desire to know more about their own parents' history – the complete version; Serafina's arrival and her impact on their beloved brother; and of course the circumstances surrounding the murder, that night when their little nephew had been cruelly taken from them. They also had a lot to say about Tina, could she really be their sister? They loved her of course, were even proud of her in an abstract kind of way, but couldn't fathom her life choices; she was just so different; it was all so bizarre.

"Mamma was talking again today about that school they worked at after they got married. I can't remember now how it came up. I had really wanted her to say something about their earlier lives in Italy, or something about their wedding up north, all we know is that she wore a pale blue suit. There seem to be no photos, none, have you ever seen any? I can't understand why she won't talk about it, it's not as though they've split up!"

"Yeh, I know what you mean. She won't even say WHY she won't talk about it. I've given up asking now. So what did she say about the school?"

"Well, stuff she's said already I suppose, but it seemed she really needed to spill it out again, as though she's still not over it. Even though it's not like her to rake up the past. But you know, how they were treated by the boarders and the other staff members, sometimes like inferior beings, life in the kitchen, those long hours, even each time she was pregnant and you know all those misunderstandings, that thing about the cheese word, getting confused with their word for kill? And also that time she thought they were letting her go early one day but she had clearly not got what they were talking about. And got into trouble for it. You know Papà won't talk about their wedding day either?"

Such rambling and idle gossip, however, never leaked out into the wider world; it was the way of certain families to keep an airtight lid on their affairs, the traditional 'omertà' kept alive and well in England, even regarding day to day

194

fairly trivial matters. As far as the De Martinos were concerned, silence was particularly safe in the minds and mouths of their two older daughters despite the fact that it was unlikely any lesson on the subject would have been openly taught by their parents. It had been a wordless learning process, non-articulated; a slowly-gained course of study, which worked like osmosis, as to how one had to behave with regard to the outside world.

The two sisters had recently been sharing stories about dreams, a recurrent family talking point they would have grown up with, since both their parents and family friends, would often have made reference to certain dreams that had threaded through their (sleeping) heads during the night not only relating to a sequence of events, but also picking up on the significance of specific words, of people and objects, colours even, which had all made their way into that same dream. Especially after someone had died.

And as the girls grew older, they became somewhat confused by this phenomenon as they witnessed their parents and others retell dreams on a regular basis and in such detail, but without ever having experienced anything quite like it themselves; their own dreams having faded by sunrise, and only a few producing hazy leftovers, which never lingered for very long and once gone, were gone forever. It never seemed possible to get them back, no matter how hard they tried. But according to witness accounts made particularly by the middle-aged and elderly, it seemed many of their dreams remained crystal-clear and would return again and again, sometimes without change, sometimes with slightly different endings or messages of warning; with numbers transferring their own powerful signs, which indicated financial gain or a turn of the wheel of fortune, the owner of each dream always speaking with great authority. There was absolutely no point trying to argue that it was all nonsense. These people made life choices (and obviously less crucial decisions) based on their dream experiences and all held a wealth of anecdotes on the subject. But were they God-given, (we all had a guardian angel!) or transmitted by the souls of deceased relatives or the workings of Fate herself?

Meanwhile, Patrizia still hadn't encountered the man of her own dreams and this was possibly the one aspect of her life she herself would never openly discuss with her younger sister nor with anyone else in the family. A growing pile of paperbacks shoved at the back of an already cluttered wardrobe, was the only clue that she was possibly leading a 'double life'. With her sister now dating a slightly younger man from Malta, she had found herself with time on her hands, time she had bit by bit learned to fill with the reading of (lightweight?) romantic fiction, and some of it often set against a historic backdrop. The secret side of it also filled her with an ongoing and unexpected thrill; for the first time in her life and just like a child, she had created her own private world she could regularly escape back into, which left her with a deliciously sweet guilt complex!

And in spite of the growing trail of romantic heroines fixed in past or present time that she had come to know, she had concluded that if an ordinary person, such as herself, were ever lucky enough to find true love, there was every chance it would stand the test of time. She had learned that the beauty of glamorous women would eventually fade, and that a life built on or around physical appearance would be doomed from the outset, just look at Marilyn Monroe, who wasn't able to face middle-age, let alone the reality of becoming old. It was the same for a wealthy woman: how could she ever be sure she was being loved only for herself? It would always be a problematic.

She knew that she wasn't as pretty as Sandra, (her mother's friends had made no bones about that) or as clever or as funny as Tina, or as beautiful or as wise as Zia Giulia and she was never going to appeal to an intellectual but neither would she have wanted that. She was waiting for someone nice and ordinary, who worked hard as she did herself and who loved her and the family they would create together, beyond anything else. It all sounded so simple so little to ask for; he didn't even have to be good-looking but alas, such a person still hadn't presented himself.

Her parents, Domenico and Carmela, were now on the point of despair that they would never see their firstborn child 'sistemata', never shed a happy tear or two as she sat facing the altar in a lavish white bridal gown. And even over the past difficult months they had each tried their best, to introduce into their daughter's life, a series of 'suitable' young men (ragazzi seri) as if she were a storybook princess: definitely no divorcees; no one out of work; preferably Italian, preferably Catholic though the bar of desirability was by now beginning to get lowered.

What they didn't know, of course, was that Patrizia also wanted marriage more than anything else in the world. Every night (like the child she once was) she knelt by the side of her bed, head bowed and palms pressed together in perfect reverence, in the hope that her prayers might soon be answered. She would then pick up her current romance and lose herself in the dreamy world of quasi-literary heroes and heroines before falling into a deep sleep.

Chapter 40
The Power of Eyes

Five Years Later

Giulia couldn't believe what she had just witnessed; it had only taken a few moments to deduce what had been going on...

Earlier that day, she had taken Carmen, Fabrizio and little Giulio (who had slept through all their adventures) to the local park and had only brought them back early because it had begun to rain quite unexpectedly, and so she hadn't thought it necessary to pack protective clothing.

The two older children were now seated at the newspaper-covered kitchen table painting idiosyncratic versions of nature's treasures set out in front of them: a variety of leaves of different shapes, sizes, shades and textures; a clutch of acorns and still-shiny horse chestnuts; a range of tatty white and grey feathers. The baby she had seated in his high chair and he was playing with his plastic pots, out of which Giulia constructed colourful towers. Giulio was having the time of his life as he smashed up each tower, enjoying the explosive sounds of the pots landing one after the other on the kitchen floor, and then seeing the ever-patient Giulia re-build them for him in a different order of colours, his laughter bubbling and gurgling over and above any chatter coming out of the mouths of his older sister and brother.

It was hard work, keeping them all amused and focussed on indoor activities and yet she always managed to come up with something. And of course she wanted to support Serafina as much as possible, now that Lorenzo spent more and more time away on business. The couple, since the tragedy, had bought a much bigger, grander house, but Serafina nearly always chose to spend part of the day with Lorenzo's family at Casa Stella: there was always something happening, and, of course, she had to admit, the stream of people coming and going, threw up many opportunities for the children to be taken off her hands if only for a few minutes.

However, by early evening all four of them were safely installed in their own home not too far away, the cruel pond at Casa Stella having been covered over five years beforehand.

Whenever adult company became too tiresome for Giulia, which now occurred more regularly these days, she found a strange kind of cure, that of spending time with the children, in spite of any resulting mess, squabbles to sort out or her own tiredness to address. It was an exhausting business but she loved the way they climbed on her, clung to her, delved deep into her eyes when trying to explain something to her. And little Giulio just melted her heart; he was the carbon copy of Dominic. No one said it but everyone knew.

On returning to the house earlier that day, she had first popped her head round the sitting-room door, expecting to find either Carmela or Serafina in there. But the room was empty except for what they and their friends had (seemingly in a hurry) left behind on the table and armchairs. A non-descript bowl, which still contained the tell-tale water; the matching little jug of olive oil; the prayer books and rosaries; a couple of little dolls, made out of wood and very basic in shape; a long dark and matted plait-like structure, which looked as though it had been cut from a woman's head many years beforehand.

The women then returned, Carmela in particular looking flushed and sheepish. "Oh, Giulia, you're back, you are usually out for much longer. Oh yes, the rain, we are just about to clear up this mess now…no I know you say that mess never bothers you, well it does me, but it'll only take a couple of minutes… just wait till I get a cloth."

Serafina and each of Carmela's friends fell silent as they picked up their own possessions and one by one made their excuses to leave the house. Giulia merely looked on words uncannily failing her, but she was soon aware that, on this occasion, silence was proving to be the most powerful and efficacious of tools.

However, appearing judgemental did not fill her with any lasting satisfaction; she was utterly horrified, bemused and disappointed in her sister's behaviour.

Later that evening, Carmela and Giulia found themselves alone in the kitchen and it was the older sister who brought up the subject.

Now for thousands of years, people living near and around the Mediterranean Sea (and, of course, come to think of it, all over the world) had participated in the practice of magic. But with the coming of Christianity nearly 2000 years ago, it seems logical to deduce that such beliefs and esoteric rites would eventually dissolve and disappear like gradually thinning mist through each new generation, as communities could unite around one true God, accessed through Holy Communion, Jesus Christ and the power of prayer and the Holy Spirit.

"Giulia, let me explain you know, about what you saw this morning. I saw your face and so knew what you were thinking. And you're probably right except we thought it would be worth a try. I hadn't done it in years, I assure you; in fact, none of us knew exactly what to do anymore; it was all a mixture of the bits we remembered from our childhoods and we're all from different parts of the South in any case. I also had some bits and pieces given to me by my mother, which, OK, I didn't forget about completely, because whenever I cleaned out my room, I would see them wrapped in newspaper at the bottom of the chest. It had often crossed my mind to just throw it all out, once and for all; that it was no longer part of my life here in England, my children's life. We've all moved on a lot but somehow that would have meant betraying my mother in some way."

"So why did you use it?" Giulia quietly cut in.

"Well, I was coming to that. Please hear me out, Giulia; it's difficult to explain and I don't fully understand it myself. But it all started a few months ago when Serafina happened to let on to me that she had been suffering from quite severe headaches. I even told her to see her G.P. as it seemed odd they had started up all of a sudden, while she was in her twenties. I always thought you were the kind of person to get headaches or not. She was tested for all sorts of things apparently. But nothing was found; well, that was good news but the headaches continued and even though there are plenty of things you can take, she really didn't like the idea of depending on pills for the rest of her life."

How strange, mused Giulia, that Serafina had never shared this information with her, especially since she knew about her own predisposition to migraines but there again her two aunts had been staying with them, helping with the new baby, so naturally she had had them to confide in.

"So one day, when we started talking about these headaches, me and my friends, one thing I suppose led to another, and, of course, we were all a bit worried about Serafina's health especially after all she's been through that one of us – I'd rather not say who at the moment – suddenly blurted out that it could be as a result of the 'malocchio', you know, the evil eye. Everyone knows it's one of the signs that someone has it in for you; my mother taught me that and believed in it completely, and yes alongside her love of Jesus Christ and the saints."

Giulia had to accept that in spite of twentieth century progress and city sophistication, it was often said in her circles that their illiterate peasant ancestors were in possession of a great store of worldly wisdom, which had been lived out and handed down to them for hundreds of years, thousands maybe, and that in a strange sort of way this made their lives almost superior to ours. We had merely lost touch with all they considered fundamental. Most of us spent whole lifetimes without even touching the soil. "*Scarpe grosse, cervello fino!*" was the saying she found ringing in her ears. With or without a formal education, man once knew how to live and breathe alongside nature; interpret the unpredictable workings of the weather; we knew how to make things grow and all about the best herbal medicines and cures; we knew how to fix things, how not to be wasteful, and make things last; our lives mirroring the regular yet sweeping changes of light and dark, day and night, heat and cold, the playing out of the seasons. We no longer live out those natural rhythms, that perpetual and intricate dance that we've lost our place in, but which still continues and yet what did all this have to do with magic and the evil eye? Perhaps she had let herself become side-tracked?

Trying hard not to detach herself too long from Carmela's rambling 'confession', she soon picked up its former thread, and continued to allow her sister to have her full say about actions, totally at odds with their Church's teaching.

She listened passively to the minutiae of the ritual they had carried out that morning, when the women had sat in a circle holding hands only letting go in order to make the sign of the cross; watching the three drops of yellow-green oil which landed in the water; how Carmela had reacted to her friends' interpretation of the forming shape on its surface; yes, it really did seem to be an EYE; the Catholic prayers which would protect Serafina from the black heart of the jealous person who was plotting her ruin. The Evil Eye how irresistible, the belief that it is possible for someone, no matter how quiet or insignificant, to inflict pain and ruin upon the person they secretly envied or even hated, without ever being caught, no arrest; no prison sentence to endure; outside of suspicion. A rush of revenge. Faith moving mountains to destroy, not create. And even better now that society at large had abandoned such primitive mumbo jumbo marking its demise.

200

That uncomfortable fusion of magic and Christianity.

Giulia said it was all mumbo jumbo, totally ridiculous and it had done nothing to explain why Dominic had been so cruelly murdered; uncover the cause of Serafina's headaches or offer a way to protect Lorenzo's family from future malice.

That night before falling asleep, however, Giulia's brain was still steeped in thoughts of the 'malocchio'.

The police had got nowhere with their apparently painstaking enquiries and five whole years had by now dragged on, with the case still remaining open. Generous sums had been offered to anyone with relevant information, but not a soul came forward, not even a sick prankster. Nothing had emerged from the hundreds of interviews and witness accounts; no one had surfaced as a possible perpetrator of the little boy's murder; little Dominic, who had incidentally been suffocated and then placed face down in the much-awaited pond; Giulia and James' lovingly designed pond with no fish within to keep out the swooping heron.

Chapter 41

Convalescence

If Giulia hadn't continued to record family and other significant events over those difficult years (and especially during the weeks and months which followed Dominic's sudden death), she would surely have forgotten huge swathes of their lives. She and the others, Carmela, Domenico, Lorenzo, Serafina, the girls, spent month after month simply clinging on to a life which often didn't seem to be worth living, but each doing so for God and for one another; the slightly easier option. Each day a re-enactment of the one before: getting up, sharing simple, quiet meals, going to bed, the nights characterised by broken sleep. But then came the whoosh of new De Martino children, arriving thick and fast, Lorenzo replenishing his wife with babies, replacing the void with lashings of family joy, but also trailing the stark message to the faceless enemy that as a family they were invincible, and ripe for a counter attack…it was just a matter of time.

None of these lovely children could, however, replace their older brother.

Sunday afternoons were kept free for family visits to the cemetery, according to the Italian tradition, and bit by bit the new children played their own part in keeping Dominic's poignantly short life in focus, being encouraged to speak aloud to him; they would even take it in turns in cleaning his gravestone home and decorating it with flowers. And just before leaving, each child would be helped up to kiss the ceramic photograph of their beloved (and smiling) brother which had been placed near the top of the marble cross, which marked his resting place, tall enough for it to be made out from the graveyard's entrance.

Lorenzo, when not away, would always accompany them, but preferred to sit in his car for the rest of their stay, always after making the sign of the cross and saying a prayer or two with his head bowed at his son's graveside. He would continue to look on from a short distance, and weather permitting, with the car door wide open. He never got involved with the flowers and other fuss.

It was a quiet comfort for the female members of the family to remember that the cemetery was located close to a Primary School; this meant that visitors were not merely made up of distraught mourners, the old, sad and bereaved, but also of lively young families, who would use the place as a short-cut on their way to and from their children's school. It was Mrs Mogden who had alerted them to this, as she would sometimes go and visit the grave herself during the week. Such passers-through would no doubt in time familiarise themselves with the various graves, which lined their route (but perhaps not the ones positioned further back) and once in a while, Serafina had actually found little coloured drawings, slightly dampened by the morning mist, secured under big stones. They had been placed with reverence on her son's grave, left by young, anonymous donors. Such bittersweet comfort, which pointed firmly to the fact that the name of their son would never be forgotten, even outside of the family.

Giulia had also been comforted by visits from loyal school friends, one or two spending long weekends with the family at Casa Stella, and others who lived a little closer, would pop round for a couple of hours whenever possible to check that she was coping.

Father John had obviously played his part, deeply saddened, however, (on top of everything else) that Giulia now appeared so distant; never rude or cold exactly, but nonetheless unreachable. As always, he kept her in his private prayers; supplied her with a regular batch of wise sayings and philosophical phrases, some of them even humorous; regularly looked in on her, (as well as the others of course), even when he himself was exhausted. He had also carefully selected his very best words for Serafina, clinging on to his belief and sometimes with great difficulty that for some mysterious reason, God had needed Dominic with Him in heaven; he was such a special child and had thus been called back early to his Maker but the kindly priest received little indication as to whether this vapid explanation, or others, had ever managed to heal, or even touch the surface of their devastated hearts.

It was all clearly going to take a good deal of time. And not only for the family.

However, within about four months of the tragedy, a long-awaited turning-point appeared on their horizon and nothing to do with Father John, once Lorenzo happened to announce one evening to a stunned family audience that Serafina was pregnant with their second child.

For many years now John had known a fair amount about Giulia's predicament, concerning her father. Such knowledge had also turned out to be problematic for him. He had, amongst many other duties, the ongoing responsibility of trying to persuade followers of the faith to give up their sinful lives, offering them a brand-new start, a slate wiped clean, provided they had shown true repentance. He had even met with Giovanni, just the once, in a secret location, where the two men had spent several hours together in deep conversation. Of course it had been Giulia who had set up the meeting; she had come to trust Father John completely, but this she knew was backed up by the knowledge that nothing a priest was told in the confessional could ever be revealed to anyone else. This understanding lay at the heart of the Sacrament of Reconciliation for priest and confessant alike.

Needless to say, John's words urging Giovanni to come out of hiding, to come clean to the authorities about his life, to feel the corrosive weight of past actions gently disappear, fell on deaf ears and a granite heart. And the possibility of speaking to him again was close to impossible. The priest's message was merely cast aside with a shrug or two of the shoulders, but he now knew many details of Giulia's father's past which in truth he had rather not been privy to. He now felt himself with a brand-new burden to carry; he too had been lured into the lion's den of Giovanni's world. But surely, he should have been aware of that when Giulia had first approached him about it?

It was then that he came to understand so much more about Giulia's situation and why she had never allowed herself the privilege of marriage and children, something she'd never really explained to him. That was it; it was as though she felt she had to permanently atone for her father's life, by serving others, spreading comfort to those in need, casting aside her own once cherished girlish dreams and lofty ambitions; to lead a life not dissimilar from his own. Not just because she was Giovanni's daughter but because of her collusion. He had invested in her future and she had allowed him to continue in his ways. Her silence kept him safe. She knew he loved her; he knew she returned his love. An awful kind of stalemate.

Father John continued to wait for her to release what was locked in her heart.

One of the first decisions Giulia made to herself, after the death of her nephew, was that she would now have to sell her beloved Casa Stella, it had become contaminated; evil had taken up residence and she could barely bring herself to look out onto the garden. But this was clearly an irrational and knee-jerk reaction, made even clearer whenever it struck her, the thought of how she came to own it in the first place. Some weeks later she knew that it simply had to stay within the family.

And she couldn't sell it now in any case because that would also have taken energy and persistence, patience and skills concerning negotiation all in scarce supply, albeit temporarily. As time went by it just became less and less of a concern. And who would want to buy a crime scene for a home?

The police were a long-standing presence.

She thought back to the early days: her leaving Fielding; her return from the Continent; the Sisters' kind invitation for her to stay on with them for a while; then that shock meeting with her father who simply told her that she was now a property-owner. She was both thrilled and horrified, that tingling sensation of freedom and adult responsibility rolled into a tightly formed ball! Something she'd previously given no thought to whatsoever.

Giulia fell in love with Casa Stella (still unnamed at that point) as soon as she had first peeped around the huge oak door, which creakily introduced her to a set of abandoned rooms which were screaming out for someone or even better, a family to pick them up, whirl them round and embrace them, restoring the building to its original purpose and fabricating other hitherto unimagined possibilities. This house would become her life's work and she was happy her father hadn't taken it upon himself to furnish or decorate it. He had, however, made sure that structural repairs had been carried out, that basic necessities were in place and a central heating system was installed for the very first time, none of which meant very much, at this point, to the house's new owner. There was a basic kitchen and bathroom on the ground floor, a well-worn rectangular table in what must have been the dining-room and a big (uninviting) wrought-iron bed in one of the first-floor rooms. That was the sum total of furniture left behind by a previous owner.

Questions as to how her father was able to purchase it or where any of his money came from in the first place were blindly pushed into the future. He was some kind of successful businessman, wasn't he?

He had also made wise investments for her, and had opened up savings accounts in her name in continental banks.

Nevertheless, she would never have been happy living exclusively off the fruits of her father's labours. Within a few months she had reached a final decision: to devote the rest of her life passing on learning to others; not in a school building but on her own 'premises'. It would mean she would be semi-independent financially and able to choose her hours giving her time for books, her writing, some travel and it would also free up time to help those in need, no matter how they might turn up in her life. Not so much an active search for the needy, as a response to those she might come to hear about locally, even though links with her new community were still in an embryonic state. All this was surely what Veronica House had prepared her for. A life of privilege, dedicated in large part, to those less well-catered for. And built into this noble plan, the odd sprinkling of hedonism: to take off once in a while and pursue her own high-minded (or more earthly) pleasures; she was not a nun after all!

As a start, there were the faces she smiled at in church each Sunday, the housekeeper she had recently employed, and within a year Father John, that priest to whom she had made a powerful confession (or non-confession), once she had heard Star House was hers.

Yes, he had returned for a much longer stay second time around.

Chapter 42
A Man's World

Somewhere in Europe

A darkened room with male voices whizzing words to and fro, to and fro, like angry ping-pong balls across a vast black table; deep, dark voices surfacing in a mix of languages; a tense, sombre atmosphere; 2 men, one young, the other much older, though not dissimilar in appearance, whose blood ties also linked their fate.

We pick up on a conversation soon after it starts to develop.

"It's all been taken care of, your peace of mind; our sense of justice can now be restored. And the message will ring out loud and clear. Come here, and let me embrace you."

The older man then pushed a couple of newspapers in the direction of the younger. They were both folded back at the pages which contained two or more grizzly photos and headlines to articles, which both contained the word MASSACRE.

"I too have been deeply shocked but I refused from the outset to lose my mind, my ability to reason; it would have given them a double victory even though betrayal is the lowest form of human behaviour and the murder of a baby, reprehensible. But our message now rings out loud and clear there will be no confusion."

"I have always been close to you, followed your pathway; it pains me to think that you couldn't know I was there. The time was not right. But and this might open your eyes I was present at your Baptism, your First Holy Communion, your Confirmation and as you know already your wedding. I have been with you, there in the shadows, a bit like here today, on the most important days of your life. I have even wept at Dominic's grave. It is now time for you to take your place beside me."

"Look let me show you, I have here a photo of you and your mother, when you yourself were a baby."

The younger man, still standing, then took up his turn to speak, his voice hard and guttural.

"But why do you not see her, why have you ripped her out of your life, when you have always been in touch with Giulia? What has my mother ever done to deserve this treatment, and she your elder daughter?"

"I understand your pain and your deep resentment, but there are so many things I still cannot explain to you. All I can divulge on this occasion and once again it means that you will have to place your trust in me and I in you, remember it is a dangerous game for us both; a dual act of courage is what's needed from now on. It's to do with the family she married into, your own family, which has given you the De Martino name. My unbroken silence has guaranteed Carmela's ongoing safety and so it must continue. My love for her is just as deep as the love I feel for Giulia; I assure you I have always helped her from a distance and often through Giulia herself; it's just a different, more distant, detached kind of love, one-sided; unreturned as she has no knowledge of me. I have made huge sacrifices for both my daughters. Ask no more of me; all will be revealed at the appropriate times."

"I don't know, I just don't know I haven't been brought up for this, not born into your world. I am full of rage, it's all still so raw. I find it absurd having to believe that my own family is actually part of this. We have always been, all because of you, in it up to our necks, it seems, but we had no idea at all. How much does Zia Giulia know? Just how am I going to explain to Papà' if I do decide to well you know what I mean?"

"Once again I fully understand your predicament 'nipote mio'. But nothing has to be rushed. As far as I know I probably have at least another 5 years of life left in me, ha ha, maybe many more. I suggest that you start thinking about moving out of your present house, it's just a bit too close. Buy something different, you know, bigger, grander, and then 'pian piano' start saying how you've been thinking of leaving the Airport; you need a complete change, a new start, after all you've been through they will understand, and then you can gradually talk of your plans to go into business, that you've possibly found a business partner. All this, one step at a time."

"I have to go now; my 'plane will be leaving in a few hours. *Posso chiamarvi Nonno allora?* How crazy that sounds, to think I've always had a grandfather. I

208

will think about everything you've told me and by the end of the week, I will have an answer for you."

At this point the older man was ready to interject, but his visitor simply continued, having gained in confidence during the incredible encounter:

"Yes I know, you would even give me a year but for my own sanity I have to decide quickly. I can't abide this state of limbo. I've always known in life what to do, which path to take. If there is anything else, you are able to tell me?"

He found himself hugging his grandfather harder and for longer than he'd first intended, not knowing whether he was also supposed to bow his head and kiss the man's right hand, (a hand which sported a showy ruby ring), just as he had seen in the movies.

However that he put off for a (possible) future occasion.

Chapter 43
Why?

The Police had launched a huge murder enquiry, soon after Giulia had first rung 999 to report the gruesome discovery of little Dominic's lifeless body. Officers working on the case were deeply moved, to such an extent that for many it became a personal quest, far and above the normal call of duty, so determined they were to find the perpetrator. They felt supernaturally energised and more often than not found themselves working late into the night.

A huge wave of disbelief at the horror of the baby's murder had in fact engulfed the whole community. People couldn't even begin to make sense of it.

But for the police such devotion to duty, both moral and civic, had come to nothing. The hundreds of enquiry lines, door to door conversations, interviews, research; the witness accounts, forensic reports, a long shelf of bulging folders and files, but none which contained a single plausible motive or the name of a possible killer. The case had touched everyone: those working on it and those who merely looked on from a distance. The murder of an 'innocent' remained unthinkable. WHY was the word most often engraved on faces and depicted in shrugged shoulders. An act of senseless cruelty. Just who was the murderer? And who was the real target? Surely that had to be the family itself. Or could it have been carried out on impulse by a crazed killer whose own child had just died and who was hell-bent on revenge? Against a family with a baby, against society at large? So odd then that they had left behind no careless clues in their frenzy!

Simply nothing had come to light.

Those first interviewed were Lorenzo and Serafina. But after hours (which turned into days) of repeated questioning, there was found to be nothing to suggest they might have been in any way involved. Both their home and Casa Stella had been thoroughly searched. Nothing! It was likewise established that there had been no kidnapping nor demands for ransom. No family links with criminal gangs; no record of illicit behaviour, not even petty in nature. Information gathered was sifted and continually revisited. No foot or fingerprints, no productive leads, no eye-witness sightings. And of course that meant there was no obvious motive to reconstruct or analyse. The lengthy and detailed psychological examinations carried out upon Lorenzo and Serafina threw up nothing new. But who exactly were the De Martinos?

Giulia Cristaldi, who owned the house had lived there for years and was a well-recognised figure in and around the local area, a little eccentric possibly but generally known for her generosity and good works. No one had anything to say against her, other than she was "a bit posh", came across as "a bit aloof or superior, until you got to know her", that she had once been "very beautiful" with many of the elder males (and one or two younger ones) of the community confessing, in full confidence of course, that they had "really fancied her for years", but it appeared that none had possessed the necessary courage to approach her! She was known for her "calm and kindness"; the fact she had taken in a family no one quite knowing how she was connected to them; her treatment of children in particular, often stopping to chat with them (far more often than she did with adults); how she always attended Mass and supported local charities. Some commented that she must have been 'very lonely' in spite of all the people who came and went at Star House and didn't understand why she of all people, had no one at her side or even a child of her own.

Even when the De Martinos had moved in, there had never been any trouble, never a whiff or whisper of anything untoward, inside or outside of the house. The police had never been called. The children had never been involved, not even indirectly, in the local drugs scene. No drunken fights or reports of anti-social behaviour. It was a hardworking family who minded their own business, literally and metaphorically; responsible, law-abiding members of society. No one knew Carmela or Domenico well, other than by sight, because of their lack of English and because they drew only from the well of support from deep within the family structure at home. The couple didn't participate in the life of the local area other than through their business and attendance at church. As Catholics they regularly attended Sunday Mass and were known to keep company with other members of the local Italian community. However, anyone who frequented the family delicatessen would have seen them at work, seen just how they interacted and worked as a team; the dynamic between husband and wife; the obvious loyalty and respect of any children who might be working there; the

211

pride in the service they were providing; the unsentimental yet obvious attention paid towards visiting children.

A simple life made up of family, daily ritual, Sunday worship and business responsibilities.

With the help of an interpreter they each explained to the Police what had brought them to England in the first place and each of their 'stories' coincided, during such interrogations. They spoke of their lives and work at St. George's College; their eventual move south; the birth of their four children coming one after the other; how they always tried to look for work which allowed them to work opposite shifts, so they could look after their growing family without having to involve anyone else. Money was never frittered away; money for the rent, and other bills, always paid on time; any necessary loans being repaid in full as quickly as possible. It meant many years of hardship and that for many years they hardly saw each other, except at night!

They spoke of the early years when Domenico would visit the fruit and vegetable market late on a Saturday afternoon and ask without shame for any available leftovers, sometimes picking up from the ground a carelessly discarded melon, partially bruised apples and pears, or a slightly damaged lettuce and so on. Everything could be cut, chopped, washed and then transformed. Who would ever have guessed? Wood for the fire was gathered by the children from the local park. And Carmela, who had always got up every morning, at least an hour or two before everyone else, in order that her husband, while still in bed, could enjoy his first espresso of the morning. She would then set about the preparation of the family meal, so there would always be something nourishing on the table, whether or not she happened to be out at work that evening.

Restaurants, the theatre, pubs, the cinema all being out of the question; television providing their only form of regular family entertainment. Holidays were a rare treat; a day out somewhere on the coast, where they could open their lungs to breathe in the salty sea air, and then eat their spaghetti-based 'Pastiera' cake on the beach, a great family favourite for such days out, which they would have prepared themselves the night before, in excited anticipation.

But surely life had begun to change for the better after they had moved to Casa Stella and Giulia had loaned them money for the delicatessen? And of course it; did. Once again, however, the old family values remained, ingrained and irremovable: thrift, hard work, loyalty, unity always saving for a rainy day, always minding one's own business.

And so the rigorous questioning and painstaking detective work continued.

Giulia herself had been interviewed many times and this had prompted her to think, not just about the case, but once again about her life in general. She had to her delight and subsequent shame become mistress of the equivoque possessing the ability to answer questions truthfully, and yet somehow phrasing responses in such a way that very little 'unnecessary' information was given, never elaborating on the essence of the question, never risking to create a situation whereby she or anyone else might become compromised or implicated. She was in complete control; her life experience to date had prepared her for precisely this moment in time. And many years beforehand the three of them: Carmela, Domenico, Giulia, although never speaking to outsiders about their family connection, had nevertheless decided upon a simple explanation should they ever been put on the spot that they had merely become friends (after discovering that they came from the same part of Southern Italy) and that eventually the children had begun to call Giulia 'Zia', and that she had subsequently invited them to live with her. Giulia said she had inherited Star House from a distant relative (another equivoque?) giving the impression that the person in question was deceased.

Always punctual, always charming in spite of the tragic loss, always an air of wanting to help.

However she knew and had always known that one day she would have to square the circle; to unravel the impossibly cumbersome knot.

A possible opportunity arose about three months after little Dominic's death; at least an opportunity for her to devise a future plan of action. Giovanni had just confided in her that he had been diagnosed with an incurable illness, a malignant tumour lodged in his brain.

She arranged to speak to Father John and use him, as ever, for a sounding board.

This was not to be a meeting as to how she might cope with her father's failing health or how best prepare for his inevitable departure from this life. That could all be dealt with later; it was to do with coming clean; the putting of things right. Might it mean a prison sentence for her? She had no idea at all and no intention of finding out in advance. Rightly or wrongly, she would deal with each situation as it arose.

"So you see John, once my father can no longer be arrested or condemned in person for whatever awful things he has allegedly carried out over the years, there will be nothing to stop me telling the police what little I do know and I'm confident that this will open the way for Dominic's killer to be found."

"I hear what you are saying, Giulia," warned Father John in a deadly serious, almost alien tone, as he played nervously with his fingers, "but I don't think you have given enough consideration to all the possible implications. I don't know exactly how the law treats people in your position; God's law is of course different. It seems natural to me that any child would want to protect a beloved parent but this case is not clear cut; you could even be implicated; you say you don't know about his life, but they may not believe you, if only because you were in regular contact with him. They might accuse you of not alerting the relevant authorities, of not preventing criminal acts he presumably was involved in. You and I know it was out of love that Giovanni has deliberately kept you in the dark, to protect you, however, as I see it, there's every chance you would be accused of keeping a tight lid on the fact that you Giulia, local do-gooder extraordinaire, just happen to be the daughter of a presumed 'uomo d'onore', a man who has always supported you financially and who has had to live most of his adult life in hiding although you have no knowledge of his precise whereabouts."

And all of a sudden, Giulia was struck by the thought that the wise Priest was speaking and reasoning just like an archetypal 'uomo d'onore' himself. Just for one giddy moment and the dual image of Giovanni's inner sanctum and the secret world of the confessional flashed by. He picked up her hands and continued.

"You are not a child, and it is of course for you to decide how to behave. The normal thing to do would be to get some legal advice, but even that means that the cat is practically out of the bag, if showing only its whiskers. Just promise me you won't get yourself into such a deep hole, that not even you can climb out of and for what? What's done is done; innocent victims cannot be brought back to life. We can only pray for their souls. Think of all the good you have achieved; how you've always put your God-given gifts, talents and privilege to good use, so many vulnerable people have benefitted. You've tracked down your sister, have helped her family, helped many others in need; you've been a loving and loyal daughter not to mention the personal sacrifices you have made due to your compromised position. But in spite of all of this and it pains me to say it I don't believe you are seeing the matter from your family's point of view, only your own. You are used to the grand gesture, the dramatic performance, the show of self-sacrifice, while everyone else sits in awe of you from the side-lines. Perhaps you should consider more fully the impact and repercussions of your actions. On top of everything else, Carmela will learn that she had a father she never knew and one who never came forward to acknowledge her; a father with a very dubious past with a life lived out in the shadows, who might even be somehow involved in the murder of her little grandson, may he rest in peace! Domenico will curse the day that he ever allowed his family to move to Star house with you. And what about poor Lorenzo? At least you always knew that your father led a – shall we say alternative kind of existence. But for Lorenzo, discovering an arch-criminal for a grandfather it would tear him apart and just as he's trying to come to terms with the death of his baby son. Not to mention the impact on Serafina."

"But I am in the wrong John don't you see? Legally and morally. I kind of always knew, but preferred to bury my head in the sand, exactly how you are behaving now. Dominic's murder has brought everything to the surface. My father has of course said nothing to me on the matter but it must have to do with some kind of ongoing clan feud, a family vendetta, maybe something that goes back years. I enabled this to happen my silence allowed it to happen. The police are getting nowhere with their investigation. I should have…"

Giulia then quite uncharacteristically burst into tears, burying her sorry and shaking head into awaiting hands, and knew in a flash that it would be better for all, that she continued to carry around this terrible burden of family truths, alone, just as she had always done. She would wait for the outcome, the workings of fate. Should the Police discover her direct link with her father, well so be it but for the sake of the De Martinos, she would stay silent for as long as it was possible.

Father John also breathed a much quieter sigh of relief, which remained hidden from Giulia, as he too had so much to keep quiet about.

Chapter 44

The Cure

James' life had progressed considerably since we last left him. In the immediate fallout of the tragedy he had proved surprisingly strong, supportive and loyal, as regards the family who had first opened out their arms and home to him. In spite of his own once delicate situation, he had not tried to run away or take cover never distancing himself even though it all had, in reality, very little to do with him. After weeks of interrogation, he had asked the Police if it was OK for him to go and spend some time with Harriet, his sister. The ongoing proceedings had by now left him emotionally exhausted. He furnished them with her Oxfordshire address and telephone number and answered all subsequent questions to their satisfaction. And of course any attempt to leave the country would have directly implicated him in the baby's murder. He had been first to discover the tiny body in the pond; he was the lodger, the outsider, the stranger and a man recovering from some sort of psychological condition. Surely first in the line of possible Prime Suspects!

They allowed him to go and in return he offered to contact them each week to keep them abreast of his comings and goings; any future plans.

He had incidentally made contact with his estranged sister only a few weeks before Dominic's death and she had, albeit with great trepidation, welcomed him back to her own family fold. They both knew there would be much 'reconstruction' work ahead of them; it would take time, energy and tears on both sides. And James knew he would have to tread carefully as regards building a meaningful relationship with her boys, his own blood yet stranger-nephews whom he had often wondered about during his long stay at Casa Stella, and long before any meetings were set up with his sister. In time he hoped to become for them what Father John now was for him, to succeed where their (and his) own father had failed. After all we don't merely learn from good examples, but all so often from the negative behaviour around us. The boys' father had abandoned them (and Harriet) a good while ago; a child-man who at the age of forty, still wasn't ready for a life of duty and adult responsibility.

Harriet would also have to take on board the fact that a baby boy had been murdered at the house her brother was occupying.

In spite of the fact James and Giulia had quietly drifted apart, he felt no need to harbour grudges. It had been a lovely interlude; part and parcel of the healing process, of that gradual awakening only Father John and a prolonged stay at Star House could deliver. As regards Giulia, he was fairly certain that he had caused her no added suffering. He felt reborn and well on the road to recovery in spite of a few inevitable disappointments on the way but that's what life dishes up to us and we have to learn to cope with it without self-destructing. James had learned a great deal about life during the last couple of years, about himself and about human nature. The murder had nevertheless struck a major blow.

For Giovanni, however, there was no cure. He had insisted on knowing the whole and terrible truth. Clumsy whispers behind doors and blinds, fake reassurances of a probable recovery, and vacuous smiles of good cheer were definitely banned now from his daily agenda. He would approach his death in the same way he had approached life before he was forced into hiding; that is, head-on. Even behind those stifling walls he had not yielded to the destructive forces of self-pity or anger. He simply made the best of his lot, rendered naturally more pleasurable by the comfort of wine and women, both of which made a regular appearance in one of a handful of elaborate bunkers.

In the early days he had slept exclusively with young women but in time came to realise that he actually preferred a woman in her 30s, who thought with her own head, and whose body although more mature, had not yet lost the firmness of youth. He equally enjoyed good food, a range of books his favourite being philosophical in nature; music (and once in a while had 'brought in' professional singers, both male and female, who offered up arias from Verdi, Puccini and Rossini or his very favourite sentimental love songs from a vast Neapolitan repertoire, singers whom he paid generously for their silence as well as for their performance!

He was the owner of fine quality suits, made to measure by one of the finest tailors, whose clients included international royalty. A local barber came every few weeks to see to the thick, wavy hair he was so vain about. His shoes and shirts arrived from an old family firm in Florence. He insisted on wearing formal attire (suit and tie) every day of his 'captivity', only changing into something more casual, when taking a walk or some other form of physical exercise. Keeping up with appearances even when there was no one there all part of his resolve to never give up or give in.

However he had expected to live longer than this; somewhere into his mid or late 80s; that would have surely been acceptable; a good deal. But had he ever asked himself if that was how octogenarians feel about it? Are they really ready to slip off life's helter-skelter? Was it not just a cowardly way, a false comfort, of pushing our inevitable disappearance from this world a bit further into the future? The most heart and mind-breaking knowledge we ever have to face in our lives is that of our own death, paradoxically something we learn from a very early age, and yet the one thing we are never ready for, that awful looming 'monstrous thing' which we cannot properly conceive. It makes no difference that we don't grow up to be Presidents and World Leaders, or rise to celebrity status. How can planet Earth continue to spin if we are no longer attached to it? How can the Sun rise tomorrow without us seeing it? Can it even ascend without us? Perhaps only when we are wracked with pain, do we ask for Death's sweet release? But we don't really mean it – we don't want to die – we just want a bit of a break and then come back with a bang, stronger than before. And if we can't deal well with the death of our loved ones, it's surely more to do with the fact we can't face our own mortality yet another poignant reminder; with each passing day we are one step closer, further along the inescapable line.

An insidious tumour was growing day by day in Giovanni's well-oiled brain spreading its evil poison, a slow-burning bullet fired from the gun of an even higher power. Cruel, derisory torture in slow-motion, each minute lasting more than an hour. A slow in and out of sleepwalk to the gallows.

Though for Giovanni there was no physical pain as yet, not even a headache…in spite of the tumour's growing size. It had all started with the falls, and then being told on one occasion that he had fainted; had been unconscious for a few hours. But he couldn't remember anything. Only the bruising down one side of his face convinced him they were telling the truth. Tufts of his hair were also starting to fall out, found in his combs and on his pillows. They kept it from him as best they could knowing just how proud he had always been of that shock of wavy Mediterranean hair. He was now aware that his memory was fading and yet he could recount certain events in full detail, things which had happened many years beforehand. He sometimes recognised those around him and

218

sometimes didn't. He began to recognise them less and less. He continued to describe the past; he was losing touch; his body and mind shutting down in turns until that morning when he didn't wake up at all. Twelve weeks they had said, and twelve weeks it was almost to the day.

The Man of Honour was no more.

Chapter 45

A Bed and a Pile of Notebooks

Giulia was leafing through the notebooks she usually kept locked away in her study. They had been growing loyally in number since her Fielding House days though the language they were written in had at some point changed from Italian to English. The older ones propelled her back into the mists of her past and today also provided an escape route away from her present pain, otherwise gaping red and raw and even that she was forced to keep locked away from those around her. She had let Carmela know earlier that morning that she had a vicious migraine and had decided to spend the day in bed (meaning of course that she was not at home to visitors, nor wanted to be disturbed.) She had then smuggled upstairs about ten of the earlier volumes; they would last her a good while; she just wasn't able to carry any more at one go. Locking the door gratefully behind her, she settled herself on the bed with the relics of her girlhood (and now somehow in her father's presence) scattered beside her.

With no children of her own, she had already made plans to bequeath the whole collection to Tina. Tina loved history and this was family history; she would be best placed to keep the notebooks safe and enjoy delving into them once in a while. They recorded the minutiae, of a life both ordinary and extraordinary, some important and of general interest, others more subtle and personal in nature; tiny treasures only Giulia, and possibly Tina, could appreciate. All proof, however, that she had lived; had been selected for that unique gift of life! And all that came with it, events, episodes and interludes, chosen or unchosen.

And they weren't just arranged as words on the page, but interspersed with pictures, sketches, cuttings, drawings, photos, maps, diagrams, leaflets, tickets, cards and so on. Life's bits and pieces, serving as a reminder (as well as evidence) of where she had been and when, signposting her interests; all that she considered meaningful and therefore worth retaining. She also wrote in verse as well as in diary-type entries. The longer she left these books dusty and unvisited, the greater her pleasure in rediscovering the by now yellowing pages, and she was often taken by surprise: all those half-forgotten cameos and other more hazy memories at once brought back into sharp focus.

Today of course she was particularly drawn towards reviewing items concerning her father. She retraced his features with gentle fingers. She stroked over his black and white photo-faces, as he stared up at her for minutes at a time so she could absorb everything they still had to offer up, any tiny detail that may have escaped her in the past. The familiar, yet frustrating gaps in her knowledge, continued to blight the memories. She didn't even know his real surname, to divulge it to her would have been inopportune; he had not sufficiently trusted her but by way of recompense, he had invented Cristaldi just for her; he'd apparently liked the sound of it. It began with the letters which made up the name of Christ. He only used it for himself during her boarding school years.

She loved him. Oh how she had loved him.

Looking back reminded her that she too had always been one of his pawns; even the search for her long-lost sister had largely been manipulated by Giovanni. She saw that now. This he could do because he knew her through and through. He knew she loved stories; was always hungry for clues which might link her with an Italian home; that she was lonely… kept herself in dark shadows; had always craved a family especially when her school friends spoke of theirs.

She had, like so many others, fallen into her father's fathomless net.

And many years beforehand he had felt compelled to ensure a permanently secure future also for his elder daughter and her growing family. He had tracked all her moves, knew where she was living; where she was working, each stop of her journey from the Scottish borders, which had eventually taken her to North London.

He'd given Giulia a big house, which she had named Casa Stella, and then set about telling her, bit by bit, that she had a sister who was also living in England and of course it was then Giulia herself who took it all on from there leading up to that first historic meeting. (And in this way Giovanni, via Giulia's involvement with the family, could also keep a close yet distant eye on the growing Lorenzo but this was something she was not privy to, something she would never have been able to contemplate herself!)

221

While flicking through the pages, Giulia also allowed herself to speculate upon Giovanni's possible crimes, but it was all a waste of time as she knew nothing, simply nothing, of his parallel world. Had he really ever taken a man's life? If so, just how many times? Did he give orders for men to die? How had it all started? Who exactly was he hiding from? There never seemed to be anything about it in the newspapers. She had always dreaded the day she might see that same face staring out at her amidst an article shot with detail connecting him to horrendous murders and disappearances.

Neither had he ever told her much about her mother, other than she was called Maria (a popular name that Giulia concluded Giovanni must have made up on the spot in order to silence her!), that she was the only woman he had genuinely loved, well more of a young girl in effect and how much she herself reminded him of her. The next flood of questions were never answered, not even in part: Who was she? Did they actually marry? Where was she now; was she dead? Was she also Carmela's mother? (She never had been able to make out a physical resemblance with her older sister.) And by now it was too late to get back in touch with Zia, her father's sister; she and Zio had both died, years ago, in a car crash. Oh surely, he could have passed onto her some of this information, as he was drifting effortlessly towards death?

Death, death yes he was dead now, she reminded herself for the umpteenth time that she would never be seeing him again, never kiss his head, no longer get swallowed up in his arms, nor even smell the sweet aroma of his pipe tobacco or cigars, that she would have to continue to face the shock of each new day, alone, in the knowledge that Giovanni was gone for good, gone to that 'undiscovered country'. He had given her life, had loved her unconditionally, and had whisked her away from imminent danger, protecting her from harm, had kept her well away from that ancient code of honour (which framed his whole being), had financed her education, and had ensured she would always live well, worlds away from the joint horrors of economic poverty and subservience. He had also loved his other daughter from afar and had silently provided for her too, and yet Carmela was doubly protected, totally oblivious to the pain. Giulia carried it around for her.

Too exhausted to cry at this point and at best, only managing to let out dry sobs, as her whole body convulsed, Giulia found temporary comfort in sleep.

And she soon found herself bystander in her own dream: a diligent police constable had taken it upon herself to scramble around in the murky remains of

Giulia's past; it had all started with a hunch; a kind of sixth sense. No one else in the Force seemed to be interested. A hunch which took her back to the girl's arrival in the UK. A couple of the nuns at Fielding, who still remembered Giulia Cristaldi, were interviewed. They spoke of a father, who came in and out of her life, always charming, always generous with his money and his words, always full of praise for the education they were providing for his beloved daughter. She was beginning to dig around more thoroughly now. Who was he exactly? Where did he live? What did he live on? Why had he brought Giulia to England in the first place?

The scraps of a strange afternoon nightmare were eventually interrupted by Carmela's shrill cries: "Giulia, Giulia, come down, come down, there's someone to see you! Oh actually no, he's coming up now. I know you'll be pleased to see who it is!"

"Oh hell," sighed Giulia, "it's got to be Father John, I'm in no mood to speak to him now, not even John! Why on earth is she letting him up? I can't cope with this! I told her I was ill!"

Even so she quickly jumped off the bed, re-arranged her bedclothes, and splashed her face a few times with cold water in the adjoining bathroom. (And that was all after she had shoved her precious notebooks down by the side of a chest of drawers.) She watched the handle of her door turn, and to her delight and genuine surprise, in strode Lorenzo. It had been so long!

"Lorenzo, Lorenzo, come in, come in! I thought I didn't want to see anyone it's been such an awful day, even more horrible than my very worst migraine no I can't tell you why but it's so good to see you." He grabbed her by the waist, long and hard, and she buried her sorry head into his warm and proud male chest.

"I know, I know exactly how you are feeling, believe me." Giulia thinking to herself that he could have no idea whatsoever as to what terrible knowledge she was grappling with, but it didn't matter. He was there. And yet she thought for a split second she also detected his own body contort with pain, mirroring her own. For some hidden reason he was just the right person to be with now and this went far beyond the fact that she hadn't seen him properly in weeks, or that he wasn't prone, like Father John, to articulate worldly-wise phrases, reminding her of God's unconditional love…

They stayed thus for quite a while, not saying or doing anything else. But she eventually came to, and started to ask him about Serafina, how the pregnancy was going.

223

"Zia, everything's going to be fine; it's all going to go away, that pain we are feeling. We've all been through so much but the worst is over. Even Serafina is now showing signs of really wanting our next child. It's a new start, a new start for us all. We can't weaken now. But what about you? How about you taking off for a while? You've been our rock for so long. Think about it at least you can always be back for the birth. What's that place you were saying you would like to visit? You know that place in France how about you planning a trip, with one of your friends perhaps? The Police must have finished with you by now and you can always let them know what you are doing?"

"Thank you, Lorenzo, thank you. I will definitely give it some thought. And even if I can't face it right now. I don't really have the energy at the moment – who knows, I might just take off one of these days."

"Just make sure you keep in touch. Let us know exactly where you are at any one time! Things will be fine, I promise, I promise."

Chapter 46

A Revelation or Two

"Oh hello James, sit down, sit down; let me draw up a chair for you. I've just poured myself a glass yes red wine, I think it's a Beaujolais and some nibbles here left over from the U.C.M.'s welcome do. Please help yourself; there are some napkins around somewhere; yes, here they are."

"So I really must say you are looking well these days; quite a different aspect from when I first saw you when was it, a good few moons ago now? You don't mind me bringing it up again, do you? Things have turned out so well thank the Lord!"

James, who hadn't really been able to speak until now – a clear sign it probably wasn't the first glass John had been savouring – eventually managed to reply that he had just got back from seeing Harriet and the boys, well more like young men now, and that they'd spent a lovely couple of blustery days in the Oxfordshire countryside.

Father John, uncharacteristically showing no signs of having listened to anything his visitor had hitherto uttered, continued to look back in time: "Yes, I must say that morning when I first picked up that piece of paper, you really had me worried, I searched for you everywhere; I went to the park."

"What piece of paper was that?" James laughed back, having judged his host to be even more 'squiffy' than he had first appeared.

"You know exactly what I'm talking about James don't try to deny it now and just look at the end result."

James chose not to continue with the nonsense and instead replied, "Well it's definitely thanks to you John, if I'm looking so well, and to your phenomenal kindness. I was a total stranger…so you'd have done the same for anyone. I wasn't even a Catholic, you became a friend, and even better you arranged for me to live at Star House."

"Why wait a minute, I must have it here somewhere, though I must say I haven't looked at it in such a while, haven't needed to, have I James, haha! Here, here it is. I suppose I should return it to you anyway; it was only ever on loan," he chuckled as he wittered on.

James was handed a sheet of paper, slightly less pristine now than when John had first spotted it, which the Priest prompted him to unfold. "I'm sorry John, but I really don't understand." And after a couple of minutes' silent perusal of the same "My goodness, this must have been churned out by a tormented soul, where did you find this?"

"Exactly where you left it young man," retorted our Priest, just beginning to lose patience, "at the back of my church!"

"Look, I'm sorry to disappoint you, John, if that's the right word, but, but I never wrote this, it's the first time I've ever set eyes on it; how come you thought I wrote it? So you actually thought all this time that; good Lord, you must have thought I was really sick in the head but come to think of it, maybe I was but you never let on, you never asked me about it."

"I decided, early on, I would merely wait for you to explain to me," his words now dropping very slowly from his lips, "and I think I'm beginning to understand why you didn't." Father John had suddenly come to, totally sobered up in couple of seconds, as though someone had just poured a bucket of icy water over his head. "Just give me a moment or two, James, I need to sort out my thoughts. This has come as quite a shock. I suppose it's a good thing, but it also begs the question as to who the desperate author of those words might have been; it obviously means I let him go; he fell through the net; I didn't help him."

Father John left the room, stroking his forehead. It felt as though he had been cheated. He also felt extremely stupid! But, of course, it was impossible to blame his friend or even blame himself come to think of it; he had acted in good faith.

John soon returned and saw that James was already on his feet, with his jacket folded over his forearm, showing all the signs of wanting to take his leave.

"No, no James, I'm sorry for my behaviour. I'm fine now it just all came as such a shock. It just goes to show how many things out there that we believe we know, whereas really… Do sit down I think you had something to tell me, didn't you?"

"Well John, if you are really sure? I feel I've already ruined your evening. Of course, I can see now how you linked it to me, it's all a question of timing isn't it?"

"Sit down, James, sit down. I've fully recovered I assure you, and am all ears! How can I be of assistance?"

"It's just that I'm bursting to tell someone that, that well it's very early days I know and that's really why I can't mention it to anyone else; it could of course all come to nothing."

"Come on, James, that's not like you, just spit it out you know your precious secret is safe with me, haha."

"Yes, of course, I know that, it's just that oh God this is so difficult and please don't laugh, I can't fully take it in myself, but I think, I think that there's a good chance that I'm falling in love for the first time ever with Tina, Immaccolata, and she with me. We haven't exactly spoken about it but all the signs are there. The right feelings. We've been spending quite a bit of time together recently, and she's just so funny, so intelligent but in a quirky, non-pompous and unexpected sort of way and we've spent hours and hours just talking over simply everything and laughing a lot too, and then one of us suddenly realises that it's 2 in the morning all quite different from when I was with Giulia that was much more carnal, desperate."

"Sorry, what was that? You and Giulia? Giulia?"

"Why, John, didn't you know? Oh you must have. I know the two of us agreed to keep it a secret, but I just supposed she would have told you or that you would have guessed; she tells you everything, doesn't she? You are her Spiritual Father; that's how she refers to you."

The Priest felt breathless all of a sudden, his collapsed insides churning, burning. He realised that his kindly face had probably turned to stone and had become as white as the cloth which covered his table. He had to recover and sharp! So he got up with a series of jokey laughs, giving James a hearty slap on the back, swiftly replying that he thought it was wonderful news about Tina, he certainly hadn't seen that one coming but he had come over quite tired, it had been such a long day and that it would be good if James could come back in a day or two, if he wanted to, to talk about his intentions.

By this time his guest was also ready to take his leave. He'd managed to put into words how he felt about Tina. That was the reason for his visit after all. But he usually looked forward to spending time in his friend's company, even when there wasn't a particular issue to discuss. However, on this occasion he'd found Father John out of salts and out of character, no doubt instigated by a few extra glasses of wine. It was a bit disappointing but we all have an off day, a day like that once in a while, James remembered. Perhaps everyone, including himself, expected far too much from Father John. He never let anyone down. And in spite of his huge vocation, actively lived out each day of the year, he was still a human being, with all the moods, the quirks and impulses that entailed. None of us could escape that and it probably became all the more apparent of an evening.

Poor Father John. Years and years of working round the clock, the emotional strain and drain; the failures and failings; he wasn't getting any younger.

Chapter 47

Opposite Sides of the Line

In the hazy days and nights leading up to Giovanni's departure from this world, many scenes of his life had risen to the brim of his consciousness, and the further they had to travel, the more clearly they appeared.

"The young man has arrived; he's in the hall. Shall I bring him through?"

He relived that initial encounter with the young man in question, that ne'er-do-well, who had stupidly impregnated his daughter, and after hasty, yet intrusive scrutiny, learned that he was not even in love with her. His guest was evidently too afraid to lie; in the presence of such a powerful man, who would have found him out in a matter of moments. The two men therefore agreed that it would be foolish to believe there might now be a future for him in the village. In truth, there never had been.

And that because Giovanni was a generous man, plans had already been put into place.

The young couple would travel to the Scottish borders, shortly after which they would get married. It would be the start of a brand-new life for them. All the necessary paperwork had been dealt with. Work and accommodation had been arranged for them. Everything had been paid for. It was a once in a lifetime opportunity, which would be extremely foolish to turn down. The older man explained to the younger, and in no uncertain terms, that it was entirely out of love for his daughter, that he too was to be in receipt of so much generosity. That he was nothing to him...a waste of space, insignificant. It all came at a price though. He had to break immediate ties with everyone he knew in their God-forsaken village; not divulge their new whereabouts to anyone; show he could be a decent husband to the naïve young woman he was about to marry. It went without saying that, if not, there would be severe consequences. The truth would always find a way of seeping out through the cracks of their pathetic lives.

And thus it transpired. Within a couple of weeks, and shrouded in a fine veil of silence, the couple had disappeared from the habitual sights and sounds of village life. No one dared openly comment or ask questions as to what might have become of them. The grief of those who mourned their absence was a purely private matter, lived out behind the walls of their heavily shuttered houses.

How much effort it took, how carefully worded everything had to be; the knowing when to act, when to wait; when to speak and when to stay silent. Giovanni now realised just how much it had taken out of him over the long dark years. Yes it had all become second nature, but the same danger lurked around every turn; it was enough to err just the once.

But he had survived, had outlived most of his enemies, he had also kept his daughters safe.

His thoughts then drifted back in time to that train journey to England, when he had accompanied Giulia to her new country and people. As he lay slumped in his bed, he grew weepy and sentimental at the thought (and image) of her beautiful heart-shaped faced, framed by the two glossy dark plaits. Always with that intense look. Such an intelligent girl. He looked back on his own stiff and passive behaviour. But that's exactly how it had to be. Everything to secure a safe golden future for her. He had put his trust in those crazy, mainly Irish nuns and they hadn't let him down: their patience and devotion to duty, their single-mindedness and welcome; and even more crucial, their absolute confidentiality. He remembered kissing Giulia on both cheeks and forehead, wishing that the circumstances might have been different – a coming home, a birthday celebration, a school prize-giving. Oh the feelings he harboured for this vulnerable, butterfly-perfect girl had once again become unbearably painful.

It was a Wednesday and Father John was grateful for that. He was also grateful to his very pro-active assistant priest, Father Daniel, and for the fact that a few years ago a small group of nuns, The Sisters of the Little Steps, inspired by the writings of St. Therese de Lisieux, had moved into town, and were supporting him and the Parish community in so many different ways. They organised the First Holy Communion meetings for parents and children. They took Communion to the housebound. They visited the sick at home and in hospital. They offered Sunday school for children not currently in receipt of a Catholic education. They had even started up some parent-craft classes for local mothers, even though as an outcome they had not yet attracted the desired target groups, being attended by those who already made up the backbone of the

Church: in the main articulate and confident women, who already invested a lot of time and energy as regards their children's upbringing and education. They were also open-minded enough to discuss different ways of doing things and trying out something new.

Well, all this and more, meant that Father John could relax a little and take some much-needed time for himself.

He was definitely in a deep state of shock that particular morning. Having discovered that James had not written the piece about the 'black holes', he knew he would eventually recover; it already seemed to be drifting away from consciousness. Yet the other matter hung about him like a suffocating shroud, not to mention just how nauseous he was feeling.

Chapter 48

Casa Stella

Star House, alias Casa Stella, has therefore stood firm throughout the many comings and goings over her eighty or so year history. It is probably with some relief, mixed with a tinge of sadness, that we will very soon have to leave her, to drag ourselves away from her high ceilings and balconies; her majestic trees and Bohemian interiors, her rug-scattered rooms whose walls bear witness to so many secrets, undercover conversations, noisy gatherings, breathless goings-on in hidey-holes, inside and outside of the house. We have to leave the family to their own future devices, but always in the knowledge that Dominic's memory will be kept alive.

The miracle of a new life; the arrival of a new houseguest; the return of a loved one; sad departures. And then of course making way for the ordinary, those seemingly trivial tasks that have to be carried out, seen to, repeated, day in day out. All this will of course continue in the quest for civilisation. This is all we have; all we are. To take forward the very best of us, leaving the errors and shame behind; that leapful step, which ultimately takes us higher; further.

Domenico, 'Menicuccio', proud Pater Familias of the De Martino clan, will remain a fixed presence at the delicatessen for as long as he can hold out, until the stubborn aches and pains of old age take root in his muscles and joints. He has no current plans to waste precious time slumped in an armchair, with a tartan rug tucked round his knees, and feet welded into carpet slippers, while he stares blankly out at a television screen, awaiting death. Likewise his loyal wife: Carmelina, who will surely stay busy all the way down to her own last gasps; such hard work, such commitment, looking after a big and ever-growing family. Cooking for them, often at all hours, dutifully helping Serafina with her own young family. Such devotion to duty, such patience. Did there even exist another way of living? If so, it had never revealed itself to Carmela, either through dream, desire or imagination.

She and Domenico do it for their children: the next generation, and the generation after that. Carrying out all those little duties so that the lives of their children might be just a little less brutal, a little less austere, less unequal than theirs had been, all in the hope that they will never need to rely on outside help, never condemned to live off the state, never have to go cap in hand.

Sandra and Patrizia, at least in the short-term, will share the looking after Serafina's children. And Patrizia will continue to enjoy playing out that sacred role of Zia, just as Giulia had done for them. (And occasionally the unforgivable thought will strike her that her nephews and niece actually prefer her to their own mother, and she will once again shoo it away with a smile.) Serafina and Sandra's future children will go on fighting and playing and falling out and regrouping and delighting in one another's company just as all children always have.

They are now allowed to occupy the garden, and the garden will benefit from their presence. Where their imaginations will once again be set alight. They will occasionally contemplate the erstwhile pond but it will not inhibit them on their journey to adulthood.

And as for Giulia, she will very soon be making that trip to France staying on, somewhere near water, until she feels ready to return.